Teachers, Education and Politics in Jamaica 1892-1972

Harry Goulbourne

for

Lisa

Harry

MACMILLAN CARIBBEAN

For
Albert and Lucy
who
Taught us much.

First published 1988

Published by *Macmillan Publishers Ltd*
London and Basingstoke
Associated companies and representatives in Accra.
Auckland, Delhi, Dublin, Gaborone, Hamburg, Harare,
Hong Kong, Kuala Lumpur, Lagos, Manzini, Melbourne,
Mexico City, Nairobi, New York, Singapore, Tokyo

ISBN 0-333-47331-0

Printed in Hong Kong

British Library Cataloguing in Publication Data
Goulbourne, Harry
   Teachers, education and politics in
   Jamaica, 1892-1972 – (Warwick University
   Caribbean series).
   1. Jamaica. Education, 1892-1972. Political aspects
   I. Title II. Series
   379.7292
ISBN 0-333-47331-0

Cover based on a painting by Aubrey Williams presented to
The Centre for Caribbean Studies, University of Warwick.

Series Preface

The Centre for Caribbean Studies at the University of Warwick was founded in 1984 in order to stimulate academic interest and research in a region which, in spite of its creative vitality and geopolitical importance, has not received the academic recognition it deserves in its own right. In the past, the Caribbean has tended to be subsumed under either Commonwealth or Latin American Studies. The purpose of the Centre is to teach and research on the region (which includes those circum-Caribbean areas sharing similar traits with the islands) from a comparative, cross-cultural and inter-disciplinary perspective. It is intended that this Pan-Caribbean approach will be reflected in the publication each year of papers from the Centre's annual symposium as well as other volumes.

This study focuses on a key social group in colonial and newly independent societies – where the teaching profession is highly regarded as a ladder of social mobility (unlike developed societies where it often suffers from low prestige). The Jamaican Union of Teachers was one of the earliest unions in that country's history, concerned not only with professional issues but also with wider questions of what sort of education was relevant to those living in a colonial society. Originating in church schools the increasing professionalization of teachers and their links with politicians (some of whom were ex-teachers) made the Jamaica Teachers' Association an influential pressure group feeding into the higher education system as well as into public life generally. This book raises pertinent questions about the role of élites, intellectuals and political processes as well as the teaching concerns of the profession, and so prepares the ground for comparison with teachers elsewhere in the Caribbean and the developing world.

Prof. Alistair Hennessy
Series Editor

Warwick University
Caribbean Studies

Andrew Sanders
The Powerless People — The Amerindians of the Corentyne River

Editors: Jean Besson and Janet Momsen
Land and Development in the Caribbean

Kelvin Singh
The Bloodstained Tombs — The Muharram Massacre in Trinidad 1884

David Nicholls
From Dessalines to Duvalier — Race, Colour and National Independence

Editors: Malcolm Cross and Gad Heuman
Labour in the Caribbean — From Emancipation to Independence

Harry Goulbourne
Teachers, Education and Politics in Jamaica, 1892-1972

Neil Price
Behind the Planter's Back — Lower Class Response to Marginality in Bequia Island, St Vincent

Douglas Hall
In Miserable Slavery — Thomas Thistlewood in Jamaica, 1750-86

Contents

Abbreviations

AAMM	Association of Assistant Masters and Mistresses
APSR	American Political Science Review
ATTI	Association of Teachers in Technical Institutions
ATTS	Association of Teacher Training Staffs
BITU	Bustamante Industrial Trade Union
CUT	Caribbean Union of Teachers
G	General
J	Jamaica
JAS	Jamaica Agricultural Society
JLP	Jamaica Labour Party
JTA	Jamaica Teachers Association
JUT	Jamaica Union of Teachers
NUDT	National Union of Democratic Teachers
NWU	National Workers Union
PNP	People's National Party
SES	Social and Economic Studies
WCOTP	World Congress of the Teaching Profession
WIRC	West India Royal Commission, 1938-9
WISCO	West Indian Sugar Company
C.O.	Colonial Office

List of tables and figures

Acknowledgements

It is not possible to acknowledge all the influences which went into the fashioning of this project nor all the debt incurred but mention must be made of some. Michael Heale not only took an interest in my undergraduate career at the University of Lancaster, but later encouraged me to carry out research on the West Indies. Robert Benewick and Donald Wood, both of the University of Sussex, formally introduced me to the study of West Indian history and politics during my years as a research student at Sussex. Without their commitment, careful and painstaking attention this work may never have came to fruition.

Intellectual stimulation also came from discussions with members of the Comparative Politics Group, School of Social Sciences, University of Sussex, and Edwin Jones, Carl Stone and Rosina Brodber, then of the Department of Government, University of the West Indies, Mona, Jamaica, who passed friendly but critical comments on early outlines of the research. Special thanks must go to Professor G. E. Mills, Department of Government, Mona, to the late Professor Aubrey Phillips, Institute of Education, Mona, and a member of the JTA executive who provided useful contacts and guidance in Jamaica, and to Euclid King, Chief Education Officer, Ministry of Education.

Of course, without the co-operation of the officers of the JTA the task would have been at best incomplete. I am very grateful to the members of the Association for their warm reception and for the opportunity they gave me to understand the nature of their activities and role in Jamaican politics. Not only was I warmly welcomed into their councils, but the executive provided me with my full requirements. The many officers of the Association at the time, who gave unsparingly of their time, included Mrs Pat Robinson, public relations officer, upon whom the task fell to cope with me. Mr Ben Hawthorne, secretary-general of the Association, Mr Desmond Gascoigne, secretary of development, Mr A. A. MacPherson and Mr Victor Edwards, president of the JTA 1974, were only some of the many JTA members who discussed crucial aspects of the Association's work with me.

From time to time it was necessary to draw on the knowledge of individuals closely associated with educational developments in Jamaica and teachers' organizations in the later decades included in this study. Included in this group were Mr Eric Frater, Attorney-at-law, Kingston, the late Elsa Walters and Sir Hugh Springer, now Governor General of Barbados, both formerly of the Institute of Education, Mona, Mr E. H. Cousins, formerly of the Ministry of Education, the late Edwin Allen, former Minister of Education, Professor R. N. Murray, Institute of Education, Mona, and the late Dr P. C. Evans, of the Institute of Education, London.

I am further indebted to the staffs of the various libraries where work was carried out. These included the Public Record Office, London; the British Museum and particularly the Newspaper Library, Colindale; the Foreign and Commonwealth Office Library, then at Smith Street, London; the libraries of the Institute of Commonwealth Studies and the Institute of Education, London University; the library of the University of the West Indies, Mona and, of course, the library of the University of Sussex, which was always warm and welcoming. Mrs Jackie Morgan, then of the West India Reference Library, Institute of Jamaica, Kingston, and her colleagues were most helpful in locating obscure material for me. I am also indebted to the Clerk of the Jamaica Parliament and to Mr Clinton Black, Archivist, Island Record Office, Spanish Town, for valuable assistance.

Transcripts of Crown-copyright records in the Public Records Office appear by permission of the Controller of Her Majesty's Stationery Office.

I remain grateful to the School of Social Sciences, University of Sussex and the SSRC (now ESRC) for the three-year award which made the research possible. I am also grateful to Andrea Thomas, Joan Lofters, Ivy Whiteman and Winnifred Murray of the Faculty of Social Science, Mona, for typing one version of the manuscript at very short notice.

My thanks to Professor Alistair Hennessy, Director of the Centre for Caribbean Studies, University of Warwick, for inviting me to rewrite this work for the Macmillan Caribbean Studies series and for his constant encouragement, and to Janey Fisher, my editor at Macmillan for her monumental effort.

To Selina Goulbourne, who not only shared at every stage the emotional anxieties while coping with her own intellectual development but also provided the necessary encouragement to enable me to go on, more than thanks is due.

Not unexpectedly, after all the assistance and encouragement received, I remain entirely responsible for all the mistakes as well as views expressed.

Harry Goulbourne
Coventry
October, 1987

Special acknowledgements

The author and publishers wish to thank the following who have kindly given permission for the use of copyright material:-
Manchester University Press for Numbers in Commercial Employment Table XXII (p. 165) and Table XXVIII (p. 173) from *Jamaica 1830–1930* by Eisner

Jamaica Publishing House Ltd for two tables from *Essays on Power and Change in Jamaica* by Gonzales and Girvan.

Every effort has been made to trace all the copyright holders but if any have been inadvertently overlooked the publishers will be pleased to make the necessary arrangement at the first opportunity.

CHAPTER 1

The colonial and commonwealth educational tradition

This is a study of teachers, education and the kinds of politics in which they participated from the 1890s to the early 1970s in the Anglophone Caribbean. Specifically, the study focuses upon the activities of the Jamaica Union of Teachers (JUT) and the Jamaica Teachers Association (JTA) within the limitations of the colonial and independent political systems. The trade union, professional and political issues which teachers raised during these decades are, therefore, closely intertwined with the general social, political and educational developments of the region.

Before turning to these, however, it is useful to offer some general remarks about what may be properly called the British colonial and Commonwealth tradition of education.

There are several interesting points of contrast and comparison to be found in the British tradition of education as it has developed in the colonies and the Commonwealth. Two aspects of this tradition, however, appear to be more important than most and they are central to an understanding of the Anglophone Caribbean experience which the following chapters analyse.

Educational decentralization

The first of these is the attempt to maintain a comparable standard of education within most of the English-speaking world whilst maintaining a system of decentralization. At the height of the British empire it was said that the sun did not set on it, but whether true or false, undoubtedly a great deal of variation existed under the general umbrella of its political authority. This was as true of the education system as of most other aspects of social life and institutional arrangements. There were, of course, important exceptions. These were concerned, however, with large policy directions rather than actual and specific implementation.

One of these was the debate over imperial preference. The general idea was that goods produced within the confines of the empire should enjoy preference in British markets over producers from outside. This was one response to the rise of new industrial countries in Europe and the steady decline of British industry. In such conditions Britain had to grope for a radical rethinking of the philosophy of the open market which so well served her interests during the heyday of her industrial might.

Another example of the grand, comprehensive policy direction was the attempt towards the end of the empire to construct a commonwealth of nations with a common British citizenship to present to a world rediscovering the 'virtues' of nationalism. A reading of the British Cabinet Papers for 1947/8 makes it clear that the 1948 British Nationality Act was an attempt both to check and control nationalism from destroying the empire by setting up rigid and fixed barriers along 'national' lines within the imperial enclosure. In the first instance this was directed primarily against the white dominions, particularly Canada which started the ball rolling in the nationality court. As nationalism made a huge surge forward in India, West Africa and elsewhere the British Government deliberately cast out a net which would haul in the emerging 'nations' with a British legacy.

These attempts to give practical form and structure to the spirit of being British, or the sense of belonging to a common tradition, never came close to the mercantilism of the first empire which enjoyed its economic, political and smug social enclosure. In some ways both attempts failed. It may be argued, of course, that although the common British nationality surrendered to nationalism both in Britain and in the new independent states the setting up of the Commonwealth gave substance to the spirit of 1948. The response, however, must be in terms of a paraphrasing of Menon; with the passing of time not much remains that is common between members, least of all the wealth of members.

But part of the strength of the post-mercantilist empire, not unlike the subsequent Commonwealth, rested in its ability to seek local answers to local problems. For example, although British law applied thoughout the empire, there were different jurisdictions within the imperial pen. The respect accorded princely states in India, the operation of the Dual Mandate in Africa, the slow development of the British legal system in the white sectors of the empire and the Caribbean were examples of this kind of variation.

But these were variations on themes regular throughout most of the empire. And these variations were particularly striking with respect to education. In England itself education has always been left, in the main, to local authorities. These authorities carry out their educational duties within a general framework of national education laws. These do not, however, set out much by way of compulsory subjects (apart from religious instruction). Such uniformity as exists is the result of evolution partly determined by the examining boards and the gradual standardization of entry requirements for the universities.[1]

In the Caribbean where crown colony governments took much more interest in education than in most parts of the non-white empire,[2] there was no role whatsoever for the local authorities (parish councils) in the formulation of education policy and administration. As we shall see in later chapters, educational policies were determined in each of these colonies by a central board of education during colonial days and by the Ministry of Education from the period of decolonization. Since independence, school boards have been established in Jamaica, for example, but these deal with specific schools (rather like boards of governors in England); they are not responsible for schools in the parishes.

The administration of education was, however, decentralized. During the colonial era it was the school manager, responsible in the first instance to the church which owned the school, who administered education in the locality. His actions with respect to education came, of course, under the critical eye of the inspector of schools. But the system operated on an understanding that the school manager and the churches must be trusted and left to do the detailed work of local management.

Of course, the Caribbean territories were sufficiently small and relatively homogenous (with the notable exceptions of Guyana and Trinidad and Tobago) for centrally directed education to operate in a decentralized manner. It is true that East Indians were reluctant to send their daughters to school out of fear that traditional values from India would be compromised. But there is no real evidence of official, deliberate, policy to institute a system of separate but equal education which was common in one form or other in the USA and in parts of the empire itself. Even in the case of East Indians, administrators were careful to insist that where schools were established for them, if there were no other schools in a specific locality, then these should be opened to all children in the neighbourhood.

A crucial aspect of decentralization has been the profound regard for high educational standards so that this could be compared favourably with the rest of the empire. Education reports of inspectors and commissioners throughout the period are replete with comparisons of education with other parts of the empire as well as with English schools themselves. For example, speaking of the Jamaica High School (later Jamaica College) the Superintending Inspector of

Schools, Thomas Capper, reported in a thoroughgoing comparative report in 1900 that

> No school in the British Empire takes a higher position than this (for its size) in the Cambridge Local Examinations.[3]

These reports were concerned to compare the quality, staffing, accommodation and syllabus particularly, but not exclusively, of elementary schools. There was little or no attempt to impose any centrally planned system of education throughout the empire. The comparisons allowed for lessons to be drawn, notes exchanged, attendance, accommodation, and so forth compared but there seems to have been no will to introduce any uniformity. Whitehall officials were particularly concerned about the levels of public expenditure and standards.

With political independence there was bound to be the usual complaint that educational standards were falling. This is a common complaint throughout the post-colonial world where the pressure on educational facilities increases massively with political independence. Like other services, there was never enough during the colonial period and, naturally enough, people came to expect that part of the reward of the struggle for independence would be significantly improved and available services. More than other services citizens of newly independent states expected that the State would be able to meet the obvious demand for education they desired for their children. Resources, however, have not grown with demand and facilities are often over-stretched.

This has been as true of the Anglophone Caribbean as any other part of the post-colonial world. Nonetheless, whilst expenditure has not been able to keep up with demand the quality of education has been maintained partly as a result of a conscious effort by teachers and parents to improve on what was inherited. Additionally, whereas in parts of Africa, for example, the content and purpose of education have been seriously questioned in the light of national developmental objectives, in the Commonwealth Caribbean education continues to be seen primarily as a prerequisite for upward social mobility and personal improvement.

In terms of popular education the region in colonial days stood somewhere between two other types of educational system within the empire. First, there were the preferred white settler colonies of Canada, white Australia and the educational provisions for pockets of whites in South Africa and the colonies of the Rhodesias, Kenya and on a smaller scale in Uganda and Tanganyika. A second type of educational order within the empire was to be found in India and Ceylon. Thus, in India the British established a variety of educational facilities, including universities, largely in accordance with Macaulay's famous 1835 Minutes. These established the purpose of English education in the sub-continent to be the conversion of the Hindu or Moslem into an Englishman in every way but colour. For the purpose of conversion, then, universities and schools teaching in English were established but principally for the very upper layers of Indian society.

In the British West Indian colonies provisions for schools were neither as adequate as those for the colonies (and dominions) settled on a large scale by white people, nor as inadequate as those provided in Africa and Asia, particularly at the pre-university level. Although the quality left much to be desired, elementary education was far more extensive than elsewhere in those parts of the empire commonly referred to as the 'tropical colonies'. According to the Colonial Office a significantly higher percentage of public funds were spent on education than elsewhere and unit costs were much lower than in Africa. In some of the islands most schools depended too heavily on pupil-teachers and suffered from a lack of proper teacher-training facilities. Arthur Mayhew, educational adviser to the Colonial Office in the 1930s, concluded, however, that at least Jamaica and Trinidad and Tobago came close to being on the same standard as England itself.

Whilst it is true that schools were well-endowed compared with the rest of the Caribbean and Britain's other 'tropical colonies', they were in the first instance established by the churches or enterprising individuals. The pattern followed was close to aspects of development in England. As we shall see in a later chapter, the church/state ownership of schools was only one aspect of a dualism in education which held back the system from developing. In some islands the State's contribution and participation in education was quite advanced by the time political independence came; in others the role of the churches continued much the same as in the nineteenth century.

Despite the limitations of the education system it at least made elementary education open to all after the 1890s. And it was embraced as an important gateway to upward social mobility as well as self-improvement by a population emerging from the shackles and degradation of slavery. It was also open to women, making the West Indies markedly different from other parts of the empire. Indeed the majority of children in schools in the Anglophone Caribbean have always been girls rather than boys.

It was crucial, therefore, that whatever standards there were should be maintained and these were of course those received from England. Thus, even after independence the Commonwealth Caribbean has been deliberately slow in replacing English examinations with national or regional ones. In recent years the Caribbean Certificate of Education (CXC) has found some favour with the schools. Not only, however, did this take a long time to develop but grammar schools continue to enter pupils for the English General Certificate of Education (GCE) O- and A- level examinations. It can hardly be the case that the region lacks the wherewithal to establish its own equivalents. Parts of the former colonial world, less fortunate in educational attainment and resources, responded soon after political independence to the pressures of nationalism by setting up national examining boards for their schools. In sharp contrast, even at the university level, West Indians have chosen to set standards which meet international rather than purely national or regional expectations. The strong insistence on maintaining the system of external examiners, for example, is an essential aspect of this tradition.

There are several factors which encouraged this desire to live up to an internationally acceptable standard. One is of course the perception that education is a necessary acquisition for successful upward social mobility as well as personal self-improvement. Another factor has been the dependence on regular migration in search of labour from as early as the 1880s. Literacy was a useful prerequisite for migrants within the empire as well as to other parts of the world, particularly the USA which, from at least the 1890s, many West Indians saw as the land of opportunity. The importance of travel for the average West Indian is such that it is generally regarded not only as a way of making a better living but is also an important part of the process of personal improvement which can make up for the lack of a formal education. Travelling, upward social mobility and education are fused together in the West Indian experience and psyche.

Education for improvement

The second relevant aspect of the colonial and Commonwealth tradition of education is the perception of education as a process of improvement of the individual rather than vocational training. The strong view has been that the primary purpose of education is to develop the individual personality rather than to impart vocational skills. Closely akin to this view, however, is the notion that a properly educated person should be able so to understand the world that he or she will most likely be able to make a living commensurate with the standard of his or her education. Indeed, the educated person should be able to put his or her mind to any task. The school, however, must not be the site of learning how to do any specific job.

It must already be obvious that this attitude tends to place a high premium on literary over practical education. Reports on education in the British West Indies are full of complaints from well-intentioned inspectors of schools and directors of education about the bookish nature of learning in the region. This was so in both secondary and elementary schools.

Expectedly, therefore, one of the crucial issues of contention between policy-makers and the JUT from the 1890s was whether elementary schools should not impart a more relevant education which would include subjects such as agricultural training and domestic science. Teachers objected strongly to these on the grounds that the elementary schoolteacher's task is to develop the intellectual capacities of the child. Training should, they argued, be left to post-elementary institutions. Of all the teachers' associations and unions which made representation, for example, to the Moyne Commission, set up in 1938 to investigate conditions in the region, only one argued for elementary schools to become more vocation oriented. The Dominica Teachers Union called for every classroom in the island to have a sewing machine so that girls could learn the art of sewing to equip themselves for work on leaving school.[4] The demand was certainly not unheard of but it was very much a minority call both in the colonial West Indies and in the empire generally.

This view of education has had profound effects on social attitudes and the question of development. The decades after the last World War which coincided with the process of decolonization in Africa, Asia and the Caribbean were characterized by the search for rapid development by many departing colonialists, liberals and nationalists alike. In this context education was seen as a key instrument to effect development. Whilst this shifted the literary tradition from its high social standing the eventual outcome in the Commonwealth Caribbean has been something of a compromise. The undervaluation of crucial areas of learning such as the natural sciences, technology and agriculture has not been entirely reversed even by the instrumentalist view of education which has gained some ground since the 1970s. It is still more fashionable, for example, for West Indians to study law than agriculture or the natural sciences. The instrumentalism of education has, it is true, given higher status to such subjects as management studies and accountancy and has helped medicine to retain its pride of place.

With respect to the Commonwealth Caribbean, it is too often forgotten that the question of development goes back to the years before the Second World War. Throughout the region the decline of sugar, the problems of labour, the emergence and development of an independent and frugal peasantry, particularly in Jamaica, gave rise to a lively debate from the 1890s over the relationship between education and development. After the turn of the century this debate more or less ceased; it revived again after the First World War and yet again during the period of assessing the demonstrations against the colonial system throughout the West Indian colonies in the 1930s. On each occasion officials raised the question of practical training and teachers responded by stressing the need to retain the Three Rs as the basis of elementary education. The lack of both funds and political will inhibited, however, crown colony governments in the region from effecting the kinds of educational reforms which would probably have retained much of the literary tradition as well as initiated post-school training. Political independence has seen the expansion of educational facilities but these have been insufficient to meet demand.

In these conditions education was bound to be very elitist. During the colonial period secondary education was very inadequate throughout the non-white colonies. Although in Jamaica, Trinidad and Tobago, and Barbados the standard of secondary education (particularly in the humanities) compared favourably with schools in England itself, it was offered to very few. This placed a great deal of demand and responsibility on the elementary schools and their teachers. Whereas in England the secondary modern school was introduced to fill the wide social and educational space between the grammar school and the junior years of the elementary school, a similar development did not occur until the post-independence period.

Moreover, there was a distinct absence of institutions of higher learning. Throughout the non-white British colonial world India was the exception in this respect. In Jamaica a university college existed from 1888 until the turn of the century but it offered degrees in classics and divinity only. In Trinidad the establishment in the 1920s of the Imperial College of Tropical Agriculture (which awarded diplomas in the subject) was also a step in the right direction. It was not, however, until 1948 that the British West Indies was to have its own university college. And it was as late as 1962 before the region which has long craved education had its own university, independent of London, its parent.

The provisions for higher education throughout the region remain, however, essentially elitist. Since the region cannot meet the demand of its people for higher education many West Indians have been going to the USA for this largely because of that country's less elitist tradition in tertiary education.

The absence of centralized control throughout the empire and the literary bias in education are aspects of the tradition of colonial education which continue to determine the direction of education in some Commonwealth countries. In no region is this more true than in the Commonwealth Caribbean. This has meant that in the colonial period education was at a premium for all classes in the region. Education was also one of the most visible areas of state action and was therefore necessarily contentious. In an ex-slave society parents could still remember how education was denied them by slavemasters. It is hardly surprising, therefore, that it should have been quickly recognized as one of the crucial things to acquire in order to succeed in life and improve the whole personality. In particular, elementary education became the vehicle whereby ambitious sons of a prosperous peasantry could hope to become upwardly mobile. Any attempts to limit educational provisions, effect unacceptably tight control, either by school owners (the churches) or the State, change its literary bias or make it any less comparable in quality to elsewhere, were likely to meet with stiff resistance. Such resistance was likely to come particularly from teachers who regarded themselves – and were regarded by others – as the pioneers and leaders of a population moving away from the barbarities of the slave past. Indeed, it is interesting that the JUT, regarded as the oldest teachers' union in the region, was founded at a time of significant reform and change in education, in 1894.

The study

A study of teachers, education and politics in the Commonwealth Caribbean demands, therefore, an approach which combines historical and political analyses. In the first place, although a number of papers have been published on aspects of education in the region there is a need for an up-to-date comparative and comprehensive history of the subject. This is surprising given the importance of education in the moulding of the modern Commonwealth Caribbean as well as the region's present preoccupation with development. The present study is an attempt to re-open this exciting subject to the debate it sporadically enjoyed in both the colonial and decolonization periods.[5]

Teachers and their activities have suffered a greater neglect than education itself. The elementary schoolteacher has found a place in the creative literature of the region[6] but, with few exceptions, the crucial role he or she has played in the building of the contemporary Commonwealth Caribbean has been largely ignored even though the debt West Indians will confess they owe to teacher is legendary. There are some exceptions to this. The works of Collins,[7] Smith and Kruijer,[8] and Foner[9] are amongst those which have tried to fill this glaring gap in the literature on the Commonwealth Caribbean experience. In each case, however, these writers were concerned with quite specific instances of the role of the teacher, or the teacher was not central to the discussion. This study places the elementary schoolteacher and his concern with education at its centre and examines his behaviour within both the limitations of the colonial order and the more complex situation which obtained after political independence in Jamaica in 1962.

In order to assess the influence of the teachers' unions on education and national politics the study examines the origins of the JUT and the JTA and the effects these had on their subsequent developments. The issues they raised, the activities they engaged in and the results they achieved are carefully examined. The study of the development of a corporate awareness amongst teachers and the activities they engaged in begins with the debate over education which resulted in the Elementary and Secondary Education Laws of 1892 and the formation of the JUT two years later. The study ends with the establishment of the JTA as a group which has gained continuous access to official, formal decision-makers but none the less a successful group faced with a challenge of leadership from the radical Teachers for a Democratic JTA which later founded the National Union of Democratic Teachers in 1976.

Many of the more important issues with which the teachers' unions were concerned ran throughout the broad historical period with which I am concerned. In view of this the study selects a number of years at different points on the historical scale for in-depth coverage of issues considered important by teachers. The selection of issues and years reflect a bias towards what I consider to be 'typical' years in the life of the unions. They represent those issues with which teachers were successful as well as those with which they were unsuccessful.

The distinction is sometimes made between 'crisis' and 'non-crisis' points in the experiences of groups. It may be preferable and more correct, however, to speak of 'overt-confrontation' and 'non-confrontation' in the behaviour of groups which attempt to influence the course of public policy. The distinction between 'crisis' and 'non-crisis' may be too sharp. It is a natural part of the relationship between decision-makers, governments and groups with specific grievances or interests to confront each other without there being any implication of crisis in the relationship. Obviously, continuous confrontation is likely to lead to crisis, or groups with legitimate demands or grievances may be forced to adopt tactics which are unacceptable in a democratic society, or they may join the casualty list of the wholly unsuccessful. In either case the outcome may be detrimental for a democratic order.

The issues raised by these groups are placed in one of three categories. The JUT and the JTA behaved simultaneously as what are usually referred to in the vast body of literature on 'pressure' or 'influence' groups[10] as 'spokesman' and 'promotional' organizations. Although the issues which they raised spread over a wide spectrum they tended, in the main, to be of a technical, professional or political kind.

Technical issues were those which arose out of the day-to-day conditions of school life in a society in which the teacher was community leader as well as the functionary who represented, along with the clergy, the exemplary life. Such issues would spread beyond the usual trade union concerns of the occupation but also include these. Examples of these issues were typical trade union matters such as conditions of work and salaries, but also playing fields for children, questions of hygiene, health and the nutrition of pupils.

The 'professional' type of issues reflects the desire of teachers to gain control of important areas of the occupation or to influence decision-makers in the formulation and implementation of educational policy. In the former situation questions such as the control of entry into the occupation, setting standards and discipline were raised. As semi-professionals teachers in Jamaica as elsewhere have been constantly attempting to develop towards full professional status.[11] This has been especially so for teachers who operate within the British colonial and Commonwealth tradition, which allocates a lowly social position to teachers yet entrusts them with the important task of educating the impressionable and vulnerable young.

In the Lasswellian or crude Marxist senses it may be thought that all these issues have a political content to them but I am using 'political' here in a rather narrow and specific manner. It is reserved for two types of issues. Those issues which involved some changes in the socio-political firmaments before they could be met even where goodwill existed on all sides, are deemed political. The second type of political issue involved party-political preferences which were likely to result in overt-confrontation between the Government and teachers' organizations.

Although these types of issues are distinguishable they are not exclusive and absolute categories. Some issues (for example, salaries) could be considered to be technical, professional or political. Much depended on the way particular issues were raised. There is, therefore, some unavoidable overlapping and the decision to place an issue into one category or another depends in part on the emphasis which teachers gave it.

Finally, something should be said about the general outline of the study. An examination of the circumstances of the origins and developments of the JUT and the JTA in 1894 and 1963/4 respectively is offered in chapter three. Chapter four is concerned with resources and competition in the colonial and independent political periods. The chapter discusses the specific targets which teachers sought to pressure as well as the channels and access opened to them. Aspects of these are then developed in the following chapters which focus on teachers' influence, the degree of their successes and failures, their ideological orientation and specific issues raised. The final chapter returns to some general questions about teachers, education and politics in the Commonwealth Caribbean.

It is necessary, however, to commence with a general depiction of Jamaican society from the 1880s to the end of the first decade of political independence in order to get an impression of the developments which were taking place over this period. Chapter two discusses therefore some relevant aspects of the economic, political, social and educational development of Jamaica within a historical framework proper to a study of this kind.

Notes

1 The widespread opposition to Kenneth Baker's proposals to establish a national curriculum for children aged five to sixteen must be understood from the perspective of this long tradition of decentralization; see, Department of Education and Science/Welsh Office, *The National Curriculum 5-16 – A consultation document* (London: July 1987).

2 Arthur Mayhew, *Colonial Office Memorandum on education in the British West Indies*, C.O. 950/51 (1938).

3 E. M. Sadler, *Great Britain: Board of Education Special Reports on educational subjects*, vol. iv, Cd. 416, (London: HMSO, 1901), p. 599.

4 Dominica Teachers Union, *Memorandum of Evidence*. C.O. 950/504.
5 See, for example, Eric Williams, *Education in the British West Indies* (Port of Spain: Guardian Commercial Printery, n.d., but presumably 1950).
6 See, for example, the novel by Earl Lovelace, *The Schoolmaster* (London: Heinemann, 1968).
7 S. Collins, Social mobility with reference to rural communities and the teaching profession, *Transactions of the Third World Congress of Sociology*, vol. iii (1956), pp. 267-75.
8 M. G. Smith and G. J. Kruijer, *A sociological manual for extension workers in the Caribbean* (Department of Extramural Studies, University College of the West Indies, Mona, 1957).
9 N. Foner, *Status and power in rural Jamaica: A study of educational and political change* (Columbia University, 1973).
10 For a detailed discussion of the literature on these groups as it relates to Third World situations see, H. Goulbourne, 'Teachers and Pressure Group Activity in Jamaica, 1894-1967' (D.Phil. Thesis, University of Sussex, 1975), chapter 1.
11 The distinction between 'professional' and 'semi-professional' occupations being implied in this discussion is meant to denote where the former controls the crucial aspects of discipline, entry to and exit from the occupation as in the cases of the clergy, medicine, law and university teaching and research. There is a distinction, therefore, between 'professionalism' and 'profession' following T. J. Johnson, *Professions and power* (London: Macmillan, 1972). I would also agree with Johnson that the status of being a 'profession' implies power on the part of the practitioners. These traditions are no longer maintained in some Commonwealth countries but they remain strong in most Commonwealth Caribbean countries. For historical and sociological discussions of the subject of professions and professionalisms, see, A. M. Carr-Saunders and P. A. Wilson, *The professions* (London: Frank and Cass, 1964), and A. Etzioni (ed.), *The semi-professions and their organizations: teachers, nurses, social workers* (London and New York: The Free Press and Collier-Macmillan, 1972).

CHAPTER 2 | Class, political economy and education

Introduction

In the middle of the nineteenth century Jamaica, according to Sir Arthur Lewis, 'was part of the modern world; as much so as Argentina or Australia; more so than Japan or Russia'.[1] Whilst she remains part of the modern world today, Jamaica's level of development certainly does not place her in the same category as Japan or the Soviet Union. On the contrary, Jamaica remains a 'developing' country and, like most of her neighbours – whether Anglophone, Francophone or Hispanic – who also experienced slavery and colonialism, she continues to struggle with the common problems of under-development and dependency.

Backwardness and the dependence on foreign capital and technology should not, however, obscure the fact that significant changes have taken place in the decades following the middle of the last century. First, although the economy has been more intricately integrated into the world system of production and exchange, and dependence, as opposed to interdependence, has been considerably increased, the national economy has been greatly diversified and development has taken place over time. Second, a complex system of differentiation based on class, race and colour has replaced one based largely on race and colour considerations. Third, a national political arena for the containment or management of class, racial, ideological, etc., contestations as well as a type of the liberal democratic state form reflecting aspects of the specificity of Jamaica, have been established.

One of the principal aims of this study is to offer an analysis of teachers' activities as articulated through their two main organizations – the Jamaica Union of Teachers (JUT) and the Jamaica Teachers' Association (JTA) – within the wider context of national politics. It is important, therefore, that from the outset this general context be explained. Such an explanation entails a broad outline of class development, economy, politics and education. In this regard the period from the 1890s, when the JUT was founded, to the first decade of political independence in the 1960s, when the various existing teachers' organizations came together to establish the JTA, is particularly relevant.

Class development and economic change

Professional historians have by and large ignored[2] the period between the Morant Bay rebellion in 1865 – which provided the old plantocracy with the occasion for requesting the introduction of direct crown rule from Whitehall – and the protests of 1938 which sounded the death knell for this system.[3] There is a similar neglect of the years since 1938 by historians. Fortunately, however, an abundance of both imperial and colonial government publications, monographs and analyses by social scientists along with publications by particular groups and individuals exist and provide the material from which a general picture of the period as a whole may be outlined.

Far from being the presumed 'dark age' the decades between 1865 and 1938 marked the important transition from slavery and its memories to contemporary Jamaica. The development and consolidation of a frugal peasantry which had emerged immediately after the emancipation of the slaves in 1838, the decline of the old and birth of a new plantocracy, the emergence of a pusillanimous manufacturing element out of both the plantocracy and the more confident commercial class as well as the birth and development of a wage-earning class were features of these years. Indeed, during the period the foundations of contemporary Jamaica were established. The changes that have come about since decolonization and political independence in 1962 may be understood to have taken the patterns they have done largely because of developments in the formative years after 1865 and especially since the 1880s. This view, then, clearly denies that contemporary Jamaica is to be understood as being the outgrowth almost entirely of the slavery past, as much of the historiography and its paucity implies. It is important, therefore, if only for this reason, to look a little more closely at aspects of the developments being suggested here.

The dominant classes

Jefferson has aptly remarked that during 'the period of slavery Jamaica was for all practical purposes a large sugar plantation'.[4] A relatively simple social formation, it follows that during slavery the

Table 2.1   Percentage share of sugar and banana of export 1850-1968

	1850	1870	1890	1910	1930	1950	1968
Sugar	58.2	44.5	14.7	8.1	12.2	32.0	16.0
Banana	–	0.1	19.1	52.0	57.3	14.3	7.7

Sources:

(i)   G. Eisner, *Jamaica 1830-1930*, Table XLI, p. 238.

(ii) O. Jefferson, *The Post-War Economic Development of Jamaica*, pp. 91, 100.

owners or those in control of the large plantation dominated those who worked on, or serviced it. For well over two centuries this dominant class, with the assistance of imperial Britain, was able to defend its interests from perceived and actual threats from within (such as attacks from the Maroons, from rebel slaves, missionary critics, etc.) and from without (for example, pirates). The combination of poor techniques and archaic relations of production, the emancipation of the slaves, an end to state protection in the British market after 1853, sharp competition from sugar producers in Cuba, Brazil and continental Europe, and the complacency of the old plantocracy led to its rapid decline after the 1850s.

The story of this decline is well known and therefore only the most salient points need be recounted here.[5] First, the refusal of the planters to diversify production in the first decades after slavery and their continued dependence upon a declining export crop (sugar) perhaps accounted more for the decline of their fortunes than any other single factor. The decline of sugar and the growth of banana production are clearly illustrated by the figures in Table 2.1 showing for selected years the percentage shares of these commodities between 1850 and 1968.

It may be noted none the less that even after the long and loud moan of the planters that the shortage of labour as a result of the freedmen fleeing the estates and the laziness of those who remained, were responsible for the decline, sugar still amounted in 1850 to well over 50 per cent of the country's export. In 1832, for example, at the beginning of the apprenticeship period sugar's share of export was 59.5 per cent.[6] From 1890 to the early 1940s banana, which had entered the export market in 1869, became the major exporting crop reaching its peak in the 1930s. This decline in sugar production may be further seen in the reduction of estates with factories between 1832 and 1968: in 1832 there were 670 decreasing to 134 in 1897, 24 in 1950 and a mere 15 in 1969.[7] This reduction reflected not only the, at first, absolute, and later, relative decline of sugar but also the outcome of attempts to rationalize production and the result of greater concentration of ownership.[8] The process was also the result of attempts, towards the end of the nineteenth century, to diversify, as commodities such as coffee, cocoa, ginger, logwood, etc. found export markets.

By 1950, and to the end of our period, sugar revived and replaced banana as this crop in its turn rapidly declined in the face of sharp competition from large-scale and more efficient producers in Latin America and West Africa.[9] Moreover, the recovery of sugar which had begun with increased demand due to disruption in beet production during World War I, was stimulated after 1950 by sugar agreements which ensured a secure market. But to paraphrase Post, King Sugar never recovered from the blow suffered in the 1840s and 1850s.[10] In 1969 there was, for example, a decline of 93,000 tons of sugar, or a 20 per cent fall from 1968, and the industry could not even meet its commitments abroad.[11]

Unlike banana production, the ability of sugar to relate to other industries, its labour-intensive techniques and its long association with the country's former fortunes helped to ensure that the voice and influence of the plantocracy remained intact well into the contemporary period. As with all social classes, however, a distinction must be made between the different elements of the plantocracy. Although much of the production of both sugar and banana was being done by small growers they did not enjoy the social and political clout that the big planters did. This was despite the fact that the big planters entered the banana industry only after it had proved a successful export commodity. None the less, the general point remained true: the greater diversification of the economy meant that landed capital became more fractionalized and this contributed to the relative decline in the power of the big planters.

Several other factors contributed to the decline of the plantocracy as a whole and thereby to the emergence and development of a variated dominant class as well as to the birth of modern Jamaica during the decades under review. First, with the diversification of the economy and particularly the development of the banana industry as an export commodity, foreign capital began to be more directly involved in production and other areas of the economy. For example, banana production and export were stimulated by the Americans Captain Busch and Captain Baker from 1869 and 1871 respectively.[12] By the turn of the century the United Fruit Company of Boston entered the banana industry as a major investor and in the late 1920s and early 1930s began investing both in the reviving sugar industry and in tourism. Tate and Lyle also became more involved when in 1937 it purchased, through its subsidiary WISCO, seven of the sugar estates in the country.[13] Another example would be the renewed interest in the insurance business following the 1907 earthquake. British and American insurance companies in partnership with Jamaican capitalists (such as the D'Costas, Lascelles DeMercado, Seymour and Pringle) established a number of subsidiaries. Post sums up the situation very well when he contends that 'just as capitalism in Jamaica was beginning to consolidate itself as the dominant mode of production, foreign private capital began to enter the picture'.[14]

This process continued into the years after the Second World War. Indeed, the presence of foreign capital in the Jamaican economy intensified, particularly in the bauxite/aluminium and tourist sectors. The mining and processing of bauxite necessitates a high ratio of capital goods over human labour and so, in terms of capital, accounted for a large slice of the economy. Table 2.2 clearly demonstrates the predominance of foreign capital in Jamaica and the prominence of US and Canadian bauxite firms. For example, of the total inflow of £145.2m between 1950 and 1966 Girvan informs us that £83.7m went into this industry as compared to £22.6m into public spending and only £5.7m into banking. By 1967 bauxite had come to account for 10 per cent of GDP, 44 per cent of merchandise export and 15 per cent of government revenue.[15] While amounting to a major sector of the economy, however, the bauxite industry engaged a negligible part of the working population precisely because of its high capital and low labour inputs.

The sizeable inflow of foreign, mainly private, capital in the years after the last World War has not only reinforced the earlier tendency for the Jamaican dominant classes to be subordinated to international capital, but in its particular effects has also contributed to the composition of the national dominant class itself: this class is not wholly Jamaican neither is it only national.

Second, the processes of the decline of the old and the emergence of the newly composed dominant class in Jamaica was contributed to by the growth of its commercial and manufacturing elements from the turn of the century onwards. The development of these elements was reflected in the modest increase in the corresponding areas of economic activities, commerce and manufactures. The increase of the latter vis-a-vis agriculture for selected years between 1850 and 1968 are shown on Table 2.3. It may be noted that although agriculture declined over time, manufacturing industry

Table 2.2   Net capital inflows to Jamaica 1950-1966 in £M

Period	Total	Main Sectors		
		Bauxite	Banking	Public
1950-57	61.1	46.2	3.9	1.5
1958-61	41.0	9.3	18.7	6.4
1962-63	0.3	9.7	14.9	3.1
1964-66	43.4	18.6	5.8	11.6
Total:	145.2	83.7	5.7	22.6

Source: N. Girvan, *Foreign Capital and Economic Underdevelopment in Jamaca*, (1971) Table 1.5, p. 13.

Table 2.3   Percentage shares of agriculture and manufacture of the GDP

	1850	1870	1890	1910	1930	1950	1956	1959	1963	1968
Agriculture	54.5	56.7	56.2	57.8	50.8	31.5	16.9	13.2	13.4	10.2
Manufacture	10.6	14.7	15.0	13.8	14.1	11.5	13.6	13.8	15.4	15.2

Sources:
(i)   Eisner, *op. cit.*, Table XXIV, p. 167.
(ii)   Jefferson, *op. cit.*, p. 125.

has not developed to the extent of significantly transforming the Jamaican social landscape. Agriculture improved from 54.5 per cent of the GDP in 1850 to 56.7 per cent in 1870 but declined sharply after the 1930s to as low as 10.2 per cent in 1968. Manufactures, on the other hand, experienced ups and downs between 1850 and 1968. Varying from as low as 10.6 per cent in 1850 to 15.2 per cent in 1968 – an increase which was far from spectacular.

The changes in the contributions of agriculture and manufactures to the GDP was a shift, none the less, from a predominantly agricultural economy to a more diversified one. The rise in manufactures from the 1890s was based largely on agricultural raw materials, however, and was largely subordinated to agriculture. Manufacturing was therefore 'limited to the processing necessary to ensure good conditions for overseas markets'[16] of what were essentially agricultural products. A second characteristic of manufactures in the period prior to the 1940s was that of substitution of personal consumer items such as beer and mineral waters.[17] These characteristics are borne out by the figures in Table 2.4 which shows the number of factories producing particular items. The large category 'other' includes the production of match, dyewood, banana and cassava starches.[18] It should be noted, however, that these factories employed very few workers: in 1931, for example, the largest of these employed a force of 100 and the average for the remainder was 21. On the other hand, those engaged in own-account employment continued to increase in numbers. In 1891, for example, there were 47,220 such persons increasing to 61,131 in 1921 and from all indications, this amorphous category has not slowed down in its growth in contemporary Jamaica.

If during the heyday of crown colony rule the State did little to encourage manufactures, following the boom experienced during the 1939-45 War, when imports were greatly constrained, the post-war governments did much to encourage the new development.[19] This new thrust stimulated the production of food and beverages, shoes, textiles and garments, furniture and fixtures, cement, metals and chemicals, adding to the earlier agricultural based manufacturing activities. It has been estimated that during these years the average annual growth rate of the manufacturing sector was over 7 per cent.[20] The major growth areas, however, all had to do with construction in one way or another, stimulated by a general demand for better-constructed houses, offices, etc. but especially the booming tourist trade from the 1950s to the early 1970s.

The increase in manufactures and the development of the industrial element of the dominant class in Jamaica have not been spectacular when we consider the period as a whole. It is true that there have been short periods of boom such as during and immediately after the last War, but these are insignificant compared to the more normal pattern of slow growth. The failure of manufacturing industry therefore is a significant failure of the dominant class radically to steer the country away from external dependence. The diversification of the economy has left the country dependent on imports for manufactured goods as well as many agricultural items such as dairy products, meals, flour, fish, etc. Moreover, established tastes in clothing, food, furniture, etc. have continued to influence the high import levels of personal consumption goods.

Apart, then, from landed, industrial and foreign capitals, these characteristics of the economy provided the sufficient conditions for the active presence of merchant, or commercial, capital. Indeed, the very diversification of the economy seems to have stimulated and encouraged commercial activities.[21] The tendency towards relative equalization of income between emancipation and 1910, Eisner

Table 2.4   Number of factories in production 1890-1929

	1890	1910	1929
Tobacco	2	17	1
Tannery	2	17	2
Beer and ale	1	7	7
Mineral waters	–	8	4
Soap	–	–	4
Copra	–	–	11
Sisal and rope	–	–	6
Other	3	13	17
Total	8	62	52

Source: Eisner, *op. cit.*, Table XXVIII, p. 173.

Table 2.5   Numbers in commercial employment

	1844	1861	1871	1881	1891	1911	1921
Merchants	433	150	203	216	239	332	376
Shopkeepers	2,216	1,166	1,774	2,339	3,131	3,649	3,587
Petty traders	2,216	437	1,594	1,175	1,167	3,573	4,164
Clerks	1,555	636	1,132	1,812	2,242	3,212	3,694
Transport workers	687	1,105	1,263	1,282	2,074	4,193	3,792
Other	–	620	342	565	1,587	4,795	5,013
	4,891	4,114	6,308	7,389	10,940	19,754	20,626

Source: Eisner, *op. cit.*, Table XXII, p. 165.

shows, resulting in increased personal consumption (principally food, clothing and other essentials as opposed to luxuries), no doubt also encouraged commercial activities of all kinds as Table 2.5 illustrates. The large numbers of shop-keepers and petty traders were, as Eisner pointed out, an indication of the lack of employment opportunities but they also indicated the attraction of commerce. It would be interesting to know something about the colour and racial composition of these shopkeepers and petty traders, and the relative sizes of their activities in order to understand better the relationship between petty and large commercial capital in these formative years. Unfortunately, also, the category 'transport workers' is rather ambiguous: it is not clear whether these are employees or owners of transportation networks or a combination of both.

The overriding importance of the figures on this Table, however, is the relatively steady growth of the mercantile element. Again, without knowing more about the sizes of undertakings, the figures may be insufficiently revealing, for example, although there were more merchants in 1844 (433) than in 1921 (376) it is doubtful that their activities were more in 1844 than in 1921 or that such activities accounted for more of the national economy. After 1850, the share of profits of merchants, Eisner found, began to increase and it is therefore not surprising that with the diversification of the economy this category grew. In 1832, for example, whereas planters' gross profits were 26.8 per cent and merchants' 11.1 per cent of the national income, in 1850 the planters' share had decreased to 5.5 per cent whilst merchants' increased to 13.1 per cent and in 1890, 7.8 per cent and 14.4 per cent respectively.[22] The increase in the numbers of merchants at the turn of the last century and during the first decades of this coincided, not surprisingly, with the establishment of some of Jamaica's largest corporate interests.[23] In the post-war years, between 1950 and 1968, the commercial sector continued to hold its own vis-a-vis manufactures and agriculture. For example, whereas manufactures accounted for £23.8m of GDP in 1950, distribution accounted for £28.0m and thereafter up to 1968 the latter increased over the former.[24]

These developments were important aspects of the emergence and development of the dominant social class and, therefore, of the social formation or society, in contemporary Jamaica. This class, or particular elements of it, not unexpectedly influenced and effected political and educational developments during the period under consideration as we shall see in later chapters. At this point, however, it is pertinent to look at the development of the subordinated social classes. After all, the development of a dominant class entails, in a capitalist society, the development of a wage-earning class and in the case of Jamaica and some of the English-speaking Caribbean countries, the development, further, of a semi-peasantry as a result of the demise of the plantation.

The subordinate classes

Speaking of the development of the peasantry in the West Indies, Woodville Marshall classified the period since slavery into three phases – that of establishment, consolidation and saturation. The first phase was marked by 'the rapid acquisition of landholdings and by a continuous increase in the number of peasants'.[25] This occurred where there was still an abundance of unused land, such as in Trinidad and Tobago, Guyana, Jamaica and the Windward islands, where sugar cane had not been grown in the mountainous interior. These lands provided many independently-minded freedmen with the opportunity to begin a new life away from the plantation. Expectedly, the planters did not welcome this development, rather they said it was a threat as labour was removed from where the planters had hitherto been able to command through force. It was against this background, therefore, that the planters sought to arrest the development of an independent peasantry by levying, through the legislature which they largely dominated, high taxes on commodities produced by the peasants, sold land expensively, etc.[26] In Jamaica, however, the rapid development of small landholding by the freedmen was dramatic and significantly assisted by the Baptists under William Knibb's leadership.

In the second phase, that of consolidation, peasants, especially in Jamaica where the Morant Bay revolt of 1865 had highlighted the land question in the sharpest terms possible, began to establish legal claims to their holdings. This was part of the general effort of the first Governor under the newly established crown colony system, Sir John Grant, to rationalize the country's administration and to recognize certain undeniable developments since emancipation to which the old plantocracy had proved incapable of adapting. The legal recognition of claims was, however, not only a process of rationalization but also a recognition of one of the most important forces which was shaping the Jamaica of the next century. For example, the numbers of holdings below 50 acres grew impressively between 1838, when there were 2,114 holdings of less than 40 acres each, to 184,444 in 1930.

Two observations of this spectacular rise may be made here. First, the holdings under five acres each rose from nearly 37,000 in 1880 to over 153,000 by 1930 and consistently this group of smallholders outstripped those with holdings between 5 and 49 acres. As late as 1962, for example, it was estimated that 83 per cent of farmers accounted for less than 25 per cent of total income from agriculture.[27] This skewed characteristic of land-ownership in Jamaica may be further illustrated by the fact that in 1954 holdings of less than five acres accounted for over 69 per cent of farms and it has always been these smallholdings, often on marginal lands, which have produced much of the food of the country that is not imported.

The second observation to be made of the development of a sizeable peasantry is the development of class differentiation within the peasantry itself. No doubt farmers with holdings of between 25 and 50 or 100 acres could accumulate sufficiently to be distinguished from those with smaller holdings both in terms of size and in terms of being able to employ others. Although the cultivation of cocoa, coconut, coffee and especially banana could provide the basis of the wherewithal of most smallholders, those with more sizeable but still manageable holdings would stand to gain the most. Certainly the middle size farmers would be clearly distinguished from the vast majority of those merely subsisting on smallholdings of, say, under five acres.

In terms of class differentiation, we should also remember that many smallholders had to work part of their time on large estates for needed cash whilst producing their own food. There were those too who had to work exclusively on the estates for a living or entered into labour relationship with others in the agrarian economy who could afford to purchase labour power, whether for productive or non-productive activities. Indeed, it was the persistence of this uncompleted, or stultified, development of wage labour throughout the countryside which encouraged the *New World Group* theorists in the 1960s to see Caribbean societies as being what they called plantation societies, that is to say, societies in which the plantation is the main focus of social, economic and political activities. Other theorists have sometimes spoken of the proletarianized peasantry in order to describe this aspect of incomplete capitalist relations in the countryside. This situation has meant that discussion over the peasantry in Jamaica, as elsewhere in the underdeveloped world, remains problematic and will therefore continue to attract the attention of reformers as well as theorists of social change.

Looking at the subordinated classes as a whole, however, the more important point is that with the development of a new dominant class based on the extraction of surplus there naturally developed a working class. In other words, one necessary effect of the consolidation of modern Jamaica has been the steady eradication of pre-capitalist relations of production which had been earlier introduced with plantation slavery. The point is not, however, that all pre-capitalist relations disappeared during the course of this development. Rather, the general point is that following the formal or legal abolition of slavery, the development of an independent peasantry and what Marshall calls its saturation (or its decline) in the mid-twentieth century, and the increase in capitalist activities, the formal and actual conditions were present for the existence of an urban wage-earning class. This must certainly be one of the most important aspects of the development of modern Jamaican society.

An appreciation of the growth of this class may be readily gained from the statistics showing the distribution of the work-force between 1844 and 1960. Table 2.5 shows that throughout this period agriculture, despite its decline, consistently provided the single largest employment opportunity. Although agriculture fell steadily from a high of 75.5 per cent in 1844 to a low of 39.0 per cent in 1960, the agricultural sector managed to maintain its importance as a source of employment. In the 1890s domestic employment accounted for over 13 per cent of the labour force and has remained an important area of employment and is therefore a reminder of the incomplete nature of capitalist development in the country. Despite this glaring fact, however, what is of crucial importance in the formation of modern Jamaican society has been the development of a class whose well-being has depended upon the selling of labour power on the market. These figures would suggest that although this development has not led to far-reaching removal of pre-capitalist practices, none the less the limited development of capitalism in Jamaica has meant that a significant part of the work-force has become a proletariat removed from the ownership of means of production or land.

The creation of a lumpenproletariat, not surprisingly, took place simultaneously. The attraction of the capital city of Kingston to the young who could not easily find employment on the land, the 'saturation', to use Marshall's word, of the peasantry, the desire to escape from rural poverty were some of the many socio-economic factors which encouraged the city-bound migration which in turn provided part of the basis for the development of a lumpenproletariat. Unemployment in Kingston has always been higher than the national average and urban poverty has always been much more striking than rural deprivation, if only because the lumpenproletariat has little or no opportunity to fall back on the land.

At the root of the creation of an urban lumpenproletariat was, of course, the failure of the economy to generate sufficient employment opportunities. Although these increased by 36.0 per cent between 1943 and 1960 and the labour force by 17.8 per cent during the same period, this growth, of itself, was insufficient to change the situation drastically.[28] This fact was partially concealed, however, because it was also during this period that mass migration to the UK and North America occurred. In terms of the rapid development of the lumpenproletariat in the 1960s, it is often argued that the emigration of parents, leaving behind children with grandparents and relatives, contributed to the breakdown of authority and is therefore related to the high incidence of violence in the late

Table 2.6 The gainfully employed labour force 1844-1960

	1844		1861		1881		1891		1911		1921		1943		1960	
	No.	%	No.	%	No.	%	No.	%	No.	%	No.	%	No.	%	No.	%
Agriculture		7.5		69.6		67.5	133827	62.8	146748	58.5	152852	55.3	228.0	45.1	236.6	39.0
Commerce	4891	3.0	4114	2.2	7389	3.0	10940	4.0	19754	5.9	20626	5.9	39.5	7.8	60.3	9.9
Manufacture	18485	11.4	31992	16.9	41962	16.8	47220	17.2	60727	18.1	61131	17.6	59.2	11.7	89.5	14.8
Construction	18485	11.4	31992	16.9	41962	16.8	47220	17.2	60727	18.1	61131	17.6	39.1	6.8	49.8	8.2
Mining													0.6	0.1	4.5	0.7
Domestic	20787	12.8	19013	10.0	26972	10.8	37086	13.5	49711	14.8	62157	17.9	81.3	16.1	88.2	14.5

Sources:

(i) G. Eisner, *op. cit.,* Chapter 10, Tables xx, xxi, xxvi, xxvii, xxiv.

(ii) O. Jefferson, *op. cit.,* Table 2.11, p. 20.

1960s.[29] Such arguments, however, tend to underplay the massive failure of the economy to create jobs for a growing youthful and mobile population.

The intermediary classes

Generally, these are the most difficult of all social classes to define. This is because the middle classes, or the *petite bourgeoisie*, constitute a very mixed social category and their relations to the dominant and the dominated social classes are problematic. These relations are likely to be unstable and often shifty. The very fact that these social groups are always spoken of in the plural indicates the empirical and especially theoretical difficulty in categorizing them. After all, they occupy the various intermediary positions between the two large social classes of modern societies, namely, the capitalist and the working classes. In contemporary advanced capitalist societies, the simple picture of clearly demarcated social classes has been immensely complicated by the sheer range of intermediary positions there are. In underdeveloped societies such as Jamaica, this situation is rendered even more complex by the less straightforward composition of social classes outlined.

Far from being, therefore, the social intermediary Marx and Engels thought in 1848 was destined to extinction, the *petite bourgeoisie* is flourishing in all kinds of conditions under contemporary capitalism. In the case of Jamaica, the particular importance of the *petite bourgeoisie* is that its development is very closely related to the development of a viable and healthy democratic system. The study of the semi-profession of teaching in colonial and independent Jamaica reveals the crucial importance of the middle classes in the development of a more or less social and political ethic. It is not possible to relate occupations to these classes in very precise terms as is possible with both the dominated classes and the dominant classes. These two classes relate in a more or less direct manner to the means of production in a given society. The *petite bourgeoisie* escapes this direct relationship. Hence the greyness of the social space it occupies.

It is none the less possible to indicate some of the intermediary classes' occupational locations in Jamaica. These are to be found in both urban and rural areas; in both the public and private sectors of the economy. Indeed, one certainty about these classes is that they are strategically located at almost every point in the socio-economic system. They engaged as they still do in small farming as well as small businesses. As elsewhere, some elements have been employed in the *servicing* of production and some have been engaged as owner-producers. Others have been employed in the management of the State.

Some locations of the Jamaican *petite bourgeoisie* are indicated on Table 2.5. Petty traders, shopkeepers, clerks and professionals accounted for very many of those gainfully employed in the Jamaican economy during most of the years with which this study is concerned. In an update analysis of the Jamaican socio-economy Stone showed that the self-employed increased during the decades of the 1970s and 1980s. This suggests that there has been an increase in the amorphous 'middle classes'. Indeed, during the period of the radical PNP administration from 1972 to 1980 the professional, technical and administrative elements of the *petite bourgeoisie* grew to 11 per cent of the gainfully employed in the country.[30] The growth of the *petite bourgeoisie* in any society depends largely, of course, on the development of the dominant and subordinate classes. The development of these two main classes also, in turn, depends to a degree on the development of the *petite bourgeoisie* because it is this collectivity of social classes which not only services the basic institutions of production but also develops the theoretical premises for socio-political legitimacy. This role of the *petite bourgeoisie* tends to be much clearer in the colonial and post-colonial situations than in developed capitalist social formations. This is so largely because, contrary to Franz Fanon's observations, the *petite bourgeoisie* in conditions of underdevelopment is forced to be more creative than seems to be the case in advanced capitalism.

These intermediary, amorphous, shifting and therefore often creative social classes provided Jamaica with the social elements which became committed to the prospects of education and democracy. In most societies these social elements are crucial in the development of an ethic of public service and the reproduction of the main values of the social order. In the Jamaican context they proved invaluable in the emergence and development of these values and the attending institutions. Members of these intermediary classes have been engaged in the development of ideologies which have sought to relate prevailing forms of domination and their contradictory aspect, that is, social and political participation in social affairs.

One of these, of course, was the teaching occupation, particularly before there was a university in the country. The social and political positions of this element of the intermediary classes and its relations to others are treated in chapter four and therefore need not be gone into here. It is perhaps more pertinent to turn our attention for the remainder of this chapter to some of the political developments which occurred over this long period.

Political change and continuity

The political order which emerged in Jamaica has been very much part of the general developments being considered here. Important changes there have certainly been, but none sufficiently dramatic to change significantly the established patterns of domination. One striking feature of the political tradition, therefore, has been the moments of spontaneous events effecting changes along with a simultaneous strengthening of some of the essential long-standing political practices. What may be called the Jamaican political tradition must none the less be seen as part of a common British (West Indian) colonial experience. The political tradition of the Anglophone Caribbean which has been in the making for well over a century since emancipation is profoundly conservative. Many radical and progressive social and political thinkers have been born in the Islands and Guyana but they have not, generally speaking, been able to articulate their views in the region. The names of Garvey and Padmore, of James and Rodney, are better known outside than within these countries, taken as a whole.

A second and related example of the conservatism of the Anglophone Caribbean political tradition has been the lack of a militant nationalism. This should not be taken to mean that there has been a total absence of nationalist feelings and aspirations in the breast of Anglophone Caribbean *homo politicus*, but rather that he is not the kind of political animal who will respond to the striking of the old nationalist chords which have moved men elsewhere to momentous political actions. It is probably true to say that he is more of a vocal nationalist abroad than at home. But this is not an unusual characteristic amongst people who have had to leave their homelands in search of employment elsewhere, or, who have had to go elsewhere in order to develop their creative powers.

Some of the positive aspects of this widely shared political tradition in the English-speaking Caribbean are the existence and acceptance of competitive politics and parties with opposing views; generally, the holding of comparatively free elections; a relative autonomy of judicial institutions from the directly political ones; an apparent absence of the military from politics; freedom of the press, etc. Of course, there are the exceptions. Guyana is a case in point.

Elections are widely believed to be a set of fraudulent exercises, a mockery of democracy, and political assassinations appear to be no longer uncommon. Many citizens feel that a dictatorship was firmly established by Forbes Burnham. Even in Guyana, however, the PNC regime has not been able to do away with an opposition because there is a widespread belief in both Guyana and the region that forces of opposition must be allowed to exist. In some of the smaller island states and Trinidad and Tobago, there tend to be one-party dominant systems instead of the two-party, turn-over, system such as exists in Barbados and Jamaica.

Expectedly, Jamaica's political practice exhibits its own particular features because of the specificities of its class configurations which have been a long time in maturing. Within the Jamaican variant of the Anglophone political tradition in the region, therefore, at least two distinct strands of politics may be identified. These are important because they inform certain political practices and institutions as well as signal the punctuations and commencements of developments in the country.

First, there has been the tendency to perceive political relations and practices in terms of the formal, legal and constitutional framework received from Britain, but increasingly modified by symbols from the USA. This perception complements the ideological hegemony of the dominant classes which is widely accepted at nearly all levels of society. This involves, among other things, a deep appreciation of the Westminster/Whitehall parliamentary and governmental models of the scope of legislative and executive powers. It should be noted, however, that since political independence traditional respect for many of the conventions developed and practised at Whitehall and Westminster has been declining.

The other strand to be found within the Jamaican political tradition is an attitude towards politics which is less strong and confident, less pervasive and consistent than the first. It has emerged out of the cumulated experience of the black working classes and the oppressed peasantry who, prior to 1944, were kept outside the pale of constitutional politics. This aspect of Jamaica's political development has therefore taken the form of a forceful 'intrusion' from without into the formal constitutional sphere of political life. Such events – principally the revolts of 1865 at Morant Bay and the great rebellion against colonialism throughout the country in 1938 – usually act as a catalyst for major political changes. It is also usually the case that precisely at such moments the apparently weakened dominant class re-asserts itself and re-establishes the *status quo ante bellum*. But dominant classes rarely if ever have things entirely their own way. On each of these occasions some gains have been made by the dominated classes and the political life of the country thereby enriched. It is at least in this sense that the interlaced pattern of change and continuity through processes of inter-class compromise appears to be an important part of a living political tradition.

Political developments in Jamaica have, therefore, been closely intertwined with the emergence and consolidation of social classes. The planters, merchants, men and women of the professions and foreign investors have all separately or jointly seized upon the State as a set of instruments for promoting or defending their often conflicting interests. The dominated classes too have tended to see the State, chiefly the Government, either as the fount of their salvation or as the source of all oppression. In any event, the State not only in its manifestation as a set of institutions and practices but as a political relation between and amongst classes, has long been viewed as a crucial area in the contestations between classes or elements of classes. It may be worthwhile elaborating this point by giving a few examples.

First, the demand for more land by the middle and richer peasantry which expressed itself with violence at Morant Bay in 1865, seemed to confirm the worst fears of a pusillanimous white plantocracy. Enveloped in the fear of a future not entirely of their making this class of men sought refuge in the British crown colony system. It would appear that of all classes in the social formation the planters were the least able to adjust to the emergence of a new Jamaica.[31] The loss of political nerve, however, was not a loss of faith in the State. On the contrary, the planters seemed to have thought that such was the pivotal importance of the State that it could be dangerous for its instruments to come under broader democratic influence. Indeed, as soon as the British had made attempts to rectify some of the neglected ills of the country and matters seemed to be under control, the planters along with other elements of the dominant class, began to press for political reforms which would strengthen their positions.

For example, the constitutional reforms of 1884 and 1895 which modified the crown colony system were attempts by the Crown to satisfy such demands. By an Order-in-Council of 1884 there were to be nine elected members of the Legislative Council, four ex-officio (senior officials), and five nominated members; expectedly, there was a deliberate attempt to ensure that the vote was given only to men of property or other means such as education, but initially this backfired.[32] In 1895 the number of elected members, after further pressure for greater representation, was increased to fourteen to coincide with the fourteen local administrative units (parishes) with a commensurate increase of nominated and official members. These steps were not meant to be a prelude to independence and the electorate was a small one but they were important because they reintroduced the elective principle into the island's politics. This modified form of the crown colony system existed until it was seriously challenged from outside its framework by the events of 1938. But, clearly, already within the womb of the modified crown colony system occurred developments which provided a political continuity between colonial and independent Jamaica, some aspects of which may be mentioned.

In this respect, the existence of elected and nominated members in the legislature encouraged considerable debate and sharpened criticism of government to an unexpected degree, particularly as the elected members came increasingly to see themselves as an 'opposition' facing the Government and the nominated members.[33] Sir David Barbour, sent to Jamaica by Joseph Chamberlain, then at the Colonial Office, to make a quiet assessment of the island's economy in 1898, noted that one of the main reasons for the declining economic situation was

> the division of responsibility between the government and the elected members which for practical purposes prevented either party from enforcing its policy in any complete or satisfactory manner.[34]

Over twenty years later in 1922 E. F. L. Wood, Under-Secretary of State for the Colonies, reporting to the Secretary of State for the Colonies, Winston Churchill, on a tour of the West Indies and British Guiana, made much the same point. He wrote about the relations between the elected members and the Government thus:

> The Government of Jamaica would at present seem largely to consist in a series of efforts to avoid a contest between the Governor and an unknown nine of fourteen men.[35]

The 1884 and 1895 Orders-in-Council provided that a two-thirds majority of the elected members could veto a financial (or other) measure of the Government; if this were to occur the Governor could use his reserved powers to declare the measure to be of 'paramount importance' to the community and later explain his action to the Secretary of State. Governors, however, careful to keep peace with those who controlled the economy and anxious to maintain the good-will of planters, refrained from frequent use of this power.[36]

One of the main problems with the modified crown colony system was that although it allowed for debate and criticism in the legislature, the elected members had no hope of forming a government. Their impotence tended to encourage a great deal of talking with few practical solutions to problems, as Wood found when he attempted to get some responses from the elected members regarding ways of reforming the legislature.[37] Governors complained that these members were irresponsible; this was of course meant in the sense that they did not always 'co-operate' with gubernatorial rule. Their lengthy debates on government measures tended to hold up the business of the legislature to the frustration of governors and the heads of departments.[38] For example, after the defeat of his pensions bill in 1928, Governor Stubbs wrote, rather cruelly, to Amery, then Secretary of State, that

> the elected members are always inclined to be suspicious
> of things which they do not understand and to take the
> safer course of throwing them out for fear lest they should
> commit themselves to something to which they would have
> objected if they had understood it ... [39]

Whether this was a true description of motive or not, the truth of the matter was that governors had some difficult times with a body of men who came to believe that their task in the legislature was largely to oppose tenaciously whatever the Government sought to do. On the positive side, it may be argued that such exercises strengthened and made more readily acceptable a political framework within which nationalist politicians were later to present and justify their nationalism.

With time too the racial and colour composition of the elected members began to change. Whereas the first elections after 1884 returned whites to the legislature, from 1900 the number of black and coloured politicians increased steadily.[40] It was not part of their vision, however, to seek fundamental changes in the system. Rather, in conformity with the established interest of the dominant class, they sought minor adjustments within the limitations imposed by the political order. After the First World War, men such as J. A. G. Smith, a prominent barrister, and D. T. Wint, an ex-teacher and journalist, were able to make politics, conducted within these boundaries, seem interesting and relevant even to elements of the subordinated or intermediary classes.[41] This kind of participation in colonial politics was to provide a basis upon which nationalists, in face of no viable alternative, would build. After all, a sense of loyalty and belonging informed the behaviour of the elected members. Wood advised in 1922 that the Crown should take advantage of this. He wrote:

> We shall be wise if ... we take steps to build upon the foundations of the remarkable loyalty to the throne by which these people are inspired and avoid the mistake of endeavouring to withhold a concession ultimately inevitable until it has been robbed by delay of most of its usefulness and of all its grace.[42]

But fundamental changes were not to come as a result of criticisms of the nuts and bolts of colonialism but as a result of the activity of those people operating outside the constitutional framework.

The events of May and June 1938 marked the decisive turning point in the island's political development. It was the first dramatic intrusion into the political life of the country by the non-franchised population since the rebellion of 1865 which had signalled the end of the Old Assembly under the declining planter oligarchy. In these months the strike which led to serious disturbances on the Frome Estate in Westmoreland at the western end of the island spread rapidly to Kingston, particularly the ports, at the eastern end and to other rural areas and urban centres.[43] According to one writer,

> the whole colonial structure was under the severest pressure, and it can be argued that not until June 5th did the administration really show signs of being able to handle the situation in terms other than the use of brute force.[44]

This brute force was applied by British troops, the police and special constables with the result that 32 persons were wounded, 8 killed and 139 'otherwise injured'.[45]

The revolt, which was one in a series of disturbances throughout the British Caribbean in the late 1930s, was the angry expression of the working class and the peasantry against their poverty under conditions of severe unemployment which plagued the island particularly in the 1930s.[46] Being a multi-class national series of events, the demands were naturally varied: some small and middle peasants wanted more land, workers wanted employment, but all wanted general improvements from their depressed conditions. The overwhelming importance of 1938 however lay in what developed out of the events of that year, which revealed the need for fundamental changes at all levels of the society. The aftermath of these events such as the development of political parties, trade unions and changes in the constitution were more closely related than the following brief account might suggest.[47]

After 1938 political parties developed, first slowly and loosely then more rapidly and coherently.[48] In September 1938 the People's National Party was founded to provide 'a more forceful and practical leadership of the middle-classes'.[49] Various reform groups were invited to affiliate with the new party which sought to be a truly 'national' party in the sense that its leaders wanted to avoid giving the impression that it represented any single interest such as labour even though its formation was greatly influenced by the events of May and June, as its leader N. W. Manley, a prominent barrister, noted.[50] In their attempt to embrace all interests the nationalist leaders promoted the Trade Union Council and courted the enigmatic and potential cacique Alexander Bustamante, a moneylender who had ridden on the crest of the 1938 events as the undisputed leader of labour.

Two events in particular helped the formation of a second political party – a development which the nationalists did not expect. First, the flirtation between the autocratic Bustamante and the reformist nationalist leaders ended in 1942.[51] Bustamante who had been interned for calling a strike early in the war was conveniently released by the Governor, A. Richards, and the labour leader could therefore contest the first elections under the new 1944 constitution. At this time he had the support of over 85 per cent of organized labour through the rapid growth of his, characteristically named, Bustamante Industrial Trade Union which was founded in 1939.[52] The Jamaica Labour Party (JLP) was founded in 1943 by Bustamante to contest the elections which he won by 19 seats to the PNP's five, and he was able to repeat his victory in 1949, with the support of the leaders of the defunct Jamaica Democratic Party which had sought to represent the conservative wings of the national bourgeoisie but was completely rejected by the newly enfranchised in 1944.

If the PNP was not really a political party between 1938 and 1945, nor was the JLP, in the first years of its existence, the relatively well organized party it was to become. The former acted more as a pressure group than a political party until its electoral defeat in 1945, for before this there was no visible political arena for it to play the role of a social democratic or any other party. It could, however, apply pressure on the Government – the 1944 constitution was largely the result of the PNP's insistence that constitutional changes be made – and it behaved as though it was in fact a loyal opposition

Table 2.7   1944-1967 Election victories

Elections	Parliamentary seats		Percentage of popular votes	
	JLP	PNP	JLP	PNP
1944	22	5	41.4	23.5
1949	17	13	42.7	43.5
1955	14	18	39.0	50.5
1959	16	29	44.3	54.8
1962	26	19	50.0	49.6
1967	33	20	50.7	49.1

Source: adapted from C. Stone, *Clientellism and Democracy*, p. 122.

within the British parliamentary tradition but from outside the legislature. The JLP, in its early years, even whilst in office, was little more than the electoral arm of the BITU, but the existence of something which called itself a political party introduced the competitive element into Jamaican politics.

This competition between political parties was to develop further and become an essential element in the new order. The intimation of a legislature divided into 'Executive' and 'Opposition' in the colonial period quickly developed in the decades following the 1944 electoral contests, as Table 2.7 indicates. These returns reveal a remarkable two-term swing between the parties' periods in office and this pattern has continued into the 1970s and will most likely continue. Perhaps, as Stone has argued, and the popular votes tend to suggest, the major party has been the PNP. This has not, however, hindered the JLP from taking office. Nor has there been a tendency towards a single-dominant party political system. This is not to say that the parties do not have their individual areas of strength and weakness. Indeed, Stone's work on voter behaviour in urban and rural Jamaica since 1944 reveals significant differences in areas of party support. For example, the PNP has enjoyed support in the Kingston and St. Andrew metropolitan area as well as in other large urban centres, whilst the JLP has had strong support from rural areas with small farmers. The majority of parishes, however, Stone contends, are competitive and the parties have had to sell their programmes to a questioning electorate and across class and racial lines.[53]

Although in the 1940s and early 1950s the two parties were

divided over the question of political independence and economic policy, by the mid-1950s they were generally agreed on the desirability of partial state direction, if not active participation, in the economy, a mixed and controlled capitalism and the need to invite foreign investment.[54] Bustamante, who had been opposed to political independence which he saw as 'brown man's rule' over the black man,[55] after experience in office between 1944 and 1955 came to accept that independence was necessary. On the other hand, the PNP's moderate leadership purged the party of its orthodox Marxists – the brothers Frank and Ken Hill, Arthur Henry and Richard Hart (known as the Four Hs) – and toned down the party's radical policies after 1952.[56] But although no fundamental ideological differences divided the parties between the mid-1950s and the 1960s – or perhaps because of this – they have continued to exist, for they not only differ in style but also maintain their original holds on followers and appear to present alternative policies when seeking a mandate. At elections they have been able to make inroads into each other's terrain but the losses are usually regained in the next turn of the wheel of fortune, as the figures in the last table indicate.

A complementary development after the 1938 protests was the emergence of labour unions upon which both parties came to depend for electoral support. In the 1890s craft unions had sprung up in Kingston but owing partly to the emigration of leaders and the unfavourable political climate (they were illegal), they soon went out of existence.[57] After the First World War an interest in unionism revived, resulting in the 1919 Trade Union Law and the formation of unions, particularly among dockers. The laws were liberalized after the events of 1938 and many groups took the opportunity to organize themselves. Following the example of Allan Coombs in Montego Bay, Bustamante succeeded in organizing various unions under the umbrella of the BITU and by January 1939 his union had over 6,000 members.[58] As the founder of both the BITU and the JLP, Bustamante was recognized as life-president of both.

The importance of unions to party fortunes was clearly demonstrated in the 1944 elections when Bustamante, with a strong support in labour, gained a resounding victory without any campaigning. This lesson was not lost on the PNP. The effort to have a base in the labour movement was redoubled and one of the main tasks of the PNP Opposition between 1945 and 1955 was to tighten its hold on the urban areas through the Trade Union Council of Jamaica (TUCJ).[59] After purging the party of its left-wing in 1952, all efforts were made to gain ground from the BITU in the rural areas which

Table 2.8 The growth of trade unions 1919-1970

Year	Number of unions	(Paid-up) union membership
1919	1	80
1934	2	80
1941	3	1,080
1944	25	46,000
1949	12	10,700
1954	13	59,410
1962	15	99,199
1970	24	146,389

Source: R. Gonzales, The Trade Union Movement in Jamaica, in Stone and Brown (eds.) *Essays in Power and Change in Jamaica*, p. 91.

had ensured Bustamante a second victory in 1949. With increased resources the PNP was able to assert itself through the National Workers' Union (NWU) to defeat the JLP-BITU combination in the 1955 elections and to repeat this in 1959.[60] The growth in unions is well illustrated by Table 2.8, but it must be borne in mind that this growth was partly party political growth as well.

This fact of trade unionism in Jamaica has had a number of far-reaching implications for the labour movement since 1938. First, leaders are professional unionists who do not share the same class or experiential background as members. In other words, trade union leaders are not drawn from the ranks of working men and women but from amongst middle-class professionals such as accountants, lawyers, etc.[61] Second, the independence, therefore, of unions has been hampered from their very origins. Many of the senior party leaders (such as Bustamante, Florizel Glasspole, Michael Manley and Hugh Shearer) have also been the country's outstanding union leaders.[62] Third, there has not been a tradition of unity of purpose in either the trade union or labour movements because positions on labour issues are determined largely by party political alignments.[63] Paradoxically, therefore, the protests of the working people in 1938 which gave rise both to trade unions and to the two major political parties have been utilized in an aggressive manner to ensure the essential continuity of forms of domination in Jamaican society. Whilst it is undoubtedly true that these developments have provided an immensely wider scope for upward social mobility for elements of the *petite bourgeoisie*, it is also true that the fundamental patterns of subordination remained very much intact during the period under review. The potentials for an independent labour movement have never been allowed to develop.

The steps towards political independence were slow and cautious but provided a period of 'apprenticeship' for the political parties to develop while still experimenting with the new political institutions. The 1944 constitution introduced universal manhood suffrage and provided for a bicameral legislature which was only slightly modified thereafter. One of the most important provisions of the constitution was the introduction of an executive council responsible for policy, thus reducing the power of the Governor although he still retained 'reserved powers' and was to do so until 1962. This body was composed of five members from the House of Representatives, who could be recalled by a two-thirds majority, three ex-officio members and two nominated members; the Governor presided.

Although political leaders were far from happy with the constitution, since it kept political power in the hands of the Crown, they all felt that they should attempt to make it work. It was, after all, the most advanced constitution in the black Commonwealth. The Foot Constitution of 1953 gave considerable administrative power to Jamaicans; seven ministries headed by members of the House of Representatives were established with Jamaican permanent secretaries. The leader of the party in power was also recognized as Chief Minister and it was now on his recommendations that the Governor dismissed members of the enlarged executive council.[64] The delay of political power made the nationalists impatient and when they came to power Manley was quick to call for full independence. In 1959 Jamaica, after yet more lengthy negotiations, received full internal autonomy. The Chief Minister became responsible for nominating members to the Legislative Council (the upper chamber), a Council of Ministers was replaced by Executive Council and the official and nominated element was replaced by fully elected representatives of the people. The independence constitution provided for 'a system of government, similar to that of Great Britain',[65] separating the roles of heads of state and government, emphasizing the place of cabinet government, retaining an upper house and the basic principles of the 1944 constitution which the 1953 and 1959 measures had modified but not fundamentally changed.

Between political independence in 1962 and the end of our

period (1972), the political order has demonstrated its maturity by its ability to channel protest within one or the other of the political parties. Party political governments have been elected and defeated with new leaders emerging in both the PNP and JLP. Between 1962 and 1972 the JLP held office, which the PNP won in 1972 and 1976, with a return of the JLP in 1980. These alternate times in office have strengthened the party system. Both remain dependent on their respective unions for electoral support. What remains to be seen, however, is whether the political order is capable of resolving the deep social and economic problems which have remained since 1938, and some which have since been created, particularly with the growth of high unemployment, the closing of the traditional outlets of excess labour, widespread anomic and political violence, increasing dependence on foreign capital and increased ideological differences between the parties themselves.

Since this study is concerned with teachers, it is important at this point in the review of the period to say something about the educational system of the country. This is necessary because the behaviour of teachers must obviously be seen within the wider context not only of economy and polity but also that of the educational system in which they had to function.

Some persistent features of the educational system

Between the 1880s and the 1960s, but especially after 1892, education received considerable attention from educationalists and governments. Unfortunately, however, the educational system continued to suffer from severe social and economic pressures resulting in the characterization of Jamaica as an educationally deprived and relatively underdeveloped country. In this regard it is worthwhile looking at the educational system in terms of the class divisions it reflected, its relevance and the relationship between education and politics. These may be usefully discussed separately.

The dualistic nature of the educational system

Perhaps the single most far-reaching aspect of the education system in Jamaica throughout the period was that of its dual characteristics, which have not been entirely changed. This was a reflection of the development of a society divided by class and colour, rather than an aspect of the social and cultural pluralism which according to M. G. Smith characterizes West Indian societies.[66] In Smith's view these societies have no 'compulsory' institutions to hold them together; they are divided into separate and complete entities, each with their own social and cultural norms such as languages, family patterns, religious beliefs and customs. Accordingly, it has been left to the political system to provide a cohesive force; the only zone of confluence, in the words of J. S. Furnivall, the originator of the plural society theory, was 'the market place, in buying and selling'.[67] West Indian societies, like those Furnivall saw in the East Indies, were not to be explained, Smith held, by any unitary model of society, and divisions in these societies are far deeper than mere social stratification.

Those who oppose this analysis of West Indian societies seek to show that they are held together by common value systems, customs and institutions. The core of this 'consensual' thesis is that far from exhibiting pluralist features, West Indian societies reveal a remarkable cohesion, given their history of fragmentation under the plantation and slavery system.[68] Thus, R. T. Smith[69] stressed the unity he saw in British Guiana despite racial tensions while L. Braithwaite sought to show that Trinidadian society is better understood from the perspective of social stratification.[70]

These societies exhibit features which would seem to give force to, and simultaneously give rise to doubts about, both theses. Although a strongly colour-conscious and white-biased society, Jamaica, with an African majority of over 75 per cent and small Asian and European minorities, has always seen a great deal of intermixing of cultures and races.[71] A strong dualism, for example, between African and European cultural values,[72] between nuclear and extended family systems,[73] town and country divisions and the inequitable distribution of resources resulting in extremes of wealth and poverty, has been evident throughout Jamaican society. This would appear, however, to be more the development of a class society within which strong colour and racial biases reinforce the class divides.[74] Furthermore, the widespread acceptance of British-derived values particularly by those, irrespective of colour or class, in pursuit of upward social mobility, gives conviction to a class analysis rather than either the limiting stratification thesis or the cultural and social pluralism perspective.

The dual features of the country's education system may best be seen then in terms of the constraints of a class society which have been evident in the structure, administration and financing of education since formal elementary education was introduced in the nineteenth century. These factors were not only to affect the performance of the system but also to condition the behaviour of teachers as articulated through their organizations.

The financing and control of the schools

The ownership and control of the schools has been, particularly since the 1860s, divided between the Government and the various churches in Jamaica. Indeed, it was the churches which introduced formal institutions for elementary education into the island during the last decades of slavery, and after 1838 they steadily pressured the State to participate actively in education. Nonetheless, although elementary education was enthusiastically greeted by the freedmen, in the 1830s, between 1838 and 1865 it was slow to develop. The initial interest of the imperial government in West Indian, especially Jamaican, education, declined suddenly after 1846,[75] and the planter oligarchy, which, during slavery, had opposed any instruction being given to the slaves, refused to assume responsibility for the education of the children of the freedmen.

After the establishment of crown colony government in 1865, elementary education developed rapidly. The first Governor under the new system, Sir John Peter Grant, a reformer alive to many of the social needs which the old Representative Assembly had ignored, acted on the recommendations of Mr Savage, then the only government inspector of schools in the country,[76] to establish a system of payment-by-results.[77] The Government undertook to pay a grant to any individual or group establishing a school able to satisfy the inspector on his annual examination of schools. The scheme stimulated tremendous interest in elementary education for by 1891 there were 912 schools receiving grants from the Government whereas between 1838 and 1868 the number of schools had only increased from 183 to 286.[78]

But the most important step the State ever took in the colonial period to involve itself in education came in 1892 when the Elementary and Secondary Education Laws were passed. Elementary education was made free for children between five and fifteen years (this underwent many changes in later years). This was the final step in a development which had been taking place since the 1860s; by 1892 the State was already spending over £40,000 on elementary education, one of the largest items on its budget, and free elementary education involved only another estimated £12,000 per annum.[79] The State not only paid the salaries of teachers, it also assisted the churches in the maintenance of their schools and in securing furniture, water catchments and providing a modicum of medical facilities. After the Report of the 1898 Education Commission (hereafter the Lumb Commission), the State also undertook to build, in future, all elementary schools. The churches (with the exception of the Catholic Church which had entered the field relatively late) were prohibited from building any more schools.[80] By the years 1928-32, however, the Government had still not built schools on any impressive scale. Of the 655 schools in the country 521 were owned by the churches and, although some of the churches wanted the State to involve itself further in education by taking over the schools,[81] the Government could not afford to do so. In the 1960s, as Table 2.9 shows, the Government still did not build many schools. In 1964/5 there were 739 primary (formerly elementary) schools, increasing steadily to 742 in 1965/6, to 757 the following year and to 767 in 1968/9. The Government continued to make grants to schools instead of assuming full responsibility.

Members of the Legislative Council called, in 1892, for the State to make substantial contributions to secondary education and although it became official policy to do so, by 1938 there were only two government-owned secondary schools in the country out of a total of 23 which were officially recognized. Of these schools, ten were established under trusts and the others owned and managed by the churches.[82] Although public funds went into secondary education, the amount was relatively small (in 1929, £7,600, while for elementary education the amount was over £183,000)[83] for priority continued to be given to elementary education. As Table 2.9 shows, in the 1960s the Government shifted considerable resources into secondary education, but the priority was not the traditional secondary schools but the new Junior Secondary Schools which were intended as the first step towards establishing comprehensive schools.[84] In 1964 there were 13 of these schools which increased to 16 in 1966/9 and suddenly to 40 in 1969/70 as a result of loans from the World Bank and North America.[85] In contrast the traditional secondary schools (renamed Secondary High Schools) remained in the private sector and constantly at 40; training colleges increased from five in the colonial period to six after independence; technical, comprehensive and vocational schools between 1964 and 1970 remained constantly at six, two and five respectively. But throughout the 1960s secondary education became increasingly the financial responsibility of the State yet when it was made free in 1973, another 15 per cent expenditure was added to the education budget with the ownership of the schools remaining in the private sector.

Table 2.9   Numbers and types of educational institutions 1965-9

	Government-aided institutions			Government institutions			
	Primary schools	Secondary high schools	Teacher training colleges	Junior Secondary (senior schools)	Technical high schools	Comprehensive high – schools	Vocational schools training colleges
	1964-5 739	1964-70	1964-70	1964-5 13	1964-70	1964-70	1964-70
	1965-6 742			1965-6 14			
	1966-7 761			1966-9 16			
	1967-8 757			1969-70 40			
	1968-70 767	40	6		6	2	5

Source: Numbers and types of Institutions by Parish, 1965-9, Statistical Section, Ministry of Education, n.d.

This gradual involvement of the State in education in Jamaica did not provoke the fury of the churches as in British Guiana (now Guyana) in the 1960s[86] because not only was the involvement slow but it was also encouraged, particularly in the colonial period, by the churches themselves which often could not afford to maintain the schools any longer. In terms of secondary education, the State kept a safe distance and entered the established schools only under pressure from the owners and only to assist with finance; where political pressure necessitated state action, Government responded by creating new types of, or new names for, these institutions.

The administration of education

The functions of the Schools Commission and the Board of Education revealed further the dualism in the administration of education in the colonial period. The former was set up in 1879 to supervise the secondary schools which had been established from the seventeenth century for the sons of planters who could not afford to send their boys to schools in England. The trusts under which these schools had been established were being mismanaged by their trustees and the Government saw the need to correct this.[87] As an executive body the Commission made direct representations to the Governor and although it was formally part of the Education Department the Commission gradually became completely independent of the Department.[88] The Board of Education was itself established under the 1892 Elementary Education Law and was responsible for elementary education, the operation of the Code of Regulations and distribution of state funds allocated to education.[89] As head of the Department the Director of Education (in the 1890s the Superintending Inspector of Schools) was also the chairman of the Board of Education and was appointed from Whitehall. The other members of the Board were appointed by the Governor on an annual basis. Unlike the Commission, the Board was not an executive but an advisory body, although covering a much wider field.

In the 1930s, H. B. Easter, the Director of Education, frequently called for the setting up of a single body to administer both the elementary and the secondary sectors of education, but this did not happen.[90] The Report of the Secondary Education Committee chaired by Professor Kandel of Columbia University, in 1943, saw this dualism as backward.[91] Kandel observed that 'from the point of view of administration and organization of education, Jamaica stands in the same position as England did in the last years of the nineteenth century.'[92]

He wanted to see Jamaica follow the example of England which, in 1899, established a central authority and thereby provided for some integration of the system of education.[93] In his view the Schools Commission was performing duties which clerks could easily do and was wasting valuable time on trivia. Easter had a second chance to put forward his viewpoint. The Secondary Education Continuation Committee chaired by him, reporting in 1949, recommended the setting up of a single Education Authority to be responsible for both sectors of education, but this did not happen until 1950.[94] In 1953 when ministerial responsibility was given to the JLP Government, the Supervising Officer, who had replaced the Director, became the Permanent Secretary in the joint Ministry of Education and Social Welfare. Jamaica's assumption of full internal self-government in 1959 meant yet another change in educational administration with the role of the Permanent Secretary being distinguished from that of the senior technical officers of the Ministry; the administration was enlarged, with the Chief Education Officer (later changed to Senior Chief Education Officer) coming immediately, in the education hierarchy, after the Permanent Secretary.[95]

Administrative dualism has largely disappeared, particularly since the 1965 Education Law which concentrated authority into the hands of the Minister of Education.[96] But there are aspects of the system which are reminiscent of the old dualism and therefore of the old class division.[97] For example, in areas where all the schools are owned by the State, the appointment to local school boards is done entirely by the Minister; where schools are leased by the Government, 'not less than two-thirds of the numbers of the members, including the chairman, shall be nominated by the owner',[98] and the rest by the Minister. Thus, although the administration of education is centralized, the State is still deferent to the private sector, not only because it remains indispensable but also because of the refusal of those who control this machinery to take steps against the very system through which they received their own education.

Structure of education

The dualism of the education structure may be explained partly by the origins of education in Jamaica and partly by the fact that education has long been closely linked with occupation and status and therefore class considerations.

Elementary education was originally envisaged as providing no more than religious instruction and teaching the Three Rs to the children of the freedmen. Indeed, for a long time elementary education in Jamaica was taken to mean 'religious' instruction since the prime motivation of the first teachers was evangelical rather than pedagogic.[99] In later years other subjects such as singing, sewing, geography and history were added to the curriculum, but generally the content of elementary education remained fairly fixed throughout the colonial period. Secondary schools, on the other hand, emphasized the classics and literary subjects.[100]

Traditionally, the two sectors of education were kept rigidly

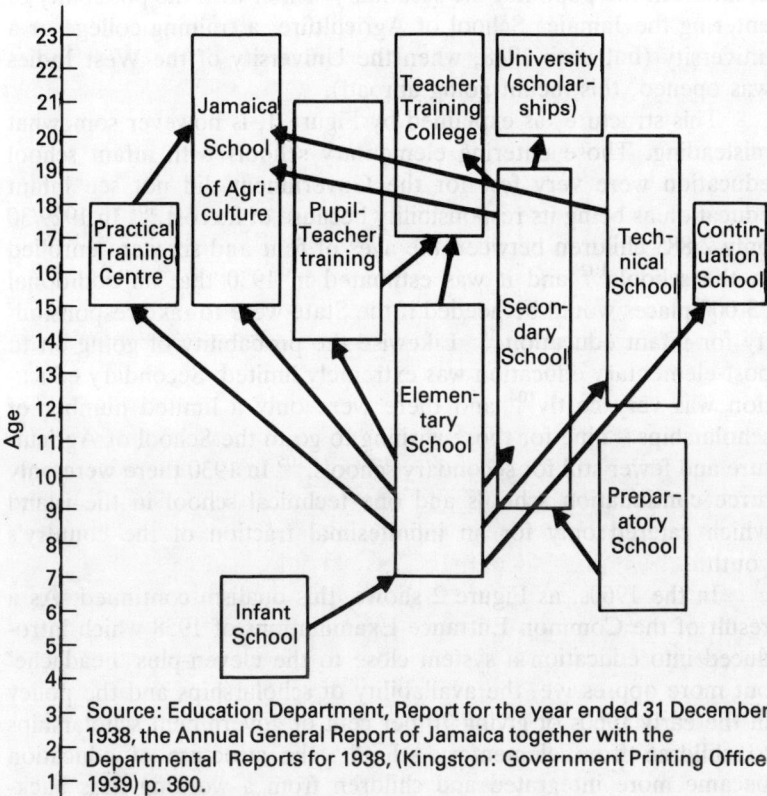

Age

University (scholarships)

Teacher Training College

Jamaica School of Agriculture

Pupil-Teacher training

Practical Training Centre

Technical School

Continuation School

Secondary School

Elementary School

Preparatory School

Infant School

Source: Education Department, Report for the year ended 31 December 1938, the Annual General Report of Jamaica together with the Departmental Reports for 1938, (Kingston: Government Printing Office 1939) p. 360.

Fig 1 The Educational Ladder

apart. Figure 1 describes the structure of education in Jamaica during a typical (education) year, 1938. It shows the types of institutions pupils were likely to attend from the age of four, after the 1890s. The child attended infant school at the age of four and elementary school at seven until the age of fifteen when the possibilities existed for him to go on to a continuation school, a practical training centre or the Jamaica School of Agriculture. At the age of twelve the successful child at the elementary school could leave to a technical school or at fourteen years of age become a pupil-teacher and at age seventeen continue to a teacher-training college; a pupil could also leave the continuation school to attend the Jamaica School of Agriculture. The second path that Figure 1 describes led from the preparatory, between the ages of six and eleven, to the secondary schools which could also be entered from the age of nine; at nineteen the pupil left the secondary school with the possibility of entering the Jamaica School of Agriculture, a training college or a university (but until 1948, when the University of the West Indies was opened, this meant going abroad).

This structure, as explained by Figure 1, is however somewhat misleading. Those entering elementary schools with infant school education were very few for the Government did not see infant education as being its responsibility because of its cost.[101] In 1929/30 only 2,885 children between the ages of four and six were enrolled in the schools[102] and it was estimated in 1930 that an additional 73,000 places would be needed if the State were to take responsibility for infant education.[103] Likewise the probability of going on to post-elementary education was extremely limited. Secondary education was very costly[104] and there were only a limited number of scholarships – nine for those wishing to go to the School of Agriculture and fewer still for secondary schools.[105] In 1930 there were only three continuation schools and one technical school in the island which catered only for an infinitesimal fraction of the country's youth.

In the 1960s, as Figure 2 shows, this dualism continued. As a result of the Common Entrance Examinations of 1958 which introduced into education a system close to the eleven-plus 'headache' but more oppressive, the availability of scholarships and the policy in the early 1960s of giving 70 per cent of government scholarships to children from elementary schools, the structure of education became more integrated and children from a working-class background had limited opportunity to receive a secondary education. But there were still a number of different streams running alongside each other, making for a very complicated system.

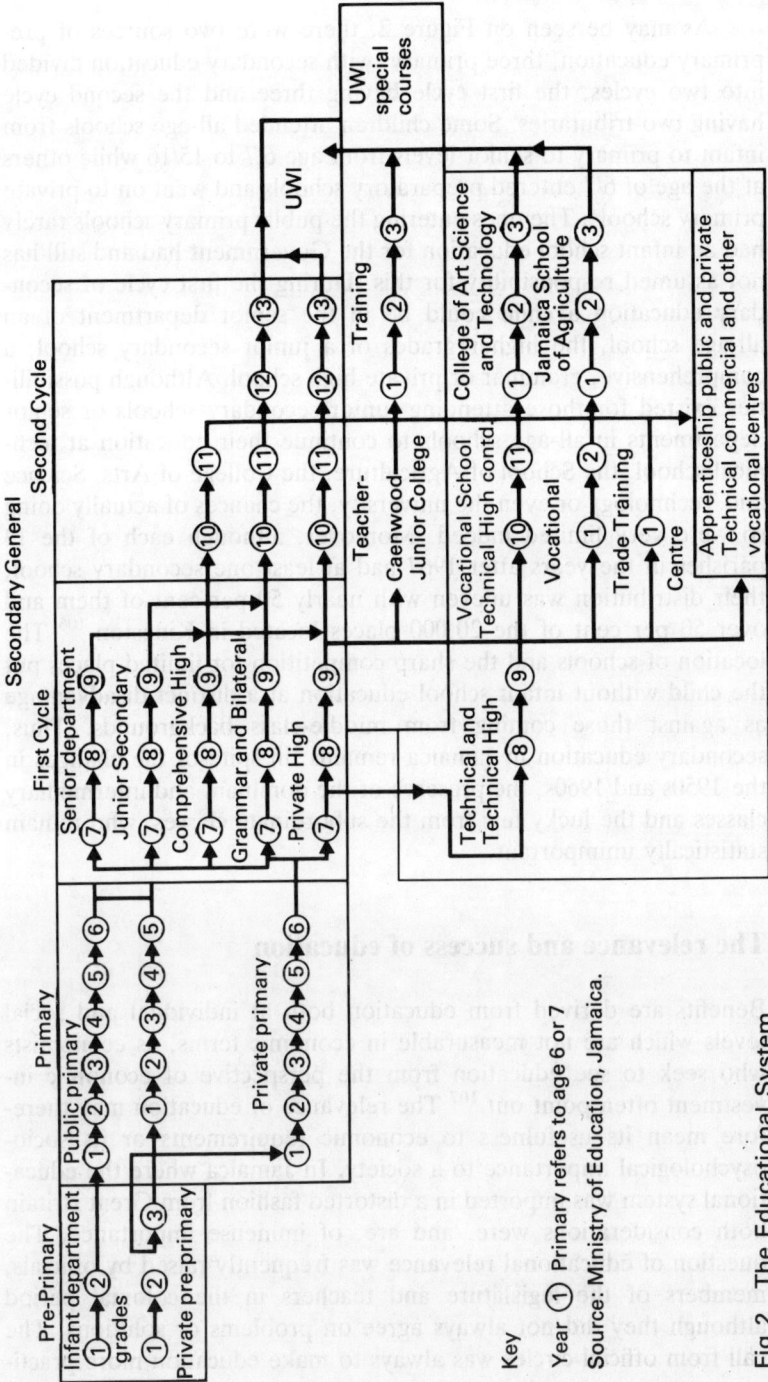

Key
Year ① Primary ① refers to age 6 or 7

Source: Ministry of Education, Jamaica.

Fig 2 The Educational System

As may be seen on Figure 2, there were two sources of pre-primary education, three primary, with secondary education divided into two cycles, the first cycle having three and the second cycle having two tributaries. Some children attended all-age schools from infant to primary to senior levels from age 6/7 to 15/16 while others at the age of 6/7 entered preparatory schools and went on to private primary schools. The ones entering the public primary schools rarely had an infant school education for the Government had and still has not assumed responsibility for this. During the first cycle of secondary education a child could be in the senior department of an all-age school, the higher grades of a junior secondary school, a comprehensive, grammar or private high school. Although possibilities existed for those attending junior secondary schools or senior departments in all-age schools to continue their education at technical school, the School of Agriculture, the College of Arts, Science and Technology or even the university, the chances of actually doing so were very limited indeed. Moreover, although each of the 14 parishes in the years after 1967 had at least one secondary school, their distribution was uneven with nearly 50 per cent of them and over 50 per cent of the 20,000 places located in Kingston.[106] The location of schools and the sharp competition for limited places put the child without infant school education at a distinct disadvantage as against those coming from middle-class backgrounds. Thus, secondary education in Jamaica remains, in spite of the changes in the 1950s and 1960s, the preserve of the dominant and intermediary classes and the lucky few from the subordinate classes, who remain statistically unimportant.

The relevance and success of education

Benefits are derived from education both at individual and social levels which are not measurable in economic terms, as economists who seek to see education from the perspective of economic investment often point out.[107] The relevance of education may therefore mean its usefulness to economic requirements or its socio-psychological importance to a society. In Jamaica where the educational system was imported in a distorted fashion from Great Britain both considerations were, and are, of immense importance. The question of educational relevance was frequently raised by officials, members of the legislature and teachers in the colonial period although they did not always agree on problems or solutions. The call from official circles was always to make education more practical and applicable to the needs of an agricultural country, particularly in the elementary schools since these were mainly in the rural areas.[108] Teachers on the other hand, and as we shall see, stressed the need to retain the existing school curriculum.[109]

Because secondary education was regarded as the chief means to a career in one of the professions or the civil service, officials often felt thwarted by the wishes of parents to have the traditional subjects taught in secondary schools.[110] In 1941, S. A. Hammond (who had been Director of Education in 1929-30), the Education Advisor to the Colonial Development and Welfare in the West Indies, stressed in a memorandum to the Financial Comptroller the irrelevance of secondary education.[111] He suggested that the whole educational system should be integrated to meet the educational needs of the country.[112] He then warned that

it is no service to a boy or girl or to their country, to lead them into that unhappy class of persons who think that the world owes them something which they cannot get.[113]

Confusion arose in the minds of the young because for them education, occupation and status had become intertwined.[114] Although it was generally understood that secondary schools prepared pupils for the civil service and the professions, Hammond was very sceptical of the contribution these schools made to the real development of the country and was therefore reluctant to recommend that any CD & W funds be allocated to them. He observed:

There is welcome evidence from the progressive elements of their staffs and authorities, and other persons interested, of dissatisfaction with the part they fill in Jamaican education, which should be resolved before the lines of development are determined upon which aid can be given.[115]

Despite these statements, education in Jamaica has been a relative success, within the limits in which it was operating. In the 1890s the expected pupil/teacher ratio was 30:1 pupil-teacher and 80:1 headmaster or assistant teacher;[116] in the 1930s this ratio was still continuing.[117] Although it was official policy in 1966 that by 1970 the average should be at 40:1,[118] in the 1970s the national average remained at 50:1; in Kingston and St. Andrew the averages were lower but in the rural parish of St. Mary it rose to as high as 80:1.[119] Many teachers were recruited after passing the Jamaica School Certificate (roughly equivalent to the CSE in Britain); in 1930, of the 1,650 elementary schoolteachers in employment 679 were untrained.[120]

Accommodation has also always been far below the requirements of the school-age population, especially after the amalgamation and closing of many schools in 1899 in response to the
recommendations of the Lumb Commission.[121] In 1929/30 there
were 107,970 places in elementary schools and 128,154 pupils on the
rolls,[122] although only about one-half of the estimated school-age
population had registered. Absenteeism has always been very high –
of those registered in 1929/30 only 54.92 per cent actually attended
on a fairly regular basis[123] – because of poverty, customs and bad
road conditions in the countryside.[124]

Even so the literacy rate in Jamaica has shown a steady increase
from 1871 when only 16 per cent of those over five years of age
could read and write;[125] the literacy rate was 52.5 per cent in 1891
and rose to 60.9 per cent in 1921.[126] The 1960 census estimated that
about 85 per cent of the population was literate,[127] but this has been
questioned on the basis that the enumerators did not assess the
extent of functional literacy which would have revealed a lower
literacy rate.[128] It is worth noting that the rate of literacy in the
Metropolitan Area of Kingston and St. Andrew has always been
higher than in the rural areas and that literacy is more widespread
among women than men.[129]

Education and politics

Education has been, at least since 1892, one of the main social
services in Jamaica which has been seen as providing a means of
upward social mobility. In both the colonial and independence
periods education was planned and executed in a situation of poverty which implied serious limitations. Accordingly, the allocation of
finances for education has been of vital concern to the community,
thus making it a sharp political issue.

Education is also important for another reason. It transmits
social and political values and in official circles it was viewed,
especially in the colonial period, as a means of solving social problems. For example, on this last point, the Commission on Housing
of the Poorer Classes of the Community, reporting in 1926, was
convinced of this. The Report stated:

> There was a general agreement of opinion that the most
> hopeful prospect of improving the health, morals and in-
> dustrial efficiency of the poorer labouring classes lay in the
> betterments of their homes, and in a well organized system

of practical instruction, especially in the country schools, in the subjects of Sanitation and Hygiene and the arousing in the minds of the children a love of health and decent home life, and a higher sense of self-respect and civic duty.[130]

Although there is no hard evidence to suggest that educational planning in Jamaica ever seriously took into account the high unemployment rate,[131] in 1932 the Director of Education warned that the 'continued existence of large masses of entirely uneducated children in a country like Jamaica is a serious menace'.[132]

Since independence education has been seen as being of potential importance for the socio-economic development of the country. Every national plan in the 1950s and 1960s stressed education as a national priority and as crucial for development. For instance, the statement from the PNP's 1957 Ten-Year Plan for Jamaica was echoed in all future 'plans' of whichever party in office:

Unless the attempt is made to train Jamaicans at all levels, economic development may be bogged down by lack of skilled personnel. A minimum of literacy and basic knowledge is essential if there is to be easy communication between officials and farmers, between producers and their customers and if science is to be applied to the land or to industry even in a small way.[133]

As early as the 1880s this point was well understood, especially by progressive governors and enlightened directors of education. Public expenditure on education has never been adequate in face of the need but it has long been one of the main areas of government spending. In 1895/6 for example, whereas the State spent £58,842 on medical services, £55,458 on the constabulary and £65,841 on public works, elementary education received £65,270 from the State besides what the churches spent and what the State also spent on the Industrial School and the Board of Supervision.[134] Only in the years immediately before the First World War did the largest Department, the Public Works, get substantially more than the Education Department. For example, in 1912-13 the Public Works Department (which has various functions) received over £280,153, and the Education Department received £91,367, but this was still a great deal more than most departments received.[135]

During the decolonizing and independence periods, for which more comparative details are available, public expenditure on education continued to be high but not as high as the boasts of politicians suggested, as Table 2.10 shows. Between 1952/3 and

Table 2.10 Public expenditure on education in relation to total public expenditure and Gross National Product

	Public expenditure on education (J$million)			Public expenditure on education as percentage of total public expenditure	Public expenditure on education as percentage of Gross National Product
	Recurrent expenditure	Development expenditure	Total		
1952/53	3.10	0.26	3.36	11.9	1.6
1953/54	3.48	0.34	3.82	12.7	1.7
1954/55	3.86	0.16	4.02	11.7	1.6
1955/56	4.76	0.32	5.08	13.6	1.8
1956/57	5.26	0.64	5.90	12.9	1.8
1957/58	5.78	1.08	6.86	12.8	1.8
1958/59	8.20	0.88	9.08	14.6	1.3
1959/60	9.08	2.08	11.16	15.1	2.6
1960/61	9.88	1.98	11.86	15.9	2.6
1961/62	11.04	1.82	12.86	15.2	2.6
1962/63	12.44	1.78	14.22	15.4	2.8
1963/64	12.70	1.76	14.46	14.6	2.7
1964/65	14.82	1.72	16.54	14.2	2.8
1965/66	16.02	1.86	17.88	14.0	2.8
1966/67	17.44	2.10	19.54	14.2	2.9
1967/68	20.48	3.34	23.82	15.3	2.3
1968/69	23.10	6.80	29.90	15.5	2.8

Source: Owen Jefferson, *the Post-War Economic Development of Jamaica* (1971) p. 267.

1968/9 public expenditure on education increased from 1.6 per cent of the Gross National Product and to 2.8 per cent at independence in 1962/3 but it fell back to 2.7 per cent the following year; only in 1966/7 did it increase to as much as 2.9 per cent of the GNP. Even this was far from achieving the 5 per cent of the GNP on education that many nations at the beginning of the 1960s had hoped to allocate to education by 1980.[136] Whereas Panama, for example, allocated 3.3 per cent of her GNP to education in 1960 and Costa Rica 3.95 per cent, Jamaica only allocated 2.6 per cent in 1959/60 to education.[137]

Expectedly most of the expenditure on education was recurrent, as the second column of Table 2.10 shows, increasing from J$3.10 million in 1952/3 to J$23.10 million in 1968/9 (J$2 = £1). Expenditure on actual development for these years were no more than J$0.26 million and J$6.80 million which was the largest amount to have been spent on development in any one year for the whole period. Throughout these years, the percentage of public expenditure allocated to education remained between 11.9 per cent in 1952/3 and 15.9 per cent in 1960/1.

There has been general agreement from all sides on the importance of education and disputes have been mainly concerned with priorities within a context of scarcity. In the colonial period the areas of dispute included, among others, the school curriculum, the role of churches in education, the position of teachers and the greater involvement of the State in education. Some of these remained contentious after independence but from 1962/3 the debate shifted to such matters as whether the State should place emphasis on primary or secondary education, the extent to which the JLP government should use education as a means of implementing a broad social policy and how the shortage of school places should be resolved.

In short, the situation of scarcity which imposed limitations on educational facilities for a population which has long regarded education as a socio-economic necessity and a right provided a background for disagreements over technical, professional and often political issues which affected education and therefore the behaviour of teachers.

Notes

1 W. Arthur Lewis, 'Foreword' to Gisela Eisner, *Jamaica 1830-1930: A study in economic growth* (Manchester University Press, 1961), p. xvi.

2 Roy Augier's The Consequences of Morant Bay, *New World Quarterly*, vol. 11, no. 2 (1966), remains an important exception.

3 The neglect by historians of the aftermaths of Morant Bay is fortunately not true with respect to the events of October 1865 themselves. See, for example, B. Semmel, *The Governor Eyre controversy* (London: Mcgibbon & Kee, 1962); D. Hall, *Free Jamaica 1836-1865: An economic history* (Yale University Press, 1959), and Don Robotham, 'The notorious riot: The socio-economic and political bases of Paul Bogle's Revolt', *ISER Working Paper no. 28* (Kingston: ISER, 1981).

4 Owen Jefferson, *The post-war economic development of Jamaica* (Kingston: ISER, 1972).

5 See, for example, Hall, *op. cit.*; also, P. D. Curtin, *Two Jamaicas: The role of ideas in a tropical colony* (Harvard University Press, 1955); and, W. G. Sewell, *The ordeal of free labour in the West Indies* (New York: Harper Brothers, 1861).

6 Eisner, *op. cit.*, p. 238.

7 Jefferson, *op. cit.* p. 92; also, K. Post, *Arise ye starvellings* (The Hague: Martinus Nijhiff, 1978), p. 30.

8 Closures in the post-1945 period did not, however, affect production, see, Jefferson, *op. cit.*, p. 94, footnote 34.

9 See, G. Beckford, The West Indian Banana Industry, *Studies in regional economic integration*, vol. 2, no. 3 (Kingston: ISER, 1967).

10 See, Post's excellent discussion of the importance of sugar and banana production in the reconstitution of a new dominant social class in late nineteenth century Jamaica, Post, *op cit.*, p. 35ff.

11 Jefferson, *op. cit.*, p. 93.

12 Post, *op. cit.*, pp. 37-8; much of the information in this part of the discussion is taken from Post's pioneering work.

13 *Ibid.*, p. 88.

14 *Ibid.*, p. 38.

15 N. Girvan, *Foreign capital and economic underdevelopment in Jamaica* (Kingston: ISER, 1971), p. 15.

16 Eisner, *op. cit.*, p. 173.

17 *Ibid.*, p. 174.

18 *Ibid.*

19 Jefferson, *op. cit.* p. 131.

20 *Ibid.*, p. 126.

21 Eisner, *op. cit.*, p. 323.

22 *Ibid.*, Table LXV, p. 332.

23 See, S. Reid, 'An introductory approach to the concentration of power in the Jamaica corporate economy and notes on its origins', in C. Stone and A. Brown (eds.) *Essays on power and change in Jamaica* (Kington: Jamaica Publishing House, 1977).

24 Girvan, *op. cit.*, p. 44.

25 W. Marshall, Notes on peasant development in the West Indies since 1838, *SES*, vol. 17, no. 3 (1968), p. 253.

26 *Ibid.*

27 Jefferson, *op. cit.*, p. 81.

28 For a discussion of unemployment and employment see, Jefferson, *op. cit.*, ch. 2, from which figures in this section are taken; see also, C. G. Clarke, *Jamaica in maps* (London University Press, 1974), ch. 15.

29 See, T. Lacey, *Violence and Politics in Jamaica 1960-70* (Manchester University Press, 1977), chs. 1-3.

30 C. Stone, *Class, state and democracy in Jamaica* (Kingston: Blackett Publishers 1985), p. 40.

31 For a discussion of this point see, W. Arthur Lewis, *Growth and fluctuations 1870-1913* (London: Allen & Unwin, 1978), p. 209.

32 A. E. Burt, The first instalment of representative government in Jamaica, 1884, *SES*, vol. ii, no. iii, (1962) p. 241ff. The original intention was to have about 15,000 on the voters list but only about 8,500 eventually qualified because of the mistakes of the Franchise Commission.

33 See, Munroe, *op. cit.*, pp. 11-16; E. F. L. Wood, *Report on a visit to the West Indies and British Guiana*, Cond. 1879, (London: HMSO, 1922); (hereafter referred to as the Wood Report).

34 Sir David Barbour, *Report on the finances of Jamaica*, (Kingston: Government Printing Office, 1899), p. 4.

35 *Wood Report*, p. 13.

36 *Ibid.*: although up to the time Wood made his report these powers had not actually been used, after 1922 they were exercised; see, J. Carnegie, *Some aspects of Jamaica's politics, 1918-38*, (Kingston: Institute of Jamaica, 1973), pp. 40, 47, 71.

37 *Wood Report*, p. 13.

38 *Ibid.* Wood noted that the sitting of the Legislative Council rose from between 12-16 days per year before the War to 70 days by 1920 and in 1921 to over 100 days because of the insistence of the elected members on using the Council to debate matters to the full. This resulted in the holding up of government business.

39 Jamaica: *Correspondence and dispatches* C.O. 137, no. 786, File 56085, (1928), Letter no. 195 dated 25 April 1928.

40 Munroe, *op. cit.*, pp. 16-18; also Carnegie, *op. cit.*, ch. iv.

41 *Ibid.*, p. 40.

42 *Wood Report*, pp. 6-7.

43 *Report of the Commission appointed to enquire into the disturbances which occurred in Jamaica between 23 May and the 8 June, 1938*, Kingston: Government Printer, 1938; (hereafter referred to as the Disturbances Commission).

44 K. W. J. Post, The politics of protest in Jamaica, 1938: Some problems of analysis and conceptualisation, *SES*, vol. xviii, no. iv (1969), p. 375. See, also, his *Arise ye starvellings*.

45 *Report of the Disturbances Commission*, 1938.

46 *W.I.R.C. 1938-9* C.O. 950, no. 152 J. 206; also G. St. J. Orde-Browne, *Labour conditions in the West Indies* (London: HMSO, 1939); 'Report of the Commission appointed to enquire into unemployment in Jamaica, 1936', (Kingston: Government Printer, 1937), Appendix XLI.; also Eric Williams, *History of the people of Trinidad and Tobago* (Port of Spain: Guardian Commercial Printery, n.d., but presumably 1950), ch. xv; Selwyn D. Ryan, *Race and nationalism in Trinidad and Tobago: A study of decolonization in a multi-racial society* (University of Toronto Press, 1972), ch. 3.

47 O. W. Phelps, The rise of the Labour Movement in Jamaica, *SES*, vol. ix no. iv (1960), p. 41ff., also Post, *op. cit.* The high incidence of

unemployment in the 1930s also affected elementary schoolteachers although this was not raised as an issue during the years 1928-32; in 1929-30 there were five Registered Assistant Teachers who had passed the Third Year Pupil Teachers' Examination who were unemployed, See, 'Education Department Report for the year ended 31 December, 1930', *The Annual General Report of Jamaica together with the Departmental Reports for 1930* (Kingston: Government Printer, 1931), p. 275; also 'Board of Education, Report for the year ended 31 December, 1934', *The Annual General Report of Jamaica together with the Departmental Reports for 1934*, (Kingston: Government Printer, 1935), p. 106.

48   See for example, Rex Nettleford (ed.), *Manley and the New Jamaica, selected speeches and writings, 1938-68*, with Notes and Introduction, (London: Longman Caribbean, 1971), p. xxviii-lxi; C. Paul Bradley, Mass parties in Jamaica: structure and organization, *SES*, vol. ix, no. 4, (1960) pp. 375-416; P. Robertson, Party 'organization' in Jamaica, *SES*, vol. xxi, no. 1 (1972), pp. 30-43; for a critical appraisal of the organization of parties in Jamaica.

49   Munroe, *op. cit.*, pp. 21-2 (quoting the PNP's 'Public Opinion').

50   Nettleford, *op. cit.*, p. 14; also T. Munroe, 'The People's National Party, 1938-44: A view of the early Nationalist Movement in Jamaica' (unpublished M.Sc. thesis, Department of Government, UWI, Mona, 1966) ch. 1.

51   Nettleford, *op. cit.*, p. xxix.

52   J. Harrod, *Trade Union foreign policy: A study of British and American Trade Union activities in Jamaica* (London: Macmillan, 1972), p. 180.

53   Carl Stone's various books, arising out of his continuous study of voter behaviour in Jamaica, have been a major contribution to the understanding of Anglophone Caribbean politics, but by far his most insightful and well argued text is *Democracy and clientellism in Jamaica* (New Brunswick: Transaction Books, 1983).

54   T. Munroe, *The Politics of constitutional decolonization* (Kingston: ISER, Mona, 1972), ch. II, pp. 36-74.

55   *Ibid.*, pp. 37-44; also G. Lewis, *The growth of the modern West Indies*, (London: Mcgibbon & Kee, 1968), pp. 182-3.

56   Nettleford, *op. cit.*, pp. lii-lxi; also, Richard Hart, *Forward to Freedom*, (Kingston: People's Educational Organization, 1952).

57   G. Eaton, Trade Union Development in Jamaica, *Caribbean Quarterly* (1963); vol. viii, no. 1, 1962, pp. 43-53 and, vol. viii, no. II, p. 69ff; (1963); also Harrod, *op. cit.*, ch. vi.

58   *Ibid.*; also, Eaton, *op. cit.*

59   Harrod, *op. cit.*, ch. vi.

60   Munroe, *The politics of constitutional decolonization*, pp. 41-5, 85 and 163-66, for discussions of electoral returns.

61   Phelps, *op. cit.*

62   *Ibid.*; also M. Manley, *A voice at the workplace*, (London: Andre Deutsch, 1975).

63   For a useful discussion see, R. Gonzales, 'The Trade Union Movement in Jamaica', in Stone and Brown, *op. cit.*

64   *Ibid.*, pp. 68-9.

65   *Ibid.*, p. 149 (quoting from 'Jamaica Constitution for Independence: basic questions').

66 M. G. Smith, *The plural society in the British West Indies* (University of California Press, 1965), especially chapters iv and viii.

67 *Ibid.*, p. 75.

68 For a discussion see, for example, D. J. Crowley, Plural and differential acculturation in Trinidad, *American Anthropologist*, vol. lix, (1957) pp. 817-24; L. A. Despres, The Development of Cultural Theory, *American Anthropologist*, vol. lxvi, (1964) pp. 1051-1077; Ivar Oxall, Race, pluralism and nationalism in the British Caribbean, *Journal of Boisoc, Sci.*, Supl. I (1969), p. 152.

69 R. T. Smith, *British Guiana,* (Oxford University Press, 1962).

70 L. Braithwaite, Social stratification in Trinidad: a preliminary analysis, *SES*, vol. ii, no. ii, (1953), pp. 5-175.

71 See, G. K. Lewis, *op. cit.*, ch. iii; D. Lowenthal, *West Indian societies,* (Oxford University Press, 1972).

72 See, for example, for the discussion around these and related issues Rex Nettleford, *Mirror, mirror: identity, race and protest in Jamaica* (Kingston: Collins & Sangster (Jamaica) Ltd., 1971); Walter Rodney, *The groundings with my brothers,* (London: Bogle-L'Ouverture, 1970); M. G. Smith, Roy Augier and Rex Nettleford, *The Rastafari Movement in Kingston, Jamaica* (Kingston: ISER, 1960); E. Braithwaite, Review of Sociology of Slavery, by O. Patterson, *Race*, vol. ix, no. iii., (1968); G. E. Simpson, Jamaican revivalist cults, *SES*, vol. v, no. iv, (1956) pp. 321ff.

73 See for example, J. Blake, *Family structure in Jamaica* (New York: Free Press of Glencoe, 1961); F. Henriques, *Family and colour in Jamaica* (London: Mcgibban & Kee, 1968); M. G. Smith, *West Indian family structure* (University of Washington Press, 1962), ch. v, and E. Clarke, *My mother who fathered me: A study of the family in three selected communities in Jamaica* (London: Allen & Unwin, 1966).

74 M. Witter, Race and class in Jamaica, *Department of Government, UWI (Mona) Seminar Series* (1981) discusses this point in a very creative manner.

75 T. Capper, 'The system of education in Jamaica', *Educational systems in the chief colonies of the British Empire*, E. M. Sadler (ed.) (Great Britain, Board of Education Special Reports on Educational Subjects, vol. iv, Cd. 416, HMSO, 1901) p. 576; also, J. J. Figueroa, *Education, society and progress in the Caribbean* (Oxford: Pergamon Press, 1972).

76 Roy D'Oyley, The Development of teacher education in Jamaica: 1835-1913, *Ontario Journal of Educational Research*, vol. 6, no. 1, (Autumn 1963) p. 43.

77 Capper, *op. cit.*

78 *W.I.R.C. 1938-9* C.C. 950, no. 204, J. 266, p. 1.

79 'Report on the proceedings of the Board of Education for the year ended 31 March 1895', *The Governor's Report on the Blue Book and Departmental Reports for 1894/5* (Kingston: Government Printing Office, 1896), p. 338-41: also 'The Hon. Legislative Council', *The Daily Gleaner*, 9 March 1892.

80 'Education Department, Report for the year ended 31 March 1899' *Departmental Reports for 1898/9* (Kingston: Government Printing Office, 1900), pp. 376-79; also, *Report of the Commission appointed to enquire into the educational system in Jamaica, 1898,* [hereafter, The

Lumb Commission] (Kingston: Government Printing Office, 1895), pp. 8-9.

81 See, *W.I.R.C. 1938-9*, C.O. 950, no. 102, J. 138, also no. 98, J. 134.
82 *Ibid.*, no. 117, J. 154.
83 'Education Department, Report for the year ended 31 December 1930', *The Annual General Report of Jamaica together with Departmental Reports for 1930* (1931), pp. 248-9.
84 *New Deal for Education in Independent Jamaica* (Kingston: Ministry of Education, Paper no. 73, 1966), p. 27.
85 *Ibid.*, pp. 1/18 Table xix; loans came from both the USA/AID and from Canada.
86 H. A. Lutchman, 'Administrative change in an ex-colonial setting: A study of education administration in Guiana, 1961-4' in G. E. Mills (ed.), *Problems of administrative change in the Commonwealth Caribbean* (Kingston: ISER, Mona, 1974), pp. 27-56.
87 *The Handbook of Jamaica for 1895* (Kingston: Government Printing Office, 1895), p. 311.
88 *W.I.R.C. 1938-9*, C.O. 950, no. 117, J. 154.
89 The Elementary Education Law, 1892, *Jamaica Laws, certified copies of Acts, 1889-93*, C.O. 139, no. 106.
90 Education Department, Report for the year ended 31 December 1932, *The Annual General Report of Jamaica together with Departmental Reports for 1932* (Kingston: Government Printing Office, 1934), p. 290); also *W.I.R.C. 1938-9*, C.O. 950, no. 117, J. 154, Oral Evidence, p. 15ff.
91 *Report of the Committee appointed to enquire into the system of secondary education in Jamaica, 1943* (Kingston: Government Printing Office, 1943).
92 *Ibid.*, p. 3.
93 *Ibid.*; G. P. W. Musgrave, *Society and education in England since 1800*, (London: Methuen & Co Ltd, 1968), chs. 1-3.
94 See, *Annual Report of the Ministry of Education year ended 31 December 1958*, (Kingston: Government Printing Office, 1961), p. 5.
95 *Ibid.*, pp. 5-7.
96 *The Education Act*, 1965 (Kingston: The Government Printer, n.d.).
97 *The Code of Regulations, 1966* (Kingston: The Government Printer, n.d. but presumably 1966 or 1967), p. 2, Art. 5.
98 *Ibid.*
99 Figueroa, *op. cit.*, ch. 1; Shirley C. Gordon, *A century of West Indian education: a source book* (London: Longmans, 1963), p. 6.
100 'The Secondary Education Law, 1892' *Jamaica Laws, certified copies of Acts, 1889-93*, C.O. 139.
101 *The Lumb Commission*, pp. 5-6.
102 'Education Department Report for 1930', *op. cit.* p. 247.
103 *Ibid.*, p. 243.
104 *W.I.R.C. 1938-9*, C.O. 950, no. 117, J. 154, Oral Evidence, p. 32.
105 'Education Department Report for 1930', *op. cit.*, p. 240.
106 Clarke, *op. cit.*, p. 34.
107 For discussions on the role of education in economic development, see, for example, J. Vaizey, *The economics of education* (London: Faber &

Faber, 1962) chapter x; W. Arthur Lewis, Education and economic development, *International Social Science Journal*, vol. xiv (1962), pp. 685-99; also T. W. Schutz, *The economic value of education* (Columbia University Press, 1967), particularly chapter iii, and for a discussion of education and political development, see J. S. Coleman (ed.) *Education and political development* (Princeton University Press, 1965), particularly, Introduction by Coleman; also S. M. Lipset, 'Some social requisites of democracy: economic development and political legitimacy', *APSR*, vol. liii. (1959), pp. 69-105.

108 For example, of the 655 elementary schools in the country in 1929-30 only 29 were located in Kingston, see, 'Education Department Report for 1930', *op. cit.*, p. 258.

109 *W.I.R.C. 1938-9* C.O. 950, no. 82, J. 117.

110 'Report of the Jamaica Schools Commission for the year ended 31 March 1899', *Departmental Reports for 1898-9* (Kingston: Government Printing Office, 1900); see, also, *Annual Report of the Ministry of Education, 1958* (Kingston: Government Printer, 1959), p. 4.

111 S. A. Hammond, 'Memorandum' to F. A. Stockdale, Comptroller of the CD & W in the West Indies, see, Stockdale, *Report on Development and Welfare in the West Indies, 1943-4*, Colonial no. 189 (London: HMSO, 1945), p. 116.

112 *Ibid.*

113 *Ibid.*

114 *Ibid.*; for a more thorough discussion of the social worth of education in Jamaica see, N. Foner, *Status and power in rural Jamaica: a study of educational and political change*, (London: Routledge & Kegan Paul 1973); M. G. Smith, *The plural society*, chapter viii, 'Community organization in rural Jamaica' and chapter ix, 'Education and occupational choice in rural Jamaica'; Edward P. G. Seaga, 'Parent-teacher relationships in a Jamaican village, *SES*, vol. iv, no. iii (1955), pp. 289-302.

115 Hammond, *op. cit.*, p. 114.

116 *The Lumb Commission*, p. 16.

117 *W.I.R.C. 1938-9*, C.O. 950, no. 82, J. 117, pp. 5-7.

118 *A New Deal for Education*, p. 24.

119 C. Clarke, *op. cit.*, p. 34.

120 'Education Department Report for 1930', *op. cit.*, p. 275.

121 *The Lumb Commission*, pp. 8-9.

122 'Education Department Report for 1930', *op. cit.*, p. 253.

123 *Ibid.*

124 Cf., C. Clarke, *op. cit.* pp. 50-90. It was customary that children stayed away from schools on Fridays to help on the land, and in areas of high banana production children would also be absent on Mondays; see, Seaga, *op. cit.*, p. 299. When it rained heavily, children were often unable to attend school because of lack of proper roads.

125 C. Clarke, *op. cit.*, p. 36.

126 Eisner, *op. cit.*, p. 333, Table lxvii.

127 C. Clarke, *op. cit.* p. 36.

128 UNESCO, *Educational Planning Mission, Jamaica September-November, 1964*, (UNESCO: Paris, January 1965), Appendix F. p. 27; also, C. N. Bolland, 'Literacy in a rural area of Jamaica', *SES*, vol. xx, no. i

(1971), particularly p. 28.

129   C. Clarke, *op. cit.*, p. 36.

130   *Report of the Commission appointed to enquire into the housing condi-*
tions of the poorer classes of the community, 1926 (Kingston: Circulars
of the Office of the Colonial Secretary, No. 11 of 1926).

131   Perhaps an exception to this was the decision in 1973 to extend the
school-leaving age from 15 to 16.

132   'Education Department Report for the year ended 31 December 1932',
*The Annual General Report of Jamaica together with the Departmental
Reports for 1932*, (Kingston: Government Printing Office, 1934), p.
290.

133   *A national plan for Jamaica, 1957-67*, (Kingston: Government Printer,
1957), p. 4; see, also, *Five year independence plan, 1963-8: a long term
development programme for Jamaica* (Central Planning Unit, Ministry
of Development and Welfare, n.d., but presumably 1963), ch. xvii, p.
157ff.

134   Cf. *The Governor's Report on the Blue Book and Departmental Reports
for 1895/6* (Kingston: Government Printing Office, 1897).

135   'Education Department Report for the Year Ended 31 March 1913',
Departmental Reports for 1912-13, (Kingston: Government Printing
Office, 1914), p. 427ff.

136   *UNESCO, Educational Planning Mission*, Appendix F, Table xii.

137   *Ibid.*

CHAPTER 3

The development of a corporate spirit among teachers

On 14 December 1963, the various teachers' organizations in Jamaica took an important decision to dissolve themselves in favour of one large association to represent all teachers in elementary and secondary schools, technical institutions and teacher-training colleges.[1] The result was that in April 1964, the Jamaica Teachers' Association was formally launched.[2]

The five associations which dissolved themselves included the Jamaica Union of Teachers (JUT), representing elementary schoolteachers; the Association of Assistant Masters and Mistresses (AAMM, sometimes referred to as A2M2); the Joint Association of Headmasters and Headmistresses (H2M2) which was composed of heads of secondary schools; the Association of Teachers in Technical Institutions (ATTI); and the Association of Teacher-Training Staffs (ATTS). Even with full memberships the ATTI, ATTS and the H2M2 were fairly small but relatively influential groups, with memberships of perhaps less than fifty.[3] In 1963 the A2M2 had just under 500 members[4] out of possibly 1,500 assistant teachers in secondary schools.[5] These associations were formed in the later 1930s and early 1940s,[6] and, mainly because of the process of decolonization and the ensuing expansion of education they quickly gained access to the relevant government bodies in the 1950s.[7] The JUT was by far the oldest and largest of the five associations with over sixty years' experience and a membership of nearly 3,000 in 1963. The existence of so many groups representing a teaching force of just over 7,000[8] indicates the division and fragmentation of the teaching community at the time. Unification in 1963/64 was therefore a tremendous achievement, overcoming much of the social prejudice and distance between elementary and secondary schoolteachers.

Perhaps, however, the more important stage in the development of the corporate spirit of teachers in Jamaica was the formation of the JUT as early as 1894. The significance of this step is partly that it took place within the formally authoritarian crown colony political system. The aim of this chapter, therefore, is to examine the two most important and interesting stages in the development of a corporate sense among Jamaican teachers in our period between 1880 and 1972 – the formations of the JUT and the JTA.

The formation of the JUT

The JUT was formally founded on 30 March 1894, with the expressed aims of uniting

> together by means of local associations, school teachers throughout the island, in order to provide a machinery by which teachers may give expression to their opinions when occasion requires, and may take action in any matter affecting their interests.[9]

It was stated that the new union would seek to 'afford' the Board of Education and the Department of Education the 'collective expreience' of teachers; it would watch over the working of the education laws (the 1892 Elementary Law and its subsequent amendments) and the Code of Regulations. The Union would, it was hoped, in time establish providential, benevolent and annuity funds for the 'scholastic profession'. It would attempt 'to secure the adequate representation of the interest of the teaching profession in the Legislative Council and on the Board of Education'.[10] It would also work to improve education generally. In short, the new union would seek to represent both what may be loosely called the professional and the more general trade union interests of teachers.

The Union was the answer to the felt needs of the more aware in the teaching occupation and the result of their own efforts. Although there were a number of Educational (sometimes referred to as Teachers') Associations, upon which the new organization hoped partly to build, the trade union and wider professional interests of teachers were not being coherently articulated. These associations started in 1882 with the encouragement of Col. George Hicks, an American who settled in Jamaica after the Civil War as an Inspector of Schools.[11] The main aims of these associations were to

> promote the efficiency of the schools and advance the interests of teachers by holding stated meetings for essays and discussions upon educational topics, by circulating among members educational periodicals and the most approved works on the art of teaching, etc., and by other suitable means.[12]

The *Gleaner* reports reveal that in 1892 the Kingston Association raised issues of more than purely educational importance, but this was unusual. The associations were only concerned with educational matters such as discussing teaching methods, and they did not involve themselves with issues of a trade union nature. They were dominated by churchmen – of the fifteen listed in the *Handbook of Jamaica for 1894* only one had a lay president. But undoubtedly these associations contributed to the founding of the JUT. They brought teachers together in centres throughout the country at regular intervals to discuss common problems. It is also interesting to note that all the elementary schoolteachers closely involved in the founding of the Union had had some experience in their local associations.[13]

A vigorous debate in the country on education between the Report of the Education Commission of 1886 and the passing of the Elementary and Secondary Education Laws of 1892 made many teachers aware of their weakness as a group. The Commission[14] had recommended that the State should subsidize teachers' housing and institute a scheme of superannuation; the State should also assume full financial responsibility for elementary education and make attendance at school compulsory. An education tax, it was recommended, should be collected to pay for these reforms. The Commissioners also wanted to see the Government establish a central Board of Education with local ones to assist in the supervision of education.[15]

These recommendations and the apparently successful Jamaica Exhibition encouraged by the progressive Governor, Sir Henry Blake, in 1891, were largely responsible for the lively debate on education in these years.[16] For many the Exhibition demonstrated the advantages which could be gained from agricultural and technical training. It was generally argued that the country would need technical and agricultural education if it were to progress,[17] and in the great debate over educational reform there was a demand to have these subjects included in the curriculum for elementary schools alongside the traditional Three Rs. By 1892 the agitation for reform had come to centre around the issues of free education (to be made possible by abolishing the fee-system and levying, for the first time, a tax specifically for education); compulsory attendance at schools; the establishment of a central Board of Education as well as boards of education in the fourteen parishes of the island; and the introduction of agricultural and technical instructions in the school curriculum. After 1891 the tax issue became particularly important when the Government made it clear that it was not prepared to pay for the reforms out of general revenue. Probably the Governor hoped thereby to gain the support of the elected members of the legislature who, true to form, were likely to oppose any new taxation.[18]

Matters of particular interest to teachers were gradually left out of the debate and the 1892 Elementary Education Law reflected this neglect. The position of the teacher, vis-a-vis his immediate employer, the school manager, remained unchanged and the teacher could expect little protection in his work. His salary continued to be dependent on his 'results' achieved at the end of the year when the inspector examined his school, and he remained without the prospect of a pension. Further, although some teachers complained that free education without compulsion would result in a fall in attendance and thus affect their salaries, the provisions for compulsory attendance were postponed.[19] On the other hand the law strengthened the position of the churches in the education system in so far as it fully institutionalized the old system whereby the State paid for education while the churches continued to own and control the schools. A central Board of Education was established and came under the strong and direct influence of the different denominations represented on it.[20] In short, the Law marked a clear victory for the churches at a time when they found it increasingly difficult to maintain, financially, the many schools that they owned.

But the churches had to fight for this victory. The Government's initial response was to let the recommendations of the Commission lapse. In 1891, when the demand for the State to take action on the recommendations was mounting, the Privy Council advised Governor Blake in no uncertain terms, as the minutes of a meeting in January of that year recorded:

1   That there was no necessity for legislation on the subject (of education).
2   That school fees should not be given up.
3   That there was no need for the central and local boards proposed.
4   That the maximum limit of age for children in Government-aided schools should be thirteen (13) with proviso that in certain cases to be determined the age should be extended for children who proposed to go on to secondary schools.
5   That it is (sic) not desirable to offer pensions to teachers.
6   That an annual grant from general revenue should be

made to pay for the fees of pauper children.
7 That the education code should be so amended as to
provide for the alterations recommended.[21]

Far from taking up the proposals for reform of the education system, the Privy Councillors advocated economic stringency. The only 'concession' they were prepared to make was to propose that the Government should make a grant available for pauper children. Although the Governor did not have to comply with the advice of the Council, it was not always wise for him to oppose the unanimous feelings of its members, particularly on this issue which at this time was a matter mainly of interest in the colony and hardly of any concern in Whitehall.[22] In April 1891, a Bill on education failed to pass the legislature and the Government was ready to drop the matter.

By February 1892, however, Blake was prepared to support a new Bill which the superintending inspector of schools, Thomas Capper, introduced.[23] On its second reading Blake, as president of the Legislative Council, took what he claimed was then an unusual step of interrupting the proceedings to explain the feeling of the Privy Council on the question. The Council, he was reported as saying,

> had adopted the bare principle that, without going into the question of the appointment of teachers, or interfering with their appointments, we simply have undertaken to assist whoever establishes a school and produces for government inspection certain results – these results we are prepared to pay for.[24]

Steadily his position on the issue had changed. Even during the course of the debate, on the second reading of the Bill, Blake's attitude underwent rapid change. He promised that if the elected members of the legislature could show him what 'the people' wanted in the Bill which was being called for, then he would be willing to see its successful passage. To ascertain public support a Select Committee was set up composed of both official and elected members with the latter in the majority. Reporting on 30 March, the Committee recommended that the State should assume financial responsibility for elementary education and to pay for this a special tax (the 'education tax' which would add £12,000 to the revenue) should be levied; a central Board of Education should also be set up, but not the proposed local ones. Attendance at schools was to be made compulsory but since the Committee disagreed strongly on the issue it was proposed that the provisions for this should not be implemented immediately.[25] The Bill was quickly passed after its third reading on 8 April.

It was the efforts of the churches to see the educational system reformed which influenced the Government and eventually forced Blake to give way on some of the more important recommendations of the 1886 Commission. In 1891-2 the churches made representations repeatedly to the Governor on the issue. Blake admitted to the emergency session of the legislature (called to consider the efforts of the McKinley Tariff on Jamaican Sugar in the US market), that:

> The question of education has been under my considera-
> tion, and I have had the advantage of having the views of
> an influential body of gentlemen interested in the
> subject.[26]

The Bill itself, it seems was 'an emasculated edition of a bill printed for private circulation some time ago, by parties interested in education',[27] according to one member of the legislature. Most of the meetings organized around the issue were called by churchmen who made up, no doubt, the 'influential body of gentlemen' who saw Blake and formed the 'parties interested in education'. Certainly, it was churchmen who also sent petitions to the Legislative Council on the matter.[28] Even the 1886 Commission was dominated by these men of the cloth, although it was chaired by the Colonial Secretary. It was not surprising therefore that the denominations should benefit handsomely from the 1892 Law. Yet it was a compromise: the Government was forced to go further than it had originally intended and the reformers accepted less than the 1886 recommendations.

Although individual teachers were involved in the agitation for reform, as a group with common interests they did not stand out. During the second reading of the Bill when Blake spoke, he attacked the teachers as being 'incompetent'. Of the 850 head teachers in the country receiving government grants-in-aid only 115, the superintending inspector of schools reported, were of the 'first grade' (there were then five grades of teachers) but the Privy Council and the Governor understood this to mean that the teachers as a whole were 'incompetent', and advanced this as their reason for refusing to levy an education tax.[29] Soon after this at a meeting at Rock River in the Parish of Clarendon, a number of teachers expressed their bitterness over the attack.[30] Many individual teachers also sent letters to the *Daily Gleaner* about the allegation and the general education question. One schoolteacher wrote to the paper in March, not merely protesting against the Governor's remarks but calling on all teachers to unite so as 'to ventilate our opinions on the educational questions of the day. If we do not speak now then it may be justly said of us that we are a body of incompetent men.'[31]

He urged teachers to take to 'pen' and 'paper' and to follow the example of teachers in England and Wales whose voices were now being listened to because they were well organized. 'In plain language', he bluntly stated, 'Mr Capper (the superintending inspector of schools and the official responsible for the Bill) is not at all in sympathy with the Jamaican schoolmaster'[32] for there was nothing in the Bill for teachers. It was soon after this that Major Plant, a prominent member of the Kingston Teachers' Association and later a president of the JUT, advertised in the *Daily Gleaner* for teachers to send their views to the Kingston association so that they could be coherently expressed to the authorities.

There was a growing awareness that elementary schoolteachers needed an organization through which they could make their views clearly heard. Whereas in the 1880s they had seen the need to form themselves into educational associations to discuss common classroom problems and had therefore responded favourably to Col. Hicks' circular, in the 1890s the public debate on elementary education and the passing of the 1892 Law brought home to many of them the glaring need for an association which would embrace both the professional and trade union concerns of teachers. The victory of the churches and the news of the activities of the NUT suggested the necessity of unity and organization as means to influence Government and to protect themselves.

Two elementary schoolteachers played particularly important parts in the formation of the JUT – J. A. Mason and W. F. Bailey. In his *History of the Jamaica Union of Teachers*, published in 1937, 'on the authority of the Executive of the Union',[33] Bailey argued that the formation of the Union was the result mainly of his own efforts. He claimed that knowledge of the activities of the NUT came to him through his many discussions with Rev. William Gillies, one of the two co-Principals of the Mico Training College. It was Gillies too, Bailey claimed, who impressed on him the necessity of a union of teachers in Jamaica. At a meeting of the North Manchester Teachers' Association Bailey mentioned that it would be desirable to do something about the formation of an island-wide association and he issued a general invitation to those teachers present to meet at his home to discuss the matter. Ten teachers accepted the invitation and seven of them sat down 'with grim determination to see this thing through'.[34]

In Bailey's words there was no 'hesitation in unanimously agreeing that the time had come for action and that this small group might do a great deal to rouse the attention of all Jamaica'; a circular was drafted, printed and sent out to 100 teachers and students 'calling for a Teachers' Convention at Spanish Town on Friday, March 30th, 1894'.[35] Since Mason was the senior member of this small gathering he was made secretary and when the new Union was inaugurated in Spanish Town he became its first General-Secretary. Bailey claimed that it ws he too, with the help of Rev. Gillies, who secured copies of the NUT's constitution and fashioned the JUT's on it. In later days this account was usually accepted as the full story of the founding of the JUT.[36]

But there is another story which described J. A. Mason as the prime mover in the formation of the Union. At the 1895 Annual Conference (the first JUT Annual Conference) at which a great deal was said about the founding of the Union, Mason was portrayed as the founder.[37] J. J. Mills, the veteran JUT member and four times president, writing in the 1960s (admittedly late in the day but no less valid for that) told the following story:

> When I joined the Jamaica Union of Teachers in 1909, shortly after I had started teaching, I was told that the real founder was Mr J. A. Mason a teacher in North Manchester. Much later on the Union officially honoured him as founder at a function at the Mico College.[38]

Addressing the JUT Annual Conference in 1903, the leading black radical of the period and a precursor of Marcus Garvey, Dr Robert Love, who had worked on the behalf of teachers,[39] strengthened this claim when he stated in his usual unabashed fashion that,

> If it is true that Mr Mason was the one who first conceived the idea of organizing the Jamaica Union of Teachers, and first attempted to give it material effect (and until now it has never been denied and therefore must be taken as true) then (sic) I am for something in the constitution of this union. I think I am safe in saying that I was the first person whom Mr Mason consulted with regard to the carrying out of his idea. He came to my room, on East Street, nearly every afternoon for a fortnight – opened his plans to me and we discussed the possibilities and methods. I did all that I could to to help him to think it out, and I impressed upon him that the chief aim ought to be about the estab-

lishment of the teaching profession in Jamaica as a department of the Civil Service. It was I who counselled him to
confer immediately with the late William Morrison, Esq.,
and to obtain his aid.[40]

Mills wrote also that there were claims that the founder was Col.
Hicks, who was by 1894 the senior chief inspector of schools in the
Education Department. This can be safely dismissed, however, for
there is no evidence to support this claim. It is possible that there
was a confusion between the encouragement given by Hicks in the
1880s to the formation of Educational Associations and the actual
founding of the JUT.

There seems little doubt that Mason played the more important
role in the founding of the Union, but, clearly, Bailey was also
closely involved. What is of even greater importance is that the
Union was the result of the efforts of the teachers themselves, unlike
the Jamaica Agricultural Society (JAS) which was founded in 1895
as a governmental response to a popular demand for state assistance
to medium and small sized farmers.[41]

This is not to deny that individual churchmen, and to a lesser
degree, state officials, had some influence on the Union in its
infancy. Certainly there was a close association between teachers
and clergymen such as Archdeacon Simms (a prominent member of
the Board of Education), Rev. W. Gillies, Rev. James Balfour (who
later became president of the Union) and of course, Col. Hicks.[42]
The strong moral tone teachers' leaders were to adopt in arguing
their briefs showed the distinct influence of the church. But even if
teachers were required to pay a price for close association with these
men, their Union gained immensely from the relationship. The JUT
was quickly accepted as a respectable and legitimate group cham-
pioning the cause of education and the interest of its members and it
gained limited and intermittent access to decision-makers through
such individual contacts.

The State welcomed the formation of the Union. It was reported at the 1895 Annual Conference that Mason, on informing the
Governor of the intention to found a union, received a letter
couched in 'encouraging terms'[43] from Blake. From all accounts
Thomas Capper, the superintending inspector of schools and head
of the Education Department, also welcomed the founding of the
Union. Another important speaker at the 1903 Conference was the
Colonial Secretary, the Fabian socialist Sydney (later Lord) Olivier
and, from the report, his address was very revealing not only about
the 'exhortatory' aspect of colonial politics, but also the official

attitude towards the Union. He posed the rhetorical question whether the Government recognized the JUT and continued:

> Any government associated with the promotion of elementary and technical education could not but welcome and recognize such an organization as this one, founded upon the model of those valuable and efficient organizations that they had in Great Britain. No system of elementary public education could be carried on satisfactorily without some such co-operative body of the teachers engaged in it. He (Olivier) was glad that there was in Jamaica such an organization with which the administrative officers of the government could meet and, to a certain extent, confer.[44]

He particularly wanted to see the JUT assist the Government in its drive to get the peasantry to work the land more efficiently and sell its products in the world and local markets. The report of his speech continued on this point:

> There was a great deal of misunderstanding ... many people regarding any activity of the government and official bodies as part of a scheme for getting money out of them in the way of taxes. The efforts of the Instructors (of the JAS) had been greatly frustrated on account of this attitude on the part of the people. *That was a feeling that must be dispelled and (sic) no body was more able to dispel it than the Union of Teachers.*[45] (Emphasis added.)

The JUT, it was hoped, would be useful to the Government as a body whose members worked among the peasantry. These encouraging words notwithstanding, it is important to remember that the JUT was the result of the initiative of elementary schoolteachers themselves.

In their efforts they were helped not only by churchmen and government officials, but also by more prestigious teachers in training colleges. Col. L. G. Gruchy, the other co-principal of the Mico Training College, gave full support to the Union and was elected to the post of president in its first three years and for a fourth later on. Another Mico man, Robert Lindsay, was the first treasurer of the Union.[46] These men were not involved in the earliest initiatives to found the Union but they were quick to give support and thus played the important role of helping to give the JUT respectability, legitimacy and a momentum.

The social position of elementary schoolteachers

Elementary schoolteachers were especially suited to being organized at this point in the development of Jamaican society and in particular the educational system in the country. In a socially and economically backward society like Jamaica, where education formed practically the only social service, it was inevitable that teachers would be a fairly pronounced group by virtue of their work. Elementary schoolteaching became one of the main – if not the main – means of upward social mobility for ambitious sons of the peasantry who saw no prospect of a satisfying future on the land and who had no way of attending secondary school which held out the possibility of going to university or into the civil service. Teachers were recruited at different levels – as pupil-teachers at the age of around 14 or 15 years, or after passing the pupil-teachers' examinations, instituted by Capper, or in their late 'teens or after attending a teachers' training college. Most entered as pupil-teachers and later progressed to taking the pupil-teachers' examinations and sometimes even going on to college. As a pupil-teacher an individual received a small grant from the Government and as a student at a college his fees were paid by the Government, with the understanding that on graduating he would teach for a minimum number of years.[47]

The system of payment-by-results made it possible for some teachers to make a decent living and a few of the more ambitious could progress into one or other of the denominations as ministers. The close links between church and school provided some means of 'promotion' for the more able. Writing in 1897, Thomas Capper saw the process thus:

> The fact that many teachers are also catechists or lay preachers undoubtedly tends to attract a higher class of men into the teaching profession, both from the addition they thus obtain to their salaries and from the hope of promotion to the Ministry of the different churches, which is in many cases recruited from the best of the teachers, whilst the religious bodies of course benefit greatly by having a living income secured to their catechists independent of anything they might get from church funds.[48]

In the 1890s elementary schoolteaching was still a male-dominated preserve, a situation which the officials of the Education Department and the Lumb Commission wished to change. Although this is suggestive of a deliberate attempt to keep salaries down,

Table 3.1   Numbers in professional employment

		1844	1861	1871	1881	1891	1911	1921
1	Doctors/Dentists	N.S.	87	84	89	107	182	197
2	Lawyers	N.S.	60	44	37	80	113	93
3	Clergy	267	278	255	261	329	344	327
4	Public servants	N.S.	624	1,203	1,481	1,501	2,241	2,521
5	Teachers	640	448	871	1,270	1,733	2,207	2,178
6	Others+	1,127	992	1,911	1,520	3,229	4,124	6,107
	Total	2,034	2,489	4,368	4,658	6,979	9,211	11,423

+Includes mainly military and naval staff in early years but in later years includes also engineers, dispensers, journalists and stenographers.
Source: Adapted from Eisner, *op. cit.*, Table XXII, p. 166.

release men for agricultural work, or even prevent teachers' militancy, the more immediate consideration seems to have been to improve the moral standing of the community and teachers themselves and to encourage the teaching of domestic subjects.[49] Since elementary schoolteaching was a main source of employment for socially ambitious men, it was not surprising that there should be some teachers who wanted to see the members of the occupation organized to defend their interests.

Moreover, elementary schoolteachers formed the largest single occupational group of those categorized as 'professionals' in the country. In 1891, as Table 3.1 shows, there were only 107 doctors and dentists in the island, 80 lawyers, 1,501 public servants (these included the constabulary, prison wardens, etc.) and 329 clergymen, whereas there were 1,733 teachers and 3,229 in the general category 'others'.[50] These figures require some qualification: for example, it seems unlikely that there were only 329 clergymen in a community as religious as Jamaica and having many religious sects.[51] It is highly probable that this number represents only clergymen of the 'respectable' denominations such as the Anglican, Methodist and Baptist churches.

The figures for teachers also call for caution, because it is not clear whether they included teachers in secondary as well as those in elementary schools. But even if these figures were inclusive, by far the largest proportion were elementary schoolteachers. In 1892/3 there were 912 elementary schools receiving government grants and in 1894/5 these had climbed to 962.[52] Each of these had a head-teacher and most had assistants or pupil-teachers, so that nearly all, if not all, of the 1,733 teachers in 1891 might be expected to have been elementary schoolteachers.

This development compares favourably with similar groups. For example, Eisner noted that the numbers of doctors and lawyers, after emancipation in 1838, 'declined sharply' in the island and that those of 'professional' workers rose from 1.9 per cent in 1881 to 2.5 per cent in 1891 and 3.3 per cent in 1921 and this was due to 'the spectacular growth in the numbers of teachers and civil servants'.[53] These were elementary schoolteachers, for the elementary sector was the only sector of education which expanded significantly in the early 1890s as a result of widespread demands from all quarters and the favourable state response.

Furthermore, this growth in the number of elementary school-teachers in the 1890s coincided with their coming more directly under government control. Indeed, the passing of the Elementary Education Law of 1892 marked the peak in this development during the colonial period. After the reforms under Sir Peter Grant and Mr Savage in 1867, teachers steadily came under the regulation of government because of the system of payment-by-results. In order to supplement the fees they received from parents, teachers had to satisfy the inspector at the end of the year when he examined their schools and the children who attended and upon which the Government's grants-in-aid depended. Under the 1892 Law the Government would pay the teacher his salary and no more fees were to be collected from parents. This brought the teacher even more directly into the clutches of the inspector upon whose findings the teachers' salaries now totally depended.

With the establishment of the Board of Education which was responsible for the allocation of the educational vote and resolving disputes between teachers and managers, and teachers and inspectors, elementary schoolteachers became more subjected than before to central control. The new and revised Code of Regulations of 1893 established exact rules regarding the 'proper' relationship between the teacher and the pupil, the Education Department and the manager. Although the teacher's relation with the Department was left ambiguous, with the churches retaining the rights of employment and dismissal and the Board being responsible for the implementation of the Codes, his contact with government officials was more frequent and definite. One consequence of this development was that grievances could now be addressed to a specific and authoritative body on such matters as terms of employment and salaries, thus promoting and facilitating an awareness amongst teachers of their particularistic interests.

In summary, therefore, it is of crucial importance in considering the general context of the emergence and development of teachers' corporate spirit at the turn of the century, to be reminded of the general texture and contours of social life at that time. First, the generation that was active in these years was removed from the harsh and inhumane realities of slavery. Men and women in active life would most likely have been born to a free life but sufficiently close to the memories of a suppressed and inhumane past to have treasured the freedom won by immediate forebears.

Moreover, the Victorian age was, as G. M. Young reminded us, an era abounding in confidence and optimism, and this spirit of the age before the Great War of 1914-18 had a positive influence even in far away Jamaica upon that body of men and women most likely to have been exposed to the ideas of the times. Thus, it may be argued, when the defeat of the Italians by black Ethiopians on the fields at Adowa, the rise of non-white Japan and her later defeat of Tzarist Russia (a white European power), the Cuban war for independence against Spain in which the majority of soldiers were black, and the abolition of slavery in the USA, Cuba and Brazil were all still fresh in the living memories of this generation of West Indians, the world must have appeared open to all and any possibilities. The period from the 1890s to the beginning of the present century was to see the conscious assertion of the Jamaican worker and the beginning of the groupings towards the forging of trade unions which were made illegal by the State. The efforts of elementary schoolteachers must be seen in this wider, general, context of social and intellectual developments.

Second, the men and women of this period were the inheritors of a long period of comparatively rising prosperity. In Europe and North America Count Bismarck's wars and unification of Germany and the Civil War, respectively, resulted in a long, if armed, peace which stimulated travel everywhere as trade expanded. In Jamaica the country moved from being a declining sugar economy to a fairly diversified one, as noted in chapter two. These developments were accompanied, as Eisner shows, by a rising GDP and an increase in per capita income. The quality of life had greatly improved after the 1850s and incomes were more equitably distributed although more was still being spent on food than on luxuries, indicating the existence of a fairly basic social formation, but one made up of freemen and therefore far removed from the painful and grossly inhumane conditions of slavery.

The formation of the JTA

The stated aims and objectives of the JTA were similar to those of the JUT in many ways but broader in scope. Apart from the expected trade union functions the Association intended to 'aid in maintaining high ethical and professional standards among all teachers';[54] it would strive to 'maintain the unity of the teaching profession, integrate its members, widen the scope of their usefulness and safeguard their interests'.[55] The JTA would seek to 'promote the educational interests of the country and keep the public informed concerning educational matters of urgency and importance'; it would 'establish friendly relationships with other teachers' organizations throughout the world and represent Jamaican teachers on these bodies'; the Association would 'receive, hold, and administer property in the interest of the teachers of the island'.[56]

It may be noted that both the JUT and the JTA came about as responses to government activity in the education system, although in very different ways. One important difference was that whereas elementary schoolteachers were not involved in an open confrontation with the colonial government when the JUT was formed, the JTA was born in a situation of conflict between teachers and the first government of independent Jamaica, that of Sir Alexander Bustamante from 1962.

The Education Bill and the Joint Executive of Teachers' Associations

On 27 April 1961, an Education Bill was introduced in the House of Representatives by the PNP Minister of Education, Mr Florizel Glasspole.[57] But taken up with such weighty matters as the negotiations for independence, the referendum in that year on the continuing membership of Jamaica in the Federation of the West Indies, followed by a general election in 1962 (both of which the PNP lost to the JLP) the Bill was, not surprisingly, pushed into the background. The new government, however, was quick to take it up. Speaking at the JUT's Annual Conference in April 1963,[58] the new Minister, Mr Edwin Allen, announced his agreement with the contents of the Bill and intimated that he would attempt to see it pass through the House. It was intended to be a comprehensive measure regulating the whole system of education, from elementary schools to teacher-training colleges. Under the direct control of the Ministry of Education in Kingston would come the regulation of schools at all levels in the system and teachers at all levels would be affected. The coming of political independence made it necessary to attempt to put an end to the dual system of administration between church and state and clarify the powers of the Minister.

The initial response of nearly all teachers to the Bill was encouraging.[59] Their associations saw the need for a ministerial and integrated system of education and the Bill was envisaged as the first step towards these ends.[60] Leaders also saw the need to present a united front with a common viewpoint on the Bill and for this purpose the various associations' executives came together to form the Joint Executive of Teachers' Associations (JETA) in 1961. The initial aim of the JETA therefore was to co-ordinate the views of the various bodies on the specific issue of the Bill and to present them in a coherent form to the Government. But this was, whether teachers realized it or not, the first important formal step towards the unification of the associations.

This event reflected the quality and vision of the leaders of the associations at this time. Many individual teachers, as might be expected, were closely associated with this development and the subsequent formation of the JTA. The more prominent of these included Edith Dalton-James. This remarkable woman was the only woman and the only assistant teacher to have become a president of the JUT, a post she held on five occasions and in 1963/4 she was also to become president of the Caribbean Union of Teachers (CUT). Then there was Ben Hawthorne, the last Secretary-General of the JUT and the first of the JTA. Eric Frater and J. Barrow (both past presidents of the Association of Assistant Masters and Mistresses) and C. C. MacArthur Ireland were all prominent in the new development. Wesley Powell, a former president of the Association of Headmasters and Headmistresses also played a significant role in the formation and development of both the JETA and the JTA, as chairman and first president, respectively.

In 1962, Dalton-James, Hawthorne and Powell represented the teachers of Jamaica at the WCOTP Conference in Rio de Janeiro and they returned to the island bent on the unification of all teachers, for they saw quite clearly the potential of a united teachers' organization and the implications of this for education policy in Jamaica.[61] Teachers had of course worked closely together in the past on the Education Authority and they were coming to see some of their problems, such as salaries, through common lenses.[62] The pious hope that one day there would be a single teachers' organization was of course longstanding among JUT leaders. The JETA marked the first formal step towards it. But it was a response to government's activity, not the result of the premeditations (even if these were aired before) of leaders.

From its beginnings the JETA had reservations about certain clauses in the Bill but only after the new Minister had taken it up did leaders express their reservations most vehemently. They were particularly worried about the concentration of power in the hands of the Minister and feared the prospects of the Minister having a stranglehold on the local education boards and over the appointment of teachers. Yet it was not the representations on the Bill which gave flesh to the skeletal JETA and brought about the JTA. By early 1963 teachers were sufficiently suspicious of the general behaviour of the JLP Minister, the ebullient Mr Edwin Allen, to be alarmed at the use he could make of the powers the Bill was proposing to concentrate in his hands.

The Byfield Case

In 1958 Mr A. G. R. Byfield, a prominent member of the PNP, was nominated by the PNP Government as one of Jamaica's two representatives at the Headquarters of the Federation of the West Indies in Trinidad, but when Jamaica voted to withdraw from the federation in 1961 Byfield returned to Jamaica without a job.[63] Before going to Port of Spain, the federal capital, Byfield had been, from all accounts, a successful headmaster of Trench Town Elementary School and when in November 1962 the Kingston school board advertised for a headmaster for the new Trench Town Senior School, he applied.[64] Although he was appointed by the board, by the beginning of the school year in January 1963 Byfield had still not received the usual confirmation from the Ministry of Education. In the ensuing court action, Byfield v the Minister of Education, it was alleged that the Minister had acted unconstitutionally by taking into account political considerations when he refused to give his formal approval of the appointment of Mr Byfield.[65]

This case was later seen by the leaders of the JTA as the single most important development in the formation of the Association. It seemed to them at the time that it was really the teachers versus the Minister of Education, Mr Edwin Allen. Although Byfield lost even his final appeal to the Supreme Court by a 2:1 verdict, the teachers continued to believe that there was 'political victimization' while Mr Allen remained convinced that they had 'no feet to stand on'.[66] There were similar cases to Byfield's in the first years of political independence but they were never taken up so spectacularly, because none involved such an important public figure as Byfield and their cases were less straightforward than his.

The concern here is not with the legal aspect of the case, but with the perception teachers had of it and the responses it stimulated in them as an occupational group. Without going into a long and intricate story, suffice it therefore to say that the political content of the case emerged particularly strongly after a deputation from the Kingston school board went to see Mr Allen on 11 January 1963, about the appointment, because rumour had it that Byfield was not wanted in the area by the JLP 'political men'. These 'men' were also, it seems, acting on an earlier rumour that Byfield, who appeared to have great influence over the parents in the vicinity, would be the PNP's candidate in the constituency in any forthcoming election. The deputation failed to get satisfaction from the Minister and eventually the members of the board resigned in protest. The Minister was reported as saying that his decision not to confirm Byfield's appointment was based on the belief that he had wanted to be placed in Trench Town so that he could carry out work for the PNP in that constituency which was controlled by the JLP.

Mr Allen defended his case mainly on educational grounds.[67] He maintained that the post demanded a man with more teaching qualifications than Byfield possessed (Byfield had failed to take his third year examinations at college) and someone who sympathized, and was willing to experiment with the new system of comprehensive education. In reply to criticism from the PNP Opposition Mr Allen argued that since the Trench Town Senior School was new he was entitled as his PNP predecessor, Mr F. Glasspole, had been to confirm or veto an appointment. This claim resulted in recriminations between Mr Allen and Mr Glasspole in the *Daily Gleaner*.[68] Although Mr Allen hotly denied that he told the deputation that he was withholding approval on political grounds and he was upheld by the courts as acting within his powers, the affair had important political overtones. In later years Mr Allen was not to deny that he knew that Byfield wanted to participate in politics in the community and it was in view of this that the Ministry offered him other posts (which were in more salubrious surroundings than Trench Town and some of which were more lucrative than the headship of Trench Town Senior School), but he refused them. This refusal seemed to confirm suspicions about Byfield's motives. On the other hand, the Minister, from Byfield's point of view, would go to any length to keep him from Trench Town.[69] In this situation the Minister and the would-be headmaster, who were both suspicious of each other's political motives, refused to compromise.

The JETA and Byfield, encouraged by the support of the PNP Opposition,[70] decided that the case had better be resolved in the courts.[71] As leaders viewed the situation the post was being withheld because of party political considerations. Allen was under pressure, it was firmly believed, from members of his party in Trench Town and even in the cabinet, to keep Byfield from the area out of fear that he might make in-roads into a JLP constituency.[72] The Minister's action, the JETA held, was a breach of the independence constitution which stated that no individual should be discriminated against on the basis of his or her race, colour, creed or political views. Thus, the argument ran, a citizen's right to employment irrespective of political opinions was being violated by the Minister. Byfield's case, which before the end of 1963 was already becoming a *cause célèbre*, was fought by some of the country's most prominent lawyers who were also prominent PNP men. These included David Coore, Q.C., later PNP Minister of Finance, Vivien Blake, Q.C., who had fought Michael Manley for the leadership of the PNP in 1969, and Eric Bell, later PNP Minister in Manley the Younger's second Ministry.[73]

Although Byfield lost the case, teachers as a whole benefited tremendously from the publicity and the unity the situation demanded of them. Whereas before Byfield the JETA was merely a body of teachers' leaders meeting sporadically around a specific issue, afterwards it met regularly, organized a defence fund, arranged meetings, wrote letters and generally provided information for teachers and the public on the issue. The case was presented as one in which the whole teaching community was involved in a conflict over essential principles with a Minister who was putting his party before the interests of education. In the campaign the JETA was able to rally a considerable number of teachers from all sectors of education around an issue which seemed to affect them all. The case developed after January 1963 into a major issue of the day and pointed the way teachers had to take if they were to be in a position to face the growing authority of government and a Minister seemingly bent on exercising his authority. Yet, it was something still more immediate to teachers' experience which forced the situation to the successful birth of the JTA.

The question of salaries and negotiations

The question of salary increases in the 1960s was nearly always a heated issue between teachers and the Labour Government.

Teachers had received salary increases in 1957 from the PNP Government but even that had come after the demands of civil servants had been satisfied.[74] Before the PNP left office in 1962, the associations had made representations for increases and when the matter was taken up with the new Government it was lukewarm and this angered teachers.[75] Moreover, whenever leaders met the Minister, they claimed that he spoke incessantly so that they had no chance actually to put their cases to him face to face. After one such occasion in 1963 the Minister reported that he and the teachers' leaders had met and they found that he and they had little over which to disagree – a remark which was to cause him great embarrassment later.[76]

The situation was complicated by the Government's doubts whether the JETA really represented the teachers and whether in fact it could negotiate on their behalf as its leaders claimed. When the Minister questioned the leaders' legitimacy he received the support of the Prime Minister, Sir Alexander Bustamante. The Government decided to break off negotiations with the JETA and both sides fought to gain the support of the public on the closely linked issues of a general salary increase for all teachers and the right of the JETA to represent the teachers.[77] The situation deteriorated in November 1963, when a letter from the Prime Minister in reply to an earlier one from the JETA, stated in the usual blunt Bustamantean terms the position of his government:

> If and when Government decides to increase wages and when the increase is settled by Government, your attention will be called to it, but I am not prepared to negotiate as to how much an increase should be given. We are the ones to decide which increase can be given to any section of employees that receive their salaries from public funds. An increase can only be given if and when a decision is made according to the financial position of the Government. Whatever increase we may decide on when the time may come, as far as I am concerned, that increase is final ...

> I am giving no guarantee that there will be any increase. If there is going to be an increase, it will be published sometime in January, 1964 ... In January a statement will be made regarding the review of salaries for certain sectors and until then you may write again but no more correspondence will serve any purpose.[78]

Earlier in a reply to another letter from the JETA, the Prime Minister wrote in a similar vein:

It must be a wonderful feeling to sit down and plan as to what increased wage Government should grant ... When the Government may decide to review the salaries of teachers, Government will decide what increases they will give and nothing will change us from that decision.[79]

The general tone of these letters reflected the cavalier, if not contemptuous, attitude of the Government towards the JETA. They reflected also an authoritarian perception of the general role of government which, if felt and acted upon, was never so clearly expressed by the colonial governors. Some teachers' leaders felt that this attitude towards them was too brusque and that the Prime Minister was insulting the whole teaching community. But this was only reflecting the Prime Minister's general attitude towards groups as a whole. When the lower grades of government workers threatened to strike in December 1963, Bustamante gave warning that his Government was prepared to take tough measures; as he boasted, characteristically – 'I am no dictator, but I am no weakling either.'[80]

The JETA felt that it had to demonstrate to the Government that the executive had considerable support from teachers. Two divergent tactics can be detected in the activities of the JETA, particularly between November and 14 December 1963. The 'moderates' wanted to explore the posssibilities of further negotiations with the Government whilst the 'militants' wanted to adopt the strike as a tactical weapon.[81] In a letter in November, the Secretary of the JETA, Mr G. W. Little, wrote:

> In our desire that this procedure be continued (i.e. negotiations between employer and employee) the Joint Executive of Teachers' Associations ... fully recognizes that in the final analysis it is Government which makes the decision according to the state of the nation's finances.[82]

The teachers were not claiming, as Bustamante thought, that they should dictate measures to the Government but that it should be prepared to listen to the representations of the JETA. The Labour Government was not treating the teachers as the previous PNP Government had in a fair manner when it came to negotiations between employer and employee. Little concluded with a suggestion:

> Finally, the association requests Government to set up, immediately, machinery to negotiate with JETA the re-

grading of the salaries of all teachers in accordance with
the mandate given by the teachers of Jamaica.[83]

Wesley Powell, who as chairman of the JETA was meeting
much of the attack from Bustamante, stated that on 'this issue of
salaries, the fundamental principle on which teachers are not prepared to yield is their right to negotiate'.[84] Clearly, the Government
was denying this right and he could only plead with them to recognize these rights.

Between 1 and 14 December, the dispute turned on whether
teachers would be led into a strike by the JETA. Wesley Powell, a
leading moderate, after his last attempts to negotiate had failed, was
forced to say: 'We will strike if the occasion demands it, having said
this let us keep cool heads.'[85] In this regard, a meeting at Excelsior
School, Kingston, on 14 December was a momentous one. Some
JTA members remember vividly how the meeting, attended by
nearly 3,000 teachers from the various schools and associations,
wanted to declare a strike immediately and how almost single-
handedly Powell turned the tide by calling for moderation. Instead
of authorizing a strike, the JETA/JTA was given a mandate to call a
three day strike throughout Jamaica if the Government did not
respond favourably to their demands in the near future.[86] By far the
most significant development at the meeting, however, was the
decision to dissolve the various associations and form the Jamaica
Teachers' Association to represent all teachers in the country.

The situation was soon defused although the demands were
not, as they rarely are, entirely met. The Government realized that
the JETA had considerable support from the teachers at all levels
and before the year had come to an end friendly overtures were
made to its leaders. The Government's attitude towards junior civil
servants and militant workers who, like the teachers, were demand-
ing increases in their salaries and wages, also underwent change.

This relaxation of Bustamante's tough policy must have come
about not only because of the JETA's agitation but also because of
the NWU and the PNP's opposition to his tough-minded approach
to resolving such issues.[87] The *Daily Gleaner* which had given general support to the Government was also prepared to criticize it for its
overbearing and negative attitude in disputes. On 4 December, the
editor criticized the Prime Minister's uncompromising policy thus:

it would appear that the Prime Minister is being vexatious
for the sheer hell of it. He cannot possibly mean that his
Government will not consult with teachers' organizations,
doctors, engineers, postmen, sewage workers, custom

guards, nurses or permanent secretaries, about their conditions of work, pay and the like. Therefore the Prime Minister's stentorian declarations that he will not negotiate are giving people the impression that he will not allow consultation.[88]

Towards the end of December the Government sent its 'plan' for proposed salary increases in the 1964/65 financial year to the JETA, the trade unions and the Civil Service Association for their consideration. Teachers' leaders responded amicably but called for the setting up of machinery whereby teachers' salaries and conditions of work would be under continuous review.[89] This was not to come about until after the strike of 1966 and the 10 per cent increase which teachers received was seen as falling far short of what was required. Nor were their leaders satisfied with the manner in which the increases were made because the increases were announced before first consulting them and they felt that the Government was attempting to undermine their authority as representatives. None the less, although the Labour Government was too rough and ready to appreciate the subtleties of a democratically-orientated group such as teachers, generally the offer served to defuse an explosive situation. The issues of salary increases and the setting up of permanent machinery to review teachers' conditions of service, became for a short while less important than the continuing Byfield Case, the Education Bill which was in Select Committee and the proposed Code of Regulations. Besides, it was necessary for the new Association to consolidate itself before showing that it was quite prepared to confront Government even by calling teachers out on strike.

Between 1961 and 1964, the political awareness of teachers in Jamaica developed significantly as a result of general changes in the political life of the country. The Government's negative attitude to teachers' leaders reinforced teachers' awareness of themselves as a distinct and important group. But it was the careful exploitation of the specific issues of the Education Bill, the Byfield Case and the negotiations over salaries which transformed the hardly more than *ad hoc* JETA into the JTA in 1963.

The JUT and the JTA

It is necessary to examine some of the issues, activities and fortunes of the JUT and the JTA before the question of how they existed in the colonial political structure and the immediate post-colonial period can be adequately answered. Before, however, embarking upon these aspects of the study it may be worthwhile to summarize the discussion of this chapter. For a number of reasons it is not at all surprising that the JUT was formed within the colonial political system. Teachers were a fairly educated and sizeable group in transition from the memories of a slavery past and groping towards the new age of modernity and some of them were very aware of their potential strength if organized. Teaching was the occupation opened to the ambitious sons of the lower *petite bourgeoisie* and elementary schoolteachers were needed by the colonial government, not only as teachers who transmitted a body of knowledge which rested on assumptions common to aspects of the ideology of empire, but also because of their close proximity to the producing peasantry. Thus they were useful as instruments of government policy in such vital areas as agriculture. The JUT was therefore a salutary development from the point of view of the State. Its usefulness was no doubt enhanced by the fact that the officials and teachers shared many common values. Of course the JUT was useful to the Government also for its guaranteed co-operation of the teaching community with Government on most of its policies and because the Union would provide information about the attitude of teachers towards official policy. None the less as teachers became increasingly subjected to the State's regulations they became more and more aware of themselves as a distinct group in the community with clear interests to protect. In these ways the contradictions of acceptance and rejection, resulting in the establishment of an area of active contestation, came to be recognized.

In the 1960s teachers in all sectors of education developed an even greater awareness of themselves as a group capable of solidarity and influence. They realized far sooner than the Labour Ministry that Government needed the co-operation of teachers' organizations if the educational system was to operate smoothly. It was to the credit of their leaders that they were quick to call what they saw as stern and brusque government into question by raising issues and organizing themselves so as not to be merely considered by the authorities but also to influence the course of education.

Of course, the two organizations were founded in different circumstances. The JTA was founded in a situation of open confrontation between the Government and teachers, unlike the JUT. Yet both were responses to the felt needs of teachers engendered largely by the activities of the Government in the educational system. In both periods teachers felt that existing organizations had become inadequate for their purposes and the requirements, on both occasions, were more of a trade union kind than professional.

The contemporary political systems profoundly influenced the groups' origins and developments. The JUT was greatly helped by the skills provided by the Mico men, Gillies, Gruchy and Lindsay, clergymen such as Gillies himself and Simms and even officials such as Hicks. Close associations with these influential men made access (although limited and intermittent), legitimacy and respectability relatively easy. Partly as a result of this and partly because the JUT was a body of schoolteachers, the Union at no time in its sixty-nine years' history became militant.

The JTA, on the other hand, adopted a militant posture from the very beginning because of the JLP Government's initial attitude towards it. This hostile attitude was partly governed by its fears or ignorance of the role of secondary groups in the political system and partly by the situation of political independence in 1962. In other words, like all party governments in Jamaica – whether PNP or JLP – the legitimate actions, demands, etc., of groups are interpreted entirely in terms of party political motives. The view that teachers could possibly have occupational and/or professional interests independently of the PNP Opposition, was beyond the comprehension of the Government. In this situation the overtones of militancy of the teachers were understandably interpreted by a relatively unpopular JLP Government to be an instigation.

In fairness, too, it should be said that there ought to be no surprise if indeed the PNP was, in Jamaican terms, 'trying a thing' by attempting to exploit the differences between teachers and the JLP. After all, the JLP came to power in 1962 in a hostile environment in which the police, the military, the civil service, urban workers and teachers, supported the PNP.

Notes

1 Dissolution of the Association of Assistant Masters and Mistresses, *AAMM Journal* Spring 1964, pp. 4-5; 'President's Message', *The New Clarion*, JTA Annual & Conference No., December 1964, p. 2; *The Minutes of the Joint Executive of Teachers' Associations*, February – December 1963, *passim*; 'Circular to Members, 2 March 1962', Joint Association of Headmasters and Headmistresses.

2 *The JTA souvenir programme* 1964; The story of the JTA, *The New Clarion*, WCOTP Special (1971), pp. 16, 17, 37.

3 For example, the largest of the five teacher-training colleges, the Mico, had only between 6 and 8 teachers during 1963; there were only 6 technical and 40 secondary schools in 1964. Cf. 'Interview with Dr Aubrey Phillips', 21 March 1954, Head of the Teaching Section of the

Education Department at the University of the West Indies (UWI) and former president of the ATTS and the JTA; also *Numbers and Types of Institutions, 1964-1970* (Kingston: Statistical Section, Ministry of Education, n.d. but presumably, 1970).

4   Cf. *AAMM Journal* Spring 1962, p. 4 and Spring 1963, p. 13.

5   Cf. *The Census of Jamaica, 1960*, vol. ii (Kingston: Department of Statistics, 1963-4), Part F. Section 2, pp. 522, 524.

6   For example, the H2M2 was founded in 1937: see, Glen Day, 'An assessment of the adequacy of teacher education in Jamaica in relation to educational needs, since 1938' (unpublished M. A. Thesis, UWI, 1972), p. 31; the Association of Training College Teachers was founded in 1946 but in 1959 this was changed to ATTS in a bid to get teachers at the UWI in the Institute of Education involved in the association, cf 'Interview with Dr A. Phillips'.

7   For example, each association had one representative, irrespective of size, on the Education Authority set up in 1953, see: *The Handbook of Jamaica for 1956* (Kingston: Government Printing Office, 1956), pp. 364-5.

8   See, Annual Report, Jamaica Teachers' Association, 1965, *The New Clarion*, December 1965, p. 6.

9   *The Handbook of Jamaica for 1895* (Kingston: Government Printing Office, 1885), p. 503.

10   *Ibid.*; W. F. Bailey, *The history of the Jamaica Union of Teachers* (Kingston: The Gleaner Co. Ltd., 1937), pp. 12-13.

11   See Vincent Roy D'Oyley, The development of teacher education in Jamaica, 1835-1913, *Ontario Journal of Educational Research*, vol. 6, no. 1, (Autumn 1963), p. 44.

12   *The Handbook of Jamaica for 1894* (Kingston: Government Printing Office, 1894), p. 501.

13   *Ibid.*; Bailey, *op. cit.*, chapters 2 and 3; see also the President of the JUT's address to the 1895 Conference, *The Daily Gleaner*, 20 May 1895.

14   For a very well informed and therefore useful discussion of the context of this Commission see S. C. Gordon, *A century of West Indian education* (London: Longmans, Green & Co. Ltd., 1963), viz. 5, 6, 7; also, Lord Olivier, *Jamaica: The Blessed Island* (London: Faber & Faber Ltd., 1936), ch. xviii.

15   *The Daily Gleaner*, 3 March 1892, p. 4; *The Colonial Standard and Jamaica Dispatch*, 12 January 1892, p. 2; see particularly, T. Capper, 'The System of Education in Jamaica', in M. E. Sadler (ed.), *Educational Systems in the Main Colonies of the British Empire*, Great Britain: Board of Education Special Reports on Educational Subjects, vol. iv, Cd 416 (London: HMSO, 1922), pp. 575-628.

16   Bailey, *op. cit.*, ch. 1; *The Daily Gleaner*, 5, 6, 9 February 1892. The Exhibition had its effects on teachers too, according to Bailey (pp. 2-5) and the *Handbook of Jamaica for 1895*. Two Americans, Dr Dickenson and Professor Boyden, were invited to give a series of lectures on elementary education and these proved immensely popular with the teachers who attended. At the close of the 'Teachers' Institute' (as the series of lectures came to be referred to) the view was expressed that it would be useful to have an island-wide teachers' organization. But it

seems that the desire was for an association which would organize similar lectures for teachers to be able to improve their classroom performance rather than one which would take up trade union and broader professional issues.

17 The *Daily Gleaner*, 5, 6, 9 February 1892.

18 There was considerable opposition to the tax, particularly after the Elementary Education Law became active, see, for example, *The Daily Gleaner*, April, May, July 1892, *passim.*, also *Minutes of the Legislative Council of Jamaica*, 1892-7 (Kingston: Government Printing Office), *passim.*

19 *The Daily Gleaner*, 18, 19 July 1892; 'Report of the proceedings of the Board of Education, for the year ended 31 March 1894', *The Blue Book and General Report of Jamaica 1893/94* (Kingston: Government Printing Office, 1895), the superintending inspector of schools wrote:

> The predictions of schoolmasters and other persons that the abolition of fees would result in the more irregular attendance of the children have been signally falsified and as has been pointed out, the reverse has been the result. (p. ix of the Report).

20 See, 'Report of the proceedings of the Board of Education, 1893/94', *op cit.*, p. 338; in 1892 only *The Colonial Standard and Jamaica Dispatch*, 17 June 1892, raised this as a point, but then only to ask why a certain Rev. Radcliffe had not been given a seat on the Board also.

21 *Jamaica, Minutes of the Privy Council, 1883-1893* C.O. 140, 22 January 1891.

22 It was not until 1898-9, when Joseph Chamberlain was Secretary of State for the Colonies, that Whitehall became concerned over education and this was only indirectly. Chamberlain's primary concern at this time was over the state of the Colony's finances and since education was one of the main areas of government expenditure it also came in for consideration. See, Sir David Barbour, *Report on the finances of Jamaica* (Kingston: Government Printing Office, 1899); also, *The Daily Gleaner*, 2 January 1900; also 'Education Department, Report for the year ended 31 March 1906', *Departmental Reports of Jamaica, 1906-7* (Kingston: Government Printing Office, 1907), for an account of how Whitehall attempted to restrict expenditure on education in the Colony to £60,000 per annum. This was successfully opposed by the Board of Education and the JUT.

23 *Jamaica, Minutes of the Privy Council 1883-1893*, C.O. 140, 22 February 1892, and *Minutes of the Legislative Council of Jamaica* (in Two Sessions) 5 November 1891, 4 August, and 16 February, 1892 (Kingston: Government Printing Office, 1892).

24 'The Hon. Legislative Council', *The Daily Gleaner*, 9 March 1892.

25 *Minutes of the Legislative Council*, 30 March 1892.

26 *Ibid.*, 5 November 1891.

27 'The Hon. Legislative Council', *The Daily Gleaner*, 9 March 1892.

28 *Minutes of the Legislative Council*, 5 and 10 March 1892.

29 'The Hon. Legislative Council', *The Daily Gleaner*, 9 March 1892.

30 *The Daily Gleaner*, 5 April 1892.

31 *The Daily Gleaner*, 23 March 1892, p. 3.

32   *Ibid.*

33   Bailey, *op. cit.*, title page.

34   *Ibid.*, p. 9.

35   *Ibid.*

36   See, for example, *Jamaica Union of Teachers 1894-1944, Celebrations* (Kingston: JTA, n.d. but presumably 1941); but particularly, J. C. Wolfe, 'History of the Jamaica Union of Teachers', *JTA souvenir programme*, 1964 (Kingston: JTA 1964) p. 28.

37   *The Daily Gleaner*, 20 May 1895.

38   R. N. Murray (ed.), *J. J. Mills: His own account of his life and times*, (Kingston: Collins & Sangster (Jamaica) Ltd., 1969), p. 60.

39   *The JUT Annual Report, 1903*, p. 25; I am also grateful to Mr Richard Hart for allowing me to see his 'Notes of the recollections of W. A. Domingo, of Dr Robert Love and S. A. (Sandy) Cox, made in the internment camp, 1942-43'.

40   *The JUT Annual Report, 1903*, (Kingston: JTA, 1903) pp. 25-6.

41   The popular demand was for the Government to do something to assist the small peasant farmer to improve his output; a good reason for comparing the JUT and the JAS in this way is that they are two of the oldest pressure groups in Jamaica and it is commonly believed that at the local level of the organization elementary schoolteachers provide considerable leadership. For an account of the origins of the JAS see *The Journal of the Jamaica Agricultural Society*, vol. i, no. i (January 1897), p. 2; also *Jamaica dispatches and correspondence 1894-1900, 1895*, C.O. 137, No. 560 Dispatch 234, Letter from Sir Henry Blake to the Secretary of State, dated 3 July 1895.

42   Bailey, *op. cit.*, pp. 15-16; after a long list of churchmen who became honorary members of the Union, Bailey wrote:

> The Education Department, while unable officially to sponsor the Union, recognized that here was something on which it could rest its lever if its plans to develop education were to meet with any measure of success.

Cf. also The *JUT Annual Report for the year closing with 30 November, 1897* (Kingston: JTA, 1897), p. 1; some of the more prominent honorary members of the Union included two members of the Legislative Council, Archbishop of the West Indies, Enos Nuttal and a number of headmasters of leading secondary schools and J. DeCorda the Managing Director of the Gleaner Company.

43   *The Daily Gleaner*, 20 May 1895. There was never any mention of the formation of the Union in the dispatches from Blake to the Secretary of State. Cf. *Jamaica, dispatches and correspondence 1893-1900*, C.O. 137, nos. 554-614.

44   *The Annual Report of the JUT 1903*, p. 22.

45   *Ibid.*

46   *The Daily Gleaner*, 20 May 1895; also Bailey, *op. cit.*, p. 11.

47   See, for example, *The Handbook of Jamaica for 1895*, p. 306 and also *Report of the Commission appointed to enquire into the system of education in Jamaica, 1898* (Kingston: Government Printing Office, 1898), pp. 12ff (hereafter referred to as The Lumb (chairman) Commission.)

48 T. Capper, *op. cit.*, p. 585.
49 *The Lumb Commission*, p. 12, also 'Education Department, Report for the year ended 31 March, 1899', *Departmental Reports 1898-1899* (Kingston: Government Printing Office, 1900), p. 367ff. One Inspector Watson, wrote for example, that:

> The introduction of an increased number of women as teachers in recent years is a step in the right direction, the benefits of which are already observed and in future years will be felt more and more. A greater respect for women is one of the first needs of our community and will do more than anything else to raise its moral tone, and the introduction of so many trained, intelligent young women as teachers in our day is bound to tell in this direction. The number of trained and even certificated women now working in our schools as Additional Teachers is a hopeful sign, and I have inspected some schools in which the advantages of this arrangement were very manifest. A capable teacher assisted by and working pleasantly with a capable self-respecting woman is in itself an object lesson for our children of the very highest value.

Cf. also, T. Capper's arguments against the low salary scales proposed by the *Lumb Commission* for Women teachers, *Jamaica dispatches and correspondence 1899*, C.O. 137, no. 599, Confidential Dispatch, 31 January 1899. Letter from Capper on the Commission's Report, dated 23 December 1898.
50 Gisela Eisner, *Jamaica 1830-1930: A study in economic growth* (Manchester University Press, 1961), p. 163, Table xxiii.
51 Although not primarily historical works, the following provide some useful insight into the role of religion or 'religiousity' in Jamaica: Madeline Keer, *Personality and conflict in Jamaica* (Liverpool University Press, 1952), ch. xiv; G. E. Simpson, Jamaican revivalist cults, *SES*, vol. v. no. iv (1956), p. 321; cf. *Press release, final reports 1960 population census* (Kingston: Government Printing Office, n.d.); M. G. Smith, Roy Augier and Rex Nettleford, *The Ras Tafari Movement in Kingston, Jamaica* (Kingston: ISER, 1960).
52 See, 'Report on the proceedings of the Board of Education for the year ended 31 March 1895', *The Governor's Report on the Blue Book and Departmental Reports 1894/95* (Kingston: Government Printing Office, 1896).
53 *Ibid.*, pp. 165-6.
54 See, *The constitution of the Jamaica Teachers' Association, 1964* (Kingston: JTA, 1964), p. 1.
55 *Ibid.*
56 *Ibid.*
57 *Proceedings of the House of Representatives*, Session: 1959-60, no. 1, 2 April 1959, p. 3; also no. 2, 25-27 April 1961, p. 314. Mr Glasspole who started off as an accountant became a leading light in the trade union movement and later, in the 1970s, became Governor-General.
58 *The Daily Gleaner*, 11 April 1963, pp. 1, 7, 11.
59 Cf. 'Interview with Mr E. H. Cousins' 12 March 1974 Chairman of the Board of Overseas Examinations and former President of the JUT

(1948) and Senior Chief Education Officer in the Ministry of Education. Mr Cousins was the key official involved in the drafting of the Education Bill under both Mr Glasspole and Mr Allen and he became a close confidant of the latter Minister.

60 'Interviews with officials of the JTA' (1974) [unpublished interviews given to the author]; also JTA's 'Memorandum to the Select Committee of the Legislature on the Education Bill, 1964', p. 1. *The files of the JTA*.

61 *The Minutes of the meetings of the JETA, 1961-64, passim*; 'Interviews with JTA officials' (1974); *The New Clarion*, WCOTP Special 1971, particularly pp. 23ff, '1964-71, seven years with WCOTP' and 'Clarion's Candid Interview', by Dr Aubrey Phillips of Edith Dalton-James and Wesley Powell, pp. 33ff.

62 'Interview with Mr Eric Frater, Attorney-at-Law' 16 January 1974. Mr Frater is a former PNP executive member, KSAC Councillor and formerly President of the AAMM and headmaster at Rusea Secondary School; 'Interview with Mr W. Powell' 6 February 1974 – Mr Powell – then headmaster of Excelsior School and former President of the H2M2 and the JTA and Chairman of the JETA.

63 'Interviews with Officials of the JTA' (1974); 'Interview with the Hon. Senator A. G. R. Byfield, 6 March 1975, then President of the Senate and Vice-President of the JAS.

64 *Ibid.*; also Wesley Powell's, 'Letter to members of the JETA', (February 1963) and, copy of his 'Open letter to the citizens of Jamaica, 4 March 1963', *The Files of the JTA*.

65 *Ibid.*; also, W. Powell, 'Letter to members' (February 1963), *op. cit.*, p. 2 and *The Daily Gleaner*, 26 February 1964.

66 'Interview with Mr Edwin Allen' 2 April 1974. Mr Allen was Opposition spokesman on education and former Minister of Education 1953-55 and 1962-72; he died in 1984 after long years of service to his Clarendon community and the country.

67 Cf. W. Powell, 'Letter to members' (February 1963), p. 2, *op. cit.*; also *The Daily Gleaner*, 25 February 1963, p. 4; and Vivien Blake's opening of Byfield's case in Court, as reported (verbatim), *The Daily Gleaner*, 26 February 1964, p. 21ff.

68 In a letter to *The Daily Gleaner*, 23 February 1963, Mr Allen defended his action, i.e. exercising 'discretion' rather than giving his confirmation or 'vetoing' the appointment of Byfield:

> In the case of the Turrant Senior School, which was opened when my predecessor was in office, the School Board was asked to nominate three teachers. The Board complied and one of the three teachers was appointed by the then Minister.

He claimed that he could not see why he could not act as Mr Glasspole had done when he was Minister. By this time the debate had turned on whether Mr Allen had the right to ask the Board to send a list of names for him to choose one. Glasspole defended himself thus:

> It is naturally impossible for a former Minister to remember every detailed act done by him in a Ministry after four and a half years in office, but I am prepared to state categorically –

1. Three Senior Schools were opened whilst I was Minister – Vauxhall, Papine and Turrants;
2. That (Sic) no request for a panel of names in the cases of Vauxhall and Papine Snr. School appointments.

He could not 'recollect' the Ministry asking for any panel of names in the case of the Turrants School and this was 'confirmed by one of the only two sources having this information'. On this basis Glasspole challenged Allen to prove his allegations. *The Daily Gleaner*, 22 February 1963, p. 2.

Cf. also, Powell, 'Letter to Members of the JETA' (February 1963), p. 3, where it is denied that the previous Government ever made requests for three names before making an appointment and concludes on the point that 'Had JETA been apprised of any case involving this breach of the law it would have protested as vigorously as it is now doing.' But the *Minutes of the JETA executive meeting of 22 February 1963*, p. 2, is suggestive;

> Mrs Clarke raised the question of the request that names of applicants be sent to the Minister. The Chairman remarked that that was a legacy of the previous administration. He reiterated that JETA is not anti-Government but pro-education.

69 'Interview with Mr Byfield'; Mr Byfield claimed that some of the posts offered were not as generous as Mr Allen and others stated.

70 Addressing a public meeting at Half-Way Tree in March, the Leader of the Opposition Mr N. W. Manley suggested that the affair could be taken to court; see *The Daily Gleaner*, 15 March 1963. The PNP bias of the JETA, particularly its leaders, reinforced the political content of the case for it is highly possible that Mr Allen was suspicious of Byfield because of the fear that he was being used by the PNP. Whether in fact the PNP actually 'used' Mr Byfield and the JETA is not clear, but both as the Opposition Party and as an ally of the teachers' associations, the PNP made political capital of the situation. This is not, however, to be confused with the teachers' particular interests.

71 *Minutes of the JETA meeting at Alvernia*, 15 January 1963, p. 1, also for 22 February and 6 March 1963, when the final decision was taken to fight the case in court; see also, *The Daily Gleaner*, 10 March 1963, p. 1. (Headlines: 'JETA to take legal action'.)

72 Cf. 'Interview with Mr D. Gascoigne' 8 January 1974, JTA Secretary of Development and former President.

73 All these gentlemen eventually became disillusioned, however, with the PNP, or its radical leadership under Manley the Younger and left the country by 1979/80. In the 1980s, some were to return to a much changed Jamaica.

74 'Annual Report, Jamaica Teachers' Association, 1965', *op. cit*, p. 7, *AAMM Journal* Spring 1963, p. 3.

75 Cf. 'Interview with Mr D. Gascoigne' 8 January 1974.

76 *Ibid.*; also, *The Daily Gleaner*, 28 May 1963, p. 10, and 3 June 1963, p. 17.

77 Cf. W. Powell, 'Circular Letters to Teachers' (March and October 1963); also *The Daily Gleaner*, 1 January 1964, p. 1.
78 Letter from the Prime Minister's Office, 6 November 1963, *The files of the JTA*. This led to a terrific quarrel between Bustamante and Powell conducted in the *Gleaner*, see for example, *The Daily Gleaner*, 13 and 14 November 1963, p. 1 and pp. 1-2 respectively.
79 Letter from the Prime Minister to the Secretary of the JETA, 14 October 1963, *The files of the JTA*; also *The Daily Gleaner*, 14 November 1963, p. 2.
80 *The Daily Gleaner*, 4 December 1963, p. 2; see p. 14 also.
81 The records of the JETA and the JTA do not reflect, strongly, the division which seemed to have existed between moderates and more militant teachers in the leadership at this time; I was made aware of this particularly through the interviews with officials and other individuals who were active at the time, particularly, E. Frater; also 'Interview with Sister Tarrissa' 28 March 1974. The Sister was the Librarian, Immaculate Conception High School and a former Secretary of the JETA; 'Interview with Mr C. C. McArthur Ireland' 16 February 1974.
82 *The Daily Gleaner*, 14 November 1963.
83 *Ibid.*
84 *Ibid.*
85 *The Daily Gleaner*, 1 December 1963, p. 1.
86 *The Daily Gleaner*, 15 December 1963, p. 1 ('Strike: 2, 164 Yes; 37 No').
87 *The Daily Gleaner*, 4 December 1963, p. 2; also 6, 7, 8 December 1963.
88 *The Daily Gleaner*, 4 December 1963, p. 14, Editorial: 'Consultation'.
89 *The Daily Gleaner*, 30 December 1963, p. 1 ('JETA would be satisfied if .... ').

CHAPTER 4

Teachers and the world of politics

A number of related factors may obviously combine to determine the degree of success or outright failure of organizations which aim to articulate the particularistic interests of occupational groups such as teachers. These include organizational and leadership capabilities, financial and membership resources which can be called upon when necessary, the collective ideological disposition of members as well as the nature of issues raised and the manner of articulating them. First and foremost of these factors, however, is the structural position occupied by members and leaders within the total social system which includes the location of the occupation in the productive, reproductive and circulation cycles of society. With respect to the formation of the JUT in the 1890s part of this point was considered in the last chapter but it is necessary to consider this in more general terms in relation to the resources available to the two organizations in both colonial and immediate post-colonial Jamaica. A useful starting point of a discussion of these points is the perception teachers had of the State and its impact on their political practice.

The teachers' perception of the State

It was inevitable that the formal structures of government and decision-making would greatly influence the political practice of groups such as the JUT and the JTA. This was particularly so since they represented semi-professionals in colonial and post-colonial societies and within the political constraints implied. Such influences were very clear in the strategies the groups adopted in the articulation of their interests and they were also seen in the ideological outlook and style of raising and presenting issues to the authorities. These will become clear in this and the following chapters but for the moment it is sufficient to point to the specific areas of state power which determined the groups' strategies in both the colonial and independent political systems.

In the colonial period, before the process of decolonization had commenced, the JUT saw the important areas of the State to be the Governor, the Director of Education and the elected members of the Legislative Council. We may consider these in reverse order of importance.

The elected members had little formal power in the legislature. They could not initiate financial bills and their control over the executive was negligible.[1] Even their two-thirds veto of government measures could be easily over-ruled by the Governor exercising his reserved powers. But from the point of view of the JUT leaders who wanted to influence the course of decisions relating to education, the elected members were men of considerable influence both inside and outside the legislature. Not only did these men have a ready forum in the Council, they also received wide publicity through the press.[2] The elected members were also men of considerable influence which they derived from their social positions in society. Moreover, since the Government often took educational matters to the legislature for its consideration it was important for the JUT to secure the support of the elected members who often wielded more influence than their constitutional role suggested.[3]

But the main target for the JUT's pressure was the Director of Education. As chairman of the Board of Education and adviser to the Governor on all aspects of education, the Director had a strong influence in deciding whether a resolution from teachers, churchmen or individuals should go before the Governor-in-Privy Council or whether legislative action should be recommended. Being a senior departmental head the Director was an ex-officio member of the legislature and acted in this capacity as a kind of 'minister of education' while at the same time he was also the civil servant responsible for the administration of the educational system throughout the country.[4]

Although the Colonial Office was ultimately responsible for the affairs of the colony, in Jamaica the Governor had the last word. He was at once the political leader and the Head of State since he represented both the Monarch and Whitehall. The formal head of the Civil Service in the colony was the Colonial Secretary but the Governor also had a strong say in administrative matters. As the 'man on the spot' his opinions carried weight in Whitehall with the Secretary of State and it would take a powerful group indeed to succeed against him at that level. Needless to say, it was important for the JUT leaders to secure the good will of such a man.

There were some relevant regions of political power and influence to which the JUT paid little attention, for good reasons. Because the education system in Jamaica was mainly of interest to people in the country and hardly of any concern to the Colonial Office, there was rarely any need for the union, unlike business groups, to make representations in London. Although contact was established with the NUT from the turn of the century only on two occasions before 1930 did the JUT request the NUT to make representation in Whitehall on its behalf.[5] The union did not concern itself with the local school boards set up in selected areas after 1920, because no decision of importance to teachers as a whole was likely to be taken at this level. Similarly, the union paid no attention to the Parish Councils (local authorities) which, unlike in England and Wales, played no part in the educational system of the country.

The structure of state authority was therefore greatly to influence the course the JUT took in mapping a strategy in its attempt to express the general interests of the teaching occupation. The striking but, being a colony, not unexpected, feature of this structure was its rejection of even a democratic facade to hide its highly authoritarian and undifferentiated mode of operation with few channels through which some groups could gain direct access to decision-makers. With decolonization and independence the lower House became fully elected and this had important implications for teachers and others. There were two comparable parties, as noted earlier, vying for governmental power.

None the less, there were new factors inhibiting the development of strong parliamentary control of the executive. Taking parliamentary control to mean the legislature's ability to scrutinize, publicize and influence government policies, Yorke found in his study of this process in Jamaica that the legislature in the 1960s was relatively weak.[6] He found that back-benchers, with an eye to their re-election, were concerned more about constituency than national matters. Sixty per cent of the motions put in the House, for example, were on constituency matters. Those in the party which was in office tended to shy away from criticizing government policies in the fear of jeopardizing their chances of promotion, which was always likely to be rapid in a small legislature (of 45 members in 1962 and 53 in 1967). The executive maintained its control of the legislature by refusing to develop a dialogue with the Government's back-benchers.

In these conditions many of the functions usually associated with back-benchers at Westminster such as the use of Question Time and the opportunity to put Private Members Bills were performed solely by the Opposition. The relative absence of fundamental ideological rifts between the parties strengthened these developments; the Opposition never disagreed with the principles behind government measures, only with the details. Only on two occasions between 1962 and 1970 did Bills go before Select Committees, the Education Bill of 1965[7] and the Income Tax (Amendment) Bill of 1970, because of the extra-parliamentary opposition to them.[8] Thus, although the legislature is more representative than it was in the colonial period it has grave limitations *vis-á-vis* the executive. This does not detract from its perceived importance to groups outside parliament who want to influence government legislation and can gain the support of one of the two parties.

The centralizing tendency which has been noticed in West Indian governments since independence has also been a feature of Jamaican politics and government.[9] In the 1960s there was the successful attempt by the Labour Government to centralize the administration of education in the Ministry of Education placed in Kingston. Nearly all decisions affecting teachers and education were taken therefore at the centre, thus making the Ministry of Education the principal target for pressure from the JTA.

Of course the Ministry had to operate within the broad guidelines laid down by the Ministry of Finance and the Minister of Education had to secure the support of his Cabinet colleagues, particularly the Prime Minister. In the 1960s the strong personalities of Sir Alexander Bustamante and his close lieutenants, the Minister of Finance and later Acting Prime Minister, Mr Donald Sangster, and the Minister of Education, Mr Edwin Allen, led them to emphasize their ministerial roles, as seen in the last chapter, which made them all the more visible targets for the Association.

The JUT and the JTA saw themselves as legitimate groups operating within the bounds of a political tradition derived from Britain. This already committed the JUT in the colonial period, ideologically, to values associated with the Westminster type of democracy. This included notions such as 'fair play', the desirability of 'compromise', and the right to 'negotiate'. The JTA was to be equally committed to institutions such as a bicameral parliament, an independent judiciary and a so-called neutral bureaucracy and the two-party system. Both groups had a generally conservative outlook and sought to promote British values as they understood them.

For example, one teacher, writing in 1930, expressed clearly the general ideological outlook of teachers in Jamaica and their union:

> We in Jamaica cannot boast anything in our educational
> life to equal the perfection of the English Elementary or
> Public School system in organizations. Jamaica has not yet
> advanced so far; but there are ideals towards which steady

progress is being made and one of the ideals is the developing of the spirit of 'playing the game' in the widest and
most varied sense. As an English-speaking people,
Jamaicans know the full significance of that term. When
Jamaicans learn to play the game there will then be less
embezzlements, bankruptcies, illegitimacy, superstition
and all the other ills to which modern society is heir.[10]

These values were still deeply held by Jamaican teachers in the
post-independence period and well reflected in the JTA's stand on
moral and public issues. Although Jamaica has, for instance, an
illegitimacy rate of over 70 per cent the JTA felt that teachers
should continue to promote what are in fact largely nineteenth
century Victorian middle-class notions of the family as an ideal. If
an unmarried female teacher became a mother the Association
insisted that she should resign.[11] There was little consideration that
this public condemnation of 'illegitimacy' might have a very damaging effect on the taught, most of whom were probably born out of
wedlock.

With regard to tactics, both groups, particularly the JUT,
generally followed a policy of moderation. At its 1896 Annual
Conference the JUT declared, to the pleasure of the *Daily
Gleaner*,[12] that

> The Union is not intended to be aggressive. It is only a
> combination of teachers to guard the interests and assert
> the dignity of their profession.[13]

Although the JTA eventually adopted militant tactics to defend
teachers its leaders were basically men of moderate persuasion.
Indeed, militant tactics were adopted largely because teachers felt
that they had to defend what they saw as an attack by the government of the day on their traditional rights and values.

For both the PNP nationalists and teachers' leaders the demand
for political independence was well within the British political
tradition.[14] They could be extremely pro-British since they recognized the merits of British institutions and at the same time demanded changes. From their own experiences leaders of the JUT
realized that the colonial system imposed great limitations on their
social and political aspirations but change for them, as with the PNP
nationalists, was not synonymous with rejection of British values
and institutions nor an abandonment of their moderate conservative
outlook. It was not surprising therefore that the PNP attempted to
get the JUT to affiliate with it.[15] Although this attempt failed it is

common knowledge that the JUT gave strong support to the party and that the JTA did so in the 1960s and continued to do so after the PNP came to power in the 1970s.[16] In the colonial period the JUT saw it as an unquestionable right to make demands on the political system and thereby to give force to what they understood as being British political values. This must be understood within the context of there being no rights of the existence of trade unions and therefore the Union was not actually a union in the usual sense of the word. In the 1960s the JTA tended to see themselves playing the role of defending political values and institutions derived from Westminster. These ideological outlooks were reflected in the issues raised by the groups and their general behaviour. These outlooks were also strongly reflected in the patterns of organization and leadership of the JUT and the JTA. It is therefore relevant to look briefly at the structures and memberships of both organizations with this general point in mind.

Structures and memberships of the JUT and the JTA

The formal structures of the JUT and the JTA had many similarities and dissimilarities. Briefly, the groups depended largely on local associations as the base of their organizational strength. From its inception the JUT sought to build on the existing Educational Associations which were founded in the 1880s, but the Union also encouraged the formation of new local associations which were to be affiliated to it. Thus, the Union was partly federal whereas the JTA was wholly unitary in structure. This was not just an organizational difference. Sometimes when local associations failed to renew their membership fees and did not appear on the list of affiliated members the representatives of the JUT were told by the authorities that the Union did not represent all organized teachers in the country.

Another difference was in their middle-ranging associations. The federated and regional associations developed haphazardly in the JUT during the First World War and the JUT's initial response was hostile because it saw the development as a threat to its position.[17] The JTA on the other hand, started out with the idea of forming not only district but also Parish and regional associations so that these became an early and integral part of the group's structure.

The central bodies – the executive and the council – were composed of both local and national representatives. There were also specialized committees on such matters as salaries, finances, scholarship, ethics and membership. Because of its greater complexity, size and needs the JTA established many more committees than the JUT ever had.

Like most groups they had annual conferences at which the executive had to account for its stewardship over the past year. Although these were formal occasions the members were sometimes very critical of their leaders' attitudes and agreements with Government.[18] Apart from one notable exception in 1953 this criticism never led to an open challenge of the executive by members.[19] News of negotiations and correspondence with the authorities were fairly well communicated to the members by various publications.[20] Partly because of the many points of contact between leaders and members – meetings of local associations, visits by national leaders, frequent meetings at national level and publications – trust and confidence generally remained mutual. This was strengthened by a common sense of purpose, promotion of incentive projects such as scholarships for the children of members and visits abroad, and, of course, recognizable results. Leaders were always careful to be sensitive to the needs of members and if necessary arrive at a compromise. Some good examples of this were the attempts of the associations in the western end of the country in 1916 to form a Western Association and the Manchester Teachers' Association's attitude to the strike of 1966 which is treated in chapter 6. Undoubtedly the JUT and the JTA were very concerned with upholding democratic values although it was partly on these grounds that the older leadership was to be challenged by some young Turks in the mid-1970s.

The concern with both democracy and continuity was perhaps best reflected in elections for the presidency. Originally, it seems, neither organization thought too seriously about this. The first president of the JUT held the post for three successive years and the first president of the JTA held the post for two. To avoid the post coming under the influence of an individual for too long the JUT followed the fairly common practice which was later adopted by the JTA, electing each year a vice-president at about the same time as the rest of the executive members. He would remain in the post for that year, taking over as president in the second year of his election and in the third year became immediate-past president of the organization. In all three capacities the individual would serve on the executive as one of three senior officers of the body. In this way both democracy and continuity were to a large extent safeguarded at the top. The person who had been through these positions would then be eligible for service on council and could later stand again for election to the presidency. Thus, J. J. Mills was elected four times, C. T. Saunders five times and Mrs Edith Dalton-James four times to the presidency of the JUT and Mrs Fay Saunders twice to that of the JTA before succeeding Ben Hawthorne as general-secretary in 1975.

However, democracy was checked, not surprisingly, in both organizations by the tendency to recruit leaders from amongst the better-off and the more fortunately placed teachers. The presidency of the JUT was sometimes held by non-elementary schoolteachers, such as Col. L. G. Gruchy its first president, who was one of the two co-principals of the Mico Training College, J. J. Mills who was, for most of his long life, a tutor at the college and A. J. Newman, an Englishman and principal of the same college later. The presidency of the JTA has been held by the late Dr Aubrey Phillips, Professor and head of the Teaching Section of the Department of Education at the University of the West Indies and by Mr Glen Owen, then principal of Mico. Neither group displayed a fondness for electing assistant teachers to the presidency. Although the number of female teachers increased after the turn of the century,[21] Mrs Dalton-James was the only female as well as the only assistant teacher to have held the post in the JUT during its nearly seventy years. The JTA in its early years had two women presidents, Mrs Saunders and Mrs Ellorine Walker but during the period this study covers no assistant teacher occupied the presidency.

The financial resources of the groups affected their respective structures. Thus, for example, as the JUT could not afford a full-time staff its president, secretary-general, treasurer, like all the other officers received only reimbursements for expenses from the Union. Teachers who occupied these posts carried out their work at great personal sacrifice and with the co-operation of their school staff. In 1955 the secretary-general upon whom, of course, the day-to-day work depended, became the first full-time salaried officer of the Union. It was not until August 1949 that the Union finally completed the building of its headquarters on Church Street, Kingston (now the headquarters of the JTA); before this it had to have its meetings in rented or offered buildings such as Mico. Only in 1928 was the *JUT Magazine* begun and teachers were able to express their views through their own publication.

The JTA was far more fortunate. The Association inherited most of the assets of the associations which came together to form it in 1963/4, and from its inception it was able to employ a full-time staff which is now augmented with a sizeable clerical staff. Although its president still does not receive a salary from the Association, after the confrontation with the Government in 1966 the Ministry agreed that the person holding the post could take a sabbatical year with pay while an additional teacher took over his/her school work. Some presidents have seen the need to do this but others have felt that they could carry out both tasks together, although by the mid-1970s this was becoming increasingly difficult as the scope of the Association's activities spreads.

The two organizations differed perhaps most significantly in their memberships. The JUT, formed with the ambitious aim of representing the whole teaching community, never came at all close to getting within its fold all elementary schoolteachers and still less the teachers in secondary and technical schools and the training colleges. From the late 1930s teachers in non-elementary schools and colleges began forming their own associations to protect themselves, which should have been expected, given the social divide even within the same occupation.

In 1894 the JUT had 100 members and this rose to 432 in 1899 but soon fell to just over 300.[22] According to the JUT's annual reports, the *Daily Gleaner* and the reports of the Department of Education, between 1928/9 and 1930 the Union's membership rose from 603 to 704 out of a teaching force of 1,650. In 1937 the Union for the first time reached a membership of over one thousand with 1,043 members out of a teaching community of 2,368. Between 1944 and 1954 teachers in elementary schools increased from 2,941 to 4,353, rising in 1962/3 to 5,227 and in 1959 the JUT reported a membership of 3,050. Although it does not appear that the Union improved on this between 1959 and 1962/3, there was a marked improvement in the 1950s in the size of the JUT at a time when education, for the first time since the 1890s, was expanding significantly in Jamaica. Interestingly enough, towards the end of its existence the Union became increasingly representative of elementary schoolteachers.

The JTA's membership was far greater than that of the JUT since the new Association was the result of the amalgamation of the various teachers' organizations in the country. It started with a membership of just over 3,000 out of a teaching force of over 7,000 in government and independent schools.[23] In 1966, the year the JTA led teachers on a strike, the Association had just over 6,000 teachers in the country. In 1974 the Association had a membership of 13,095 and reported: 'This is approximately 90 per cent of our teacher population and can be regarded as very good ... '.[24]

Every year throughout the 1960s (and in the 1970s) the Association has had a Membership Drive Committee and has waged campaigns to achieve the desired 100 per cent voluntary membership; there have been times too when it seemed that leaders would like to have even university teachers in the JTA. As might be expected, by far the largest element in the Association is from the primary (formerly the elementary) sector with between 90 and 99 per cent membership as against only 50-60 per cent of teachers in secondary schools and further education in the years 1966-74.[25] This success has not prevented the JTA from asking that membership be compulsory as a step towards full professionalization.[26]

The growth and development of the teaching occupation

The socio-economic position of teachers underwent important changes throughout the period with which we are concerned from the late nineteenth century and this was reflected in the growing strength of their associations. Before the process of decolonization began elementary schoolteachers did not enjoy a position of prestige in the social system of the country taken as a whole. Elementary schools were geared towards providing children of the peasantry and the working class with a basic knowledge of the traditional Three Rs of reading, writing and arithmetic. Inevitably such education was inferior to that received by the children of the various elements of the dominant class and in some cases the intermediate classes. Elementary schoolteaching was also seen as an inferior occupation as compared to the law, medicine and the civil service by the dominant social elements who insulated these areas as their particular preserves.

At the local level, however, and especially in the rural areas, the elementary schoolteacher received the respect of the community he served. He bridged the local community and the wider society; he was adviser to parents and adolescents alike and he was looked to for Christian leadership, much as when his work as a teacher and a missionary were one.[27] In a society where practical and ideal types or forms of values and behaviour were always in conflict, the teacher was expected to set an example by the way he was believed or seen to organize his private life. For example, although the people spoke a dialect derived from a mixture of English and African words, 'Teacher', who had himself most likely come from a similar background to his pupils', was expected to speak 'proper' and this meant speaking standard English in and outside the classroom.

Some teachers in Jamaica continue to believe that they must behave in the way they were expected to behave.[28] In brief, the elementary schoolteacher in the community was an adviser, an exemplary figure and a useful agent for government departments.[29] For example, at the 1903 Annual Conference of the JUT, Alexander Dixon, an elected member of the Legislative Council, was reported in the following manner:

> No class of men, at this stage of civilization in Jamaica, could do more for the advancement of the people of this country than the teacher of the elementary class. The teacher but little knew the influence they had on the minds of the peasant population from which many were taken.[30]

Although Dixon was correct in his depiction of the elementary schoolteacher as crucial in the forging of a new Jamaica, he was wrong to assume that the teacher did not know that he had a strong influence on the peasantry. The very formation of the JUT in 1894 demonstrated that teachers were aware of their importance. The years immediately after the First World War also saw the emergence of the elementary schoolteacher as politician. In that year G. L. Young, A. A. Barclay, D. T. Wint and T. J. Cawley were elected to the Legislative Council as the first of many elementary school-teachers who were to become members in the future. Young had been president of the Union at the turn of the century and again held the post in 1921; at the time of this election Wint was occupying that position. At the 1919 Annual Conference a motion was passed to the effect that the Union should elect men to the legislature 'who would look after the educational interests of the island'.[31] This interest in politics following the War was not restricted to Jamaica. Wood noted, soon after this, the new development and stated that

> Practically all the elementary schoolteachers in the West Indies are of unmixed negro descent. They are extremely interested in politics and in Jamaica and British Guiana are, in the opinion of some, inclined to take an excessive part in political disputation and organization.[32]

He further noted that although the teachers in Jamaica were making a demand for pensions on the basis granted to civil servants, he doubted whether this would be met because teachers ' ... would be the first to resent the prohibitions applicable to civil servants in regard to taking part in politics ... '.[33]

In the elections of 1930 and 1935 many elementary school-teachers stood for election and some, such as Harold Allen (later Sir Harold), were successful.[34] In 1930, C. C. Campbell, later the first Governor-General of independent Jamaica, told the Western Federation of Teachers of which he was President, that

> The time has come when the teacher's opinion carries weight in matters educational, industrial and political. His action with regard to these are watched with very keen interest by his friends and with great fear by his enemies.[35]

He went on in his address:

> You are directly and indirectly taxpayers and your true position towards the political interest of the country must be exercised. It is right that every citizen should take an intelligent interest in the political affairs of his country.[36]

He called upon the teachers to exercise their influence in the coming elections for the legislature. But before the coming of universal manhood suffrage schoolteachers were not in a position to make maximum political use of their local strength. Not many would have the resources to compete for entry into the legislature although many would have had the vote after 1895. After 1944 they were able to make their presence felt in the legislature and the Government, whether PNP or JLP. This was mostly, however, the activity of individual teachers not teachers acting in concert or being directed by their associations. Nevertheless, increasingly teachers came to realize and exploit their local base for successful political activity which strengthened the position of the JUT and later the JTA.

The JTA was composed of teachers who enjoyed a more influential position in the island than did the JUT members. Teachers were seen to have played an important part in the struggle for political independence and they were believed to have a significant part to play in the development of the country, such as forging a 'national' image, promoting education for development, etc. The JTA members were also drawn from a much broader social spectrum than those of the JUT. The new Association had in its fold headmasters of secondary schools, training colleges and technical institutions and they had useful social connections with individuals in administration and government. In the late 1950s and the early 1960s teachers were proud that many ex-elementary schoolteachers were now prominent men. For example, there were: R. N. Murray,

Table 4.1   Grant-In-Aid, awarded by Government on the principle of payment for results

	1st Class Schools		2nd Class Schools		3rd Class Schools		Exceptional Schools Half of 3rd Class Schools	
	s.	d.	s.	d.	s.	d.	s.	d.
First – Capital Grant for each pupil in average attendance during the year	6	0	5	0	4	0	2	0
Second – Class Grant for each mark obtained at the annual examinations	8	0	7	0	6	0	3	0

the first local man to occupy the most senior civil servant position in the Ministry of Education, E. H. Cousins who succeeded him, Dr A. Phillips of the University, Edwin Allen, the Minister of Education from 1953 to 1955 and again from 1962 to 1972, and C. C. Campbell.

This social change was accompanied by economic changes in the position of teachers. In the colonial period, as a whole, elementary schoolteachers were badly paid whereas after 1962 the salaries of both elementary and post-elementary schoolteachers increased as a result of successful pressure. Of course, as the last chapter indicated and a later one will elaborate, the story is not as simple as this.

Until 1921, when fixed salaries were introduced, teachers in elementary schools were paid by the famous (or infamous) system of payment-by-results. This was a fairly intricate system, as practised in Jamaica, whereby the teacher was paid only after his school had been examined by the government inspector. Table 4.1 shows the two main ways in which the school was awarded grants by government towards teachers' salaries. There were three classes into which schools were placed depending on the amount of marks gained in the subjects tested, and according to the class of the school it would receive 8/– (8 shillings: 40p), 7/–, 6/– (or 3/– for 'exceptional' schools) for each mark obtained at the examination. This was called the 'class grant'. There was also, as the Table shows, a 'capitation grant' which could fetch the school 6/–, 5/–, 4/– (or 2/– for 'exceptional' schools) for each pupil depending on the class of the school. Some schools could gain additional sums: before the 1892 Elementary Education Law which made elementary education free, the teacher would charge parents a 'fee' for teaching their children, after 1892 the Government paid a 'fee grant' of 4/– per child in average attendance per annum to the school; 3/– was paid also for each girl taking instruction in sewing.

Teachers who held a first-class certificate were allowed to employ a pupil-teacher for whom the teacher would receive £3 per annum and £1.10.0 (£1 10 shillings) for any additional pupil-teachers. The teacher had to prepare the pupil-teacher for his examinations although there was no way of really enforcing this.[37] Headmasters who had passed their third year examinations at college were granted personal payments of £15, £10, and £5, depending on the class of their schools. Some teachers also preached for their religious denominations and received allowances for this. The amount earned by a school depended therefore on the performance of the headmaster and his luck in getting children to overcome such obstacles as heavy rainfalls, bad road conditions, the poverty of their families and customary practices such as keeping children away from school on certain days to help on the land.[38] It is not possible therefore to say exactly how much teachers received as 'salaries'.

In 1897, Thomas Capper, the superintending inspector of schools, estimated that the salaries of headteachers varied from £22.10.0 per annum in the case of a small school to £120 in the case of the largest school. Salaries for assistant teachers varied from between £35 and £40 per annum; women, who were just entering the occupation, received between £16 per annum and £20 but they were likely to benefit also from the sewing grant which varied from £5 to £12 per annum.[39] These estimates and the opposition of teachers to the system of payment were well borne out by the testimony of teachers themselves.

J. J. Mills who started teaching in 1909 (although he soon returned to Mico as a tutor) wrote of the days before 1921 in very revealing terms. He recalled:

> Up to the year 1920, everything that was worthwhile for primary (elementary) education had to be bitterly fought for and gained inch by inch ...
>
> The system (of payment-by-results) generally worked out that the best paid teacher drew about £130 from all official sources for the year. Those who read these figures will put forward the threadbare justification – living in 1909 was

much less expensive than the decade following. Yes, but living was not that cheaper proportionately.[40]

In his Inaugural Address to the 1919 Annual Conference of the JUT, W. F. Bailey pointed out that the average salary of a teacher was £70 per annum. In his characteristically lively way he went on:

> And with this he (the teacher) must be tidy, bring up and maintain a family in the respectability becoming his position! Let there be no twaddle. The financial status of the man counts! And this country cannot expect to get its best brains submit to years of training and giving themselves with devotion to teaching with the prospect of earning less than a headman on a plantation or a stone mason at his trade.[41]

In 'An open letter to young men about the teaching profession' one teacher announced that he could not encourage any young man to enter the occupation for after three years training he could only hope for about £80 per annum whereas a police constable starting his career after leaving school at the third or fourth standard received as much as £91.5.0 per annum.[42] In an earlier debate in 1900 at a meeting of the Board of Education, Archdeacon Simms attacked the system because it made the teacher 'naturally sanguine', since it was grossly unfair to him; the teacher was likely to 'overestimate his probable results',[43] and this would later make him

> sanguine even in his own mind and more so to the shopkeeper whom he has to ask for credit. If the school does badly the teacher finds himself (sic) what is for him heavily in debt and he starts the next year with this debt and a diminished salary to pay it. It is all very well to say he should not get into debt, but how is he to help it? He has a very small salary, with he thinks, reasonable anticipations of a substantial addition at the end of the school year, and then finds that he does not get it.[44]

Apart from this injustice, the 'teacher practically pays for the process'[45] whereby the new inspector learned his job, and it was wrong to make a man's salary depend on a one day inspection, sometimes by a novice.

To remedy some of these ills Simms suggested a scheme of fixed salaries for all grades of teachers. There should be a minimum of £25 per annum and a maximum of £120 with incremental scales which differentiated his scheme from that suggested by the Lumb

Commission in 1898. A fixed salary scheme was not, however, to come until after the reforms of 1920.

Between 1898 and 1920 the JUT made repeated representations to the Government to establish a scheme of fixed salaries for teachers. It was successful only after a great deal of dissatisfaction was expressed by teachers in the years immediately after the First World War. Teachers were fortunate to have strong support in the Legislative Council for the first time – D. T. Wint, then President of the JUT, G. L. Young, its Vice-President, A. A. Barclay and T. J. Cawley who were close to the JUT, and the outstanding politician of the era, J. A. G. Smith. It was fortunate too that the Governor, Sir Leslie Probyn, took a sympathetic stand on the question.[46]

Teachers were not entirely satisfied with the new scales which went through many revisions as the *Gleaner* reports of December show. Before giving the new system a trial, Wint called a Special Conference of the Union to consider the scales in September 1920.[47] Even after this the JUT's leaders expressed some reservations, but generally the new system was seen as a great improvement over the old. A minimum of £24 for assistant teachers and a maximum of £100 was established; headmasters' minimum and maximum salaries were fixed at £80 and £200 per annum. Table 4.2 shows the average salary of the various grades of teachers in 1929 and 1930. Pupil-teachers received £6 when they passed the preliminary pupil-teachers' examinations; this increased by £2 for each of the three grades of the examinations. The average salaries of assistant teachers ranged from between £27.0.0 and £94.15.6 while those of headmasters were between £85.17.0 and £177.12.0 per annum.

The only change in the scales of teachers' pay before the 1940s was an increase amounting to a total of £7,700 in 1932 for assistant teachers but the minimum salary increased only to £36 per annum while the maximum remained. The headteachers' salaries compared, for example, unfavourably with those of the Jamaica Agricultural Society's instructors; after four years the instructor received a salary of £200 per annum, rising within fifteen years to £400 per annum.[48] It was not surprising therefore that nearly all the Society's field instructors were, in 1938, ex-elementary schoolmasters, even though the Society's scales were not adequate to attract men who had been trained at the Imperial College of Agriculture in Trinidad which was founded in the mid-twenties and later became the foundation for the faculty of Agriculture in the University of the West Indies.

Throughout the years before the decolonization period teachers felt particularly ill-rewarded for the work they did. They often

Table 4.2 Average salaries of teachers of all grades in 1929 and 1930

Grades	Average salary per annum 1929 and 1930 £
Pupil-Teachers – Passed Preliminary Examinations	8. 0.0
– Passed First Year Examinations	10. 0.0
– Passed Second Year Examinations	12. 0.0
– Passed Third Year Examinations	27. 0.0
Unregistered Assistants	32. 9.6
Registered Assistants 2nd Class	44. 6.9
Registered Assistants 1st Class	63.11.6
Registered Principal Teachers employed as Assistants, 2nd Class Certificate	77. 6.3
Registered Principal Teachers employed as Assistants, 1st Class Certificate	94.15.6
Registered Principal Teachers employed as Headteachers – Grade E	85. 3.6
Registered Principal Teachers employed as Headteachers – Grade D	109. 9.9
Registered Principal Teachers employed as Headteachers – Grade C	134. 9.6
Registered Principal Teachers employed as Headteachers – Grade B	153.15.3
Registered Principal Teachers employed as Headteachers – Grade A	177.11.9

Source: 'Education Department, Report for the Year ended 31 December 1930', *The Annual General Report of Jamaica together with Departmental Reports for 1930* (Kingston: Government Printing Office, 1931) General Table VA, p. 275.

compared themselves with civil servants who received much more than themselves even though teachers were better trained. From the memoranda of the JUT and the NUT to the 1938 Moyne Commission, established to investigate the protests throughout the Anglophone Caribbean in the late 1930s, it is clear that this was a regular pattern throughout the British West Indies.[49] The JUT estimated that the best-paid teacher received an average of £3.17.0 per week in 1938 and the average teacher received only 13/– per week. Not only were elementary schoolteachers well below the average civil servant in salary scales but the purchasing power of the artisan, particularly in Kingston, and that of the better-paid worker was greater than that of the teachers, as Table 4.3 shows. The average artisan in Kingston with 7/– per day in 1927, 5/7d in 1932 and 7/– in 1937 was undoubtedly better off than the average teacher. Of course, the elementary schoolteacher was in a better position than the domestic worker who earned only an average of 8/8d per week outside Kingston during his best year in 1932 but this could hardly have been of any comfort to the teacher. Even messengers in 1928/9 in civil service departments received (male) 14/– per week and (female) 8/– per week minimum.[50]

In 1929 most civil servants received increases to face the depression in the country whereas the demands of teachers did not meet with the same success.[51] For example, a clerk in charge of parcels in the Post Office department received an increase from £150 to £160 at the point of starting; district postmistresses and telegraph clerks were to receive between £30 and £200 per annum. The JUT deputation to the Moyne Commission complained that clerks, typists, transport workers and policemen received much more than the elementary schoolteacher. Yet teachers were expected to lead exemplary lives – 'the standard of living demanded by the public of teachers is much higher than that demanded from members of the other services around them.'[52]

Nor was the pension of the teacher high when compared with those of some other services. It was recommended by the Education Commissions of 1886 and 1898 that teachers should receive a non-contributory pension but only in 1914 did this happen.[53] Of the 11 teachers who retired in 1929 only one received as much as £61 per annum (the next highest was £57) at the age of 75 with 35 years' service. A first-grade clerk retiring the same year with 17 years' service at the age of 63 received £71 per annum. Another teacher retiring after 28 years' service at the age of 58 received £36 per annum whilst an office cleaner in the Railways at the age of 77 with 21 years' service, received £6 per annum and another, a carpenter

Table 4.3 Average wage of artisans and sundry labourers compiled from annual reports of collector of taxes

Type of employee		Kingston (Average rates paid)						Other parishes					
		1915	1920	1927	1932	1957	1938	1915	1920	1927	1932	1957	1938
Artisans	Per day	4/–	6/9	7/–	5/7	7/–	–	3/8	7/3	5/10	5/5	4/10	–
Labourers:													
Male	Per day	1/5	2/9	2/–	2/4	3/3	–	1/6	3/6	2/4	1/9	1/10	–
Female	Per day	1/–	1/4	1/2	1/3	1/3	–	1/–	1/4	1/2	1/–	1/2	–
Domestics:													
Male	Per week	6/3	8/–	6/6	7/6	9/–	–	5/11	11/4	9/1	8/8	7/6	–
Female	Per week	4/6	5/–	6/6	7/6	7/6	–	4/1	5/9	6/1	6/–	6/–	–

Source: W.I.R.C., 1938-9, C.O. 950, no. 152, J. 206, 'Statement V'.

Table 4.4   Salary scales of elementary schoolteachers, 1955

Position	Scales at 31 March 1954	Scales current April 1954	Scales proposed from 1 April 1955
H.T. I (601−) A	£530 × 20 − 630	£575 × 25 − 750	£650 × 30 − 860
H.T. II (201 − 600) A	410 × 20 − 570	450 × 25 − 650	550 × 30 − 760
H.T. III (152 − 200) B	320 × 15 − 425	350 × 20 − 490	450 × 25 − 650
H.T. IV (81 − 150)	275 × 15 − 380	310 × 20 − 450	380 × 25 − 600
H.T. S (−80)	275	290 × 20 − 430	360 × 25 − 580
Senior Assistant	275 × 15 − 380	310 × 20 − 450	380 × 25 − 600
Al Assistant	290 × 15 − 360	270 × 20 − 410	350 × 20 − 570
A2 Assistants	192 × 12 − 228	215 × 15 − 260	260 × 20 − 340
A3 Assistants	156 × 12 − 192	168 × 12 − 216	210 × 20 − 250
Probationers	125	137	150
Pupil-teachers	£30; 42; 54	£36; 48; 60	£48; 60; 72
Manual training instructors:			
Grade I	−	−	380 × 25 − 600
Grade II	−	−	260 × 20 − 400
Senior school Principal	570 × 20 − 670	615 × 25 − 790	690 × 30 − 900
S.A. instructors	320 × 15 − 425	355 × 20 − 495	450 × 25 − 650
Assistant instructors	260 × 15 − 365	290 × 20 − 430	380 × 25 − 600
A1 and A2 instructors	As in other elementary schools	As in other elementary schools	As in other elementary schools

Source: Ministry of Education and Social Welfare, Paper presented to the House of Representatives, 6 March 1956, in *The JUT Clarion*, vol. xxviii, no. 1, January/April, 1956.

from the same department, received £34 per annum after 21½ years' service at the age of 62. Teachers were better-off than some others but not, as they saw the situation, and, perhaps correctly, suficiently so.

Teachers' salaries increased significantly, however, in Jamaica during the decolonization and independence periods so that by the 1970s the occupation could compete in terms of salaries, if not other perks, with the civil service for well-trained young people with a good chance of success. Table 4.4 shows the salary scales of elementary schoolteachers in 1954 and the increases received in 1954/5. The grades of headteachers, assistants and probationers, pupil-teachers and instructors improved. Table 4.4 also reflects on the contemporary expansion in education with the addition of instructors and teachers in senior schools – features which were to develop even more in the independence period.

Naturally, teachers in post-primary schools also received increases during this period as Table 4.5 shows. For example, non-graduates received a minimum of £180 (plus £24 for married men) and a maximum of £540 (plus a married allowance for men of £30) in early 1954 which rose in April to £240 and £650 and to £280 and £700 in 1955 with proportionate increases in allowances to married men. The 1955 increases were granted in March 1956[54] but by April of that year the Association of Assistant Masters and Mistresses was expressing its dissatisfaction with the scales.[55] The Association's brief was that teachers' salaries were still not comparable with those of members of the civil service with the same qualifications and teachers did not enjoy the same protection in their work. They felt that the salary scale £650 × 30 − 920 × 40 − 1120, with additional benefits for special qualifications could bring the teacher with a degree into a comparable scale with civil servants who had the same qualification. Thus, although secondary schoolteachers were far better off than elementary schoolteachers, they were also, understandably, far from satisfied with their new increases.

As indicated in the last chapter, in 1964 a general increase of 10 per cent was granted to teachers after another demand to bring up the salaries to compare with those of civil servants. Table 4.6 shows the scales received by the highest- and the lowest-paid teachers in the 1967/8 increases although it fails to show clearly the strong differentials between the various grades of teachers which existed between 'pre-trained teachers' training college.[56] The figures under 'Present Salary' are those which existed after the 1964 increases. One of the aims of the teachers and the Ministries involved (Education and Finance) was to establish more grades so as to encourage untrained teachers to qualify and thereby improve the standard of the teaching occupation. But these grades also provided promotions for teachers already in the occupation. There was therefore a wide gap between the minimum for 'pre-trained teacher IV' at £320 × 20 − 360 and that of a 'Grade A' principal at £2,500.[57]

These salary increases are best assessed by the teachers' responses to them. Between 1954 and 1967/8 every increase was followed almost immediately by a fresh demand for the Government to establish salary scales comparable to those of civil servants. Apart from those with a degree (such as secondary schoolteachers) it is not always clear which section of the teaching force was being compared

Table 4.5   Salary scales of secondary school teachers, 1954-6

Position	Salary scales at 31 March 1954	Salary scales current since April 1954	Salary proposed from 1 April 1955
Principal: men	820 – 1195 (+50 M.A.)	£1025 – 1300 (+100)	£1200 × 1600 (plus 100 allowance for married men)
women	770 – 1045		
Sen. Graduate: men	545 × 25 – 845	750 × 25 – 1000 (+100)	840 × 40 – 1200 (£100 M.A.)
women	495 × 25 – 795		
Sen. Graduate: men	495 × 25 – 795 (+£50 M.A.)	700 × 25 – 950 (+100)	750 × 40 – 1110 (£100 M.A.)
women	445 × 25 – 745		
Graduate I: men	445 × 25 – 720 (+£50 M.A.)	550 × 25 – 900 (+100)	600 × 30 – 1020 (£100 M.A.)
women	395 × 25 – 670		
Non-Graduate I: men and women	300 × 20 – 540 (+£30 M.A.)	350 × 25 – 650 (+£60)	400 × 25 – 700 (+£60 M.A.)
Non-Graduate II: men and women	250 × 20 – 410 (£24 M.A.)	300 × 20 – 500 (+£48)	330 × 25 – 580 (+£48 M.A.)
Non-Graduate II: men and women	180 × 15 – 330 (+£24 M.A.)	240 × 20 – 400 (+£48)	280 × 25 – 480 (+£48 M.A.)

Notes: *M.A.* refers to allowance for married men.

Principals: Not incremental scales. Salary to be fixed for each school within above limits by the Education Authority and subject to review every three years.

Graduates: On appointment, graduates receive additional increments: (a) two increments (£60) for a 1st or 2nd Class Honours Degree; (b) two increments (£60) for a 1st Division Gen. or Pass Degree; (c) one increment (£30) for a 3rd Class Hons. Degree; (d) one increment (£30) for a 2nd Gen/Pass Degree; (e) a further two increments (£60) for Teacher's Diploma.

Non-Graduates: Personal Allowances payable to non-graduates with long service in special circumstances.

Source: Ministry of Education and Social Welfare, Paper presented to the House of Representatives, 6 March 1956, in *The JUT Clarion*, vol. xxvii, no. i, January/April 1956.

Table 4.6 Regarding and revision of salaries, 1967/8

Post	Present	Proposed regrading posts	Proposed salaries
Pre-trained teacher IV	270 × 20 – 290	Probationer	£ 320 × 20 – 360
Senior graduate I	£1100 × 50 – 1500	Senior graduate (Merged with senior graduate I)	£1100 × 50 – 1500 × 75 – 1650
Deputy headteacher:			
Primary	£ 600 × 30 – 900 × 40 – 980	Vice-principal	£ 750 × 30 – 900 × 40 – 1100 × 50 – 1159
Teacher-training college	£ 400 × 50 – 1650	Vice-principal	£1575 – 1875
Principals:			
Headteacher Grade IV	£ 600 × 30 – 900 × 40 – 940	Principal Class 4	£ 750 × 30 – 900 × 40 – 1100 × 50 – 1150
Teacher-training college Grade A	£2200	No change	£2500

Source: Ministry of Finance and Planning, Ministry Paper no. 49, 1967, Appendix I.

with which section of the civil service, for qualifications differed widely. Teachers' responses to the 1967/8 increases were very warm and they viewed the 1973/4 increases as marking a milestone in the history of settlements over teachers' salaries in the country.[58] The best evaluation of the financial position of teachers therefore is the fact that teachers in the early 1970s felt that a young person could turn to teacher for a reasonable career in public service instead of looking only to the civil service. This is a long way from the time when teachers struggled to enter the Education Department or other departments because the civil servant was financially superior to the teacher.[59]

Undoubtedly the economic position of teachers in the independence period has been far better than it had been in the colonial period. The JUT thus had a much weaker economic base than the JTA. The former spoke of its assets in terms of hundreds[60] but the latter could refer to them in terms of thousands, running as it did in the early 1970s the Jamaica Printing House, a large bookshop, a credit union and initiating various avenues of investments for members. The JTA had, therefore, in the period 1963/4 to 1967, the resources to make a mark on decision-makers whereas the resources of the JUT were less impressive. Indeed, given the limitations of the JUT and the political system in which it operated it is surprising that the Union managed to keep afloat for as long as it did. Of course, the changes which teachers underwent in the 1950s and 1960s came about largely because of the process of decolonization and independence and not as a result of teachers' efforts alone.

Competition and access

It remains now to consider the related questions of competition between unequally endowed groups and the access the teachers have had to the identified areas of the State responsible for decisions affecting education. There can be no doubt that a world existed in the colonial political system in which the JUT had to compete. In his study of pressure groups in the British West Indies between 1935 and 1945, E. S. Jones[61] placed the groups he found into six distinct categories: the business lobby, consisting of planters and merchants, the labour lobby, consisting of the trade unions; the professional associations which comprised teachers, doctors and lawyers; the religious bodies; community associations whose members included influential individuals and groups such as the Jamaica Progressive League and the National Reform Association and ethnic groups in Trinidad and Tobago and in British Guiana; and lastly the peasantry. Jones' findings on each of these rather loosely defined groups nonetheless reveal something about the nature of groups in the colonial period which were trying to influence the course of decision-making in their own favour.

The business lobby in Jamaica was closely associated with elites at various points in the society with whom they shared common values, colour and traditions. With their formal and informal contacts and combined efforts the groups had no difficulty in exerting an influence on decision-makers. For example, some of the members of the powerful Sugar Manufacturers Association were nominated members of the legislature and in London contacts were maintained chiefly through the West India Committee which had continued to exist since its founding during the struggle over the slave trade. These groups were very successful in blocking other groups from gaining access to decision-makers and they were particularly aggressive towards labour. In 1919, for example, they were successful in making the Trade Union Act less progressive than intended by making pickets responsible for damage to property.

The labour lobby, after the 1938 disturbances, was of course able to gain concessions for its members in spite of opposition by the business lobby. Jones remarked on the noticeable lack of organizations among the peasantry and the resulting high level of interest latency. The community groups he noted, tended to be organized from Kingston and other urban centres and in Trinidad and Tobago and British Guiana they were, additionally, organized along ethnic lines.

These groups fell into two categories: those seeking changes in the political 'boundaries' and concerned with status and political questions; the other type sought greater opportunities in government services and were concerned with economic, social and welfare questions. Of the 'professional' groups Jones considered the teachers and doctors as the more impressive in terms of organization compared with the lawyers. Doctors, he observed, were not opposed to the colonial structure; their prime concern was to control entry into the profession. They, of course, enjoyed a high status and had good connections and their co-operation was seen as indispensable by the Government in implementing policies.

Teachers, Jones correctly saw, were concerned with their trade union responsibilities and although strong locally they were weak nationally because of the nature of the franchise; there were, of course, more reasons why teachers were weak nationally, as indicated earlier. The JUT differed, however, from the other groups in so far as it had trade union as well as 'professional' responsibilities and could be regarded as falling into both of Jones' types of groups referred to above. Being a teachers' organization the JUT did not come into direct contact or conflict with the other groups except with the churches and sometimes with the bureaucracy which was not always as unified as may have been thought by actors engaged in contestations.[62]

Jones' general point is of course readily acceptable: groups which enjoyed high status in society were likely to gain access to decision-makers whereas others were not likely to do so. Certainly, in the colonial period the JUT was effectively blocked by its competitors. The churches sought to defend their position in the education system which they correctly saw as one of their main sources of strength in the community. Teachers did not constitute a high enough status group and their Union could not command the hearing it deserved. Although the Government needed the co-operation of the teachers and the JUT, when disputes arose between the Union and the churches the Government was more likely to give its support to the latter because of their indispensability and because they were more influential than the teachers. The churches also enjoyed the advantage of having strong links outside the colony. Furthermore, the churches owned nearly all the schools in the country. A Governor once wrote to the Secretary of State, confidentially, stating that,

> in a small colonial community where there is no leisure class, the Government cannot afford to deprive itself of the advice of active leaders of commercial and professional committees .... While the Governor would be expected to use his discretion to maintain public confidence by taking on himself any responsibility which cannot properly be shared with his unofficial advisers.[63]

In Jamaica the position of the churches was quickly recognized by the Board of Education. This was in marked contrast with its reply to the JUT, on its demand to nominate a representative on the Board, that it did

> not think that any public advantage would be gained by the appointment of any person representing any special section of the community and therefore does not recommend the appointment of a second elementary schoolteacher.[64]

The elementary schoolteacher referred to here was one appointed by the Governor without any reference to the JUT as the Union wished. The position of the JUT as a group seeking to apply press-ure on the Education Department was further weakened by the fact that the JUT's own resources were so limited that it had to depend on the Department's reports for a great deal of its information.[65] With these disadvantages the JUT in the colonial period found only limited access to decision-makers and it had to adapt or accommo-date itself to the whims of the colonial establishment to achieve even this minimum attention.

The politics of the post-independent period and the place occu-pied by the JTA was substantially different from those of the colo-nial period. The development of political parties in the 1940s and 1950s and the necessity to accept certain changes by the strong support and entrenched business groups in the Colonial Office and Whitehall forced old and new groups to seek new allies. The defeat of the Jamaica Democratic Party, which was formed by members of the more conservative and traditional socio-economic elements of the dominant class to defend their interests, and the independent candidates in the 1944 elections, revealed the need for the old – and new – socio-economic groups to seek representation within one of the two major political parties. After 1944 representation was sought within the JLP which was less hostile to the established economic interests but after the PNP 'purged' itself of its orthodox Marxists in 1952, it too came to represent these interests, thereby dividing the political articulation of the dominant class. The econo-mic groups, which had not in any event responded uniformly to the changes which the country underwent after 1938 were, by the 1960s, adequately represented within one, and often both, political parties.

As noted earlier, the powerful trade unions which emerged after 1938 were closely linked to the parties. Professional and semi-professional groups, such as teachers, were able to remain relatively free of any formal association with either of the parties; teachers' leaders had developed a keen sense of their 'professional' responsi-bilities. But to a far more significant degree than other groups in these categories, teachers conceived of their interests in terms of political nationalism and continued to give their informal support to the PNP which had led the early nationalist movement in Jamaica. Thus, although a semi-professional group, the JTA followed, to some extent, the trade unions in the support they gave to one or the other, but not both, political parties.

With greater resources and better social and political contacts with government and the administration the JTA was in a position to be far more successful than the JUT could. It was not formally blocked by any group for the churches came to see that in the new re-alignment their interests were best served by siding with the teachers who had proved that they were capable of reorganizing themselves to face the post-colonial state. In the changing conditions of the period immediately after independence teachers became a fairly high status group. They were now able to translate their local power into national power so that they could command a hearing and gain the desired access to government departments. And, occasionally, some of their leaders could walk the corridors of power.

Notes

1   See for example, A. E. Burt, The first instalment of representative government in Jamaica, 1884, *SES*, vol. ii, no. iii (1962), p. 245.

2   The proceedings of the Legislative Council were reported by the *Daily Gleaner* in this period and some of the elected members notably D. T. Wint (*The Jamaica Critic* which later became *The West Indian Critic and Review*) and J. A. G. Smith (started his *Searchlight* in 1936), were themselves publicists. For a discussion see, J. Carnegie, *Some aspects of Jamaica's politics, 1918-38* (Kingston: Institute of Jamaica, 1974), chapters 4-5; also R. N. Murray (ed.), *J. J. Mills: his own account of his life and times*, (Kingston: Collins and Sangster (Jamaica) Ltd., 1969), pp. 123-5.

3   E. F. L. Wood, *Report on a Visit to the West Indies and British Guiana*, Cmd. 1879 (London, HMSO, 1922), p. 13.

4   *Jamaica Laws, certified copies of Acts 1889-1893*, C.O. 139, no. 106 Law 32 of 1892; *W.I.R.C. 1938-9*, C.O. 950, no. 117, J. 154, Oral Evidence, p. 15ff.

5   At the 1929 Annual Conference the executive was asked whether there were any benefits to be derived from being affiliated to the NUT such as representation being made in London on behalf of the JUT; the reply was that the JUT had asked the NUT in 1906 and in 1923 to make representation on the behalf of Jamaican teachers. In 1939 the NUT also made representation to the Moyne Commission in London on the behalf of West Indian teachers. See, *The Daily Gleaner*, 9 January 1929, p. 14; also, 10 January 1929, p. 16.

6   Stephen J. Yorke, 'Parliamentary control in a small developing country: Jamaica 1962-1970', (Unpublished M.Sc. Thesis, Department of Government, University of the West Indies, Mona, January 1972.)

7   *Ibid.*; both the Education Bill and the Code of Regulations went before Select Committees although the second was a continuation of the first.

8   The weakness of the legislature was further demonstrated in 1974 when the Prime Minister, Mr Michael Manley, was able to have the Gun Court and Suppression of Crime (Special Provisions) Acts passed within a few days, thereby overriding provisions in the Constitution for debate on legislation. See for example, *The Jamaica Daily News*, 22 March 1974, p. 7; for a brief but fair discussion see, Jacqueline Kaye and Mary Turner, Jamaican Gun Courts, *New Society*, vol. 29, no. 620

(22 August 1974), pp. 469-70.

9 G. E. Mills, Public administration in the Commonwealth Caribbean: evolution, conflicts and challenges, *SES*, vol. xix, no. i (March 1970). Reprinted 1974, Special Number, *Problems of Administrative Change in the Commonwealth Caribbean*, G. E. Mills (ed.), p. 5ff.

10 *The JUT Magazine*, vol. ii, no. v (August/September 1930), pp. 1–2.

11 Cf. *The New Clarion*, vol. ix, no. i (January/February 1973), p. 7; also, 'Interviews with officials of the JTA', (1974).

12 *The Daily Gleaner*, 15 January 1896, editorial read:

> We are pleased to note the reasonable demands and the moderate tone of the union in approaching the Board of Education and the Education Department.

The editor, DeCordova, was also a member of the Board of Education and became an honorary member of the JUT.

13 *The Daily Gleaner*, 14 January 1896, p. 4. 'Interviews with officials of the JTA', (1974).

14 Cf. Trevor Munroe, 'The People's National Party 1938-1944: a view of the early Nationalist Movement in Jamaica', (Unpublished M.Sc. thesis, Department of Government, University of the West Indies, Mona, Jamaica, 1966), particularly chapter 3.

15 The JUT was one of the groups listed in the 1940 Constitution of the PNP which was eligible to affiliate with the party, *Ibid.*, pp. 19-33; in 1938-9 the JUT carefully considered being affiliated to the PNP but eventually did not do so. See, 'The Annual Report of the JUT for the year ending 1939' *The files of the JTA*, p. 4; also 'Interview with Mr A. A. Macpherson' 16 January 1974.

16 For example, in 1938 H. F. Cooke (One of a series of Ministers of Education in the PNP 1972-80 Government) was elected to the PNP's General Council; so too were other prominent JUT members such as V. A. Bailey, Amy Bailey and O. H. Cameron; in the 1944 elections Edith Dalton-James, V. A. Bailey and W. W. Benjamin stood for the party. See, Munroe, *op. cit*; 'Interviews with JTA officials' (1974). It is generally assumed that at least 75 per cent of teachers support the PNP and although the JLP would quote a higher figure it must be noted that no systematic work has been done to show the extent to which these assertions are correct. What is clear, however, is that the PNP gets strong support from the teaching community and that the JTA is very strongly pro-PNP.

17 *The Daily Gleaner*, 5 September 1929, p. 21.

18 The best example of this was the critical response of teachers to the salary negotiations in 1952; in 1974 teachers in secondary schools were also critical of Mrs Fay Saunders' handling of the salary negotiations and raised serious questions at Conference.

19 Widespread dissatisfaction with the executive over the negotiations of the new salary scales went as far as some assistant teachers leaving the JUT and forming a new union which existed for one year before folding up and members returning to the JUT. The assistant teachers who broke away were mainly female teachers; they felt that the new scales would benefit only the headteachers. *The Daily Gleaner* gave good coverage to the event, see for example, *The Daily Gleaner*, 10,

15, 18, 19, 21 April, 11 August and 25 September 1952 and 7 January 1953; and 'Interview with Mr A. A. MacPherson', 14 March 1974. Mr MacPherson succeeded Mrs Dalton-James in 1953 as President of the JUT and was responsible for handling the situation.

20 For example, *The JUT Magazine* and the *The JUT Clarion* which it later became, changing after the JTA was formed into *The New Clarion*; the JTA published some newsletters, particularly during times of crisis.

21 For example, whereas in 1897 there were only 255 women teachers in 1930 there were 965 which was a majority of elementary school-teachers in the country. See, T. Capper, 'The system of education in Jamaica', E. M. Sadler (ed.) *Educational systems in the chief colonies of the British Empire*, Great Britain: Board of Education Special Reports on educational subjects, vol. iv. Cd. 416, (London: HMSO 1901), p. 567; and Education Department, 'Report for the year ended 31 December 1930', the *Annual General Report of Jamaica togehter with Departmental Reports for 1930* (Kingston: Government Printing Office, 1931).

22 Bailey, *op. cit.* ch. 2; 'Annual Report of the JUT for the year ended 30 November 1899', p. 1; also *The Daily Gleaner*, 8 October 1894; and *The Teacher*, vol. ii, no. x, 13 October 1902, p. 85. The aim of this paper was to 'help teachers in difficulties of school work' and advise them on the best methods of teaching. Its editor, A. L. Walcott, who worked from Kingston, was later to become a president of the Union.

23 *The New Clarion*, Annual and Conference No., December 1964, p. 6.

24 'The JTA membership and organization', (December, 1973), p. 2, *The files of the JTA*.

25 *The Jamaica Teachers' Association, 10 years, 1964-74*, (Kingston: JTA, 1974), pp. 2-3.

26 The question of compulsory membership was considered at the 1973/4 Annual Conference and many young teachers expressed the view that the Association should take steps to secure the Ministry's approval.

27 I am grateful to the late Dr P. C. C. Evans, formerly of the Institute of Education, London University, for allowing me to see his unpublished MS on teachers in rural Jamaica, particularly chapters 8/9 'The role of the teacher in Jamaican rural society' and 'Changing patterns of rural leadership'; see also M. G. Smith, *The plural society in the British West Indies* (University of California Press, 1965), chapter vii, and, Edward P. G. Seaga, Parent-teacher relationships in a Jamaican village, *SES* vol. iv, no. iii (1955), pp. 289-302.

28 See, Sydney Collins, Social mobility in Jamaica, with reference to rural committees and the teaching profession, *Transactions of the Third World Congress of Sociology*, vol. iii (1956), pp. 267-75; also Ivy Reid, What a way him talk bad, *The JUT Clarion*, vol. xxxv (June 1963), p. 5.

29 P. C. C. Evans, *op. cit.* ch. 7, 'Formal and informal rural associations'; also Seaga, *op. cit.*; M. G. Smith and G. J. Kruiger, *A sociological manual for extension workers in the Caribbean*, (1957), particularly, Sydney Collins, 'The teacher in rural Jamaica', pp. 45-52.

30 'The Annual Report of the JUT, 1903', p. 24, *The files of the JTA*.

31 *The Daily Gleaner*, 11 January 1919, p. 21; also, 4 January 1921.

32 *The Wood Report*, p. 66.
33 *Ibid.*
34 R. N. Murray, *op. cit.*; *The Jamaican Critic*, vol. iv, no. i (January 1929), pp. 4-5; also *The West Indian Critic and Review*, vol. iv, no. xi, (November 1920), pp. 12-29.
35 *The Daily Gleaner*, 28 March 1929, p. 10.
36 *Ibid.*
37 'Education Department Report for 1930', *op. cit.*, p. 222; also *The Handbook for Jamaica 1895*, (Kingston: Government Printing Office, 1895), pp. 307-11.
38 'Board of Education, Report for the year ended 31 December 1932', *The Annual General Report of Jamaica together with Departmental Reports for 1932* (Kingston: Government Printing Office, 1934), pp. 19-20.
39 T. Capper, *op. cit.*, p. 596.
40 R. N. Murray, *op. cit.*, pp. 62-3.
41 *The Daily Gleaner*, 8 January 1919, p. 11.
42 *The Daily Gleaner*, 15 January 1920, p. 11.
43 'Report of a meeting of the Board of Education, 23 and 24 October 1900', p. 2, *The Annual General Report of Jamaica together with Departmental Reports for 1900*, (Kingston: Government Printing Office, 1901).
44 *Ibid.*
45 *Ibid.*, p. 3.
46 *The Daily Gleaner*, 10 January 1919, p. 3.
47 *The Daily Gleaner*, 27 September 1920, p. 4; January 4 1921.
48 *W.I.R.C. 1938-9*, C.O. 950, no. 97, J. 113, 'Exhibit C'.
49 *W.I.R.C. 1938-9*, C.O. 950, no. 901, G. 7041, p. 2 and no. 82, J. 117, p. 3.
50 'Report of the Commission appointed to enquire into the staffing of government offices and the emoluments of public officers and employees, 1928', *The Minutes of the Legislative Council of Jamaica for the Year 1929*, vol. 70 (1930), Appendix xiv., Appendix A. Sometimes referred to as the 'Report of the Salaries Commission'.
51 *Ibid.*; also 'Board of Education Report for the year ended 31 December 1930', *The Annual General Report of Jamaica together with Departmental Reports for 1930*, (Kingston: Government Printing Office, 1931), p. 16.
52 *W.I.R.C. 1938-9* C.O. 950, no. 82, J. 117, p. 3.
53 See, *The Minutes of the Legislative Council of Jamaica for the Year 1930* (Kingston: Government Printing Office, 1931).
54 *The JUT Magazine*, vol. xxviii, no. 1 (January/April 1956), pp. 5-9; *The Daily Gleaner*, 7 March 1956.
55 Memorandum on Teachers' Salaries submitted by the President of the AAMM to the Minister of Education and Social Welfare, 30 April 1956, *AAMM Journal*, Summer 1956, p. 7-8.
56 'Regrading and revision of salaries of teachers, 1967/8', *Ministry Paper no. 49*, 10 July 1967 (Kingston: Ministry of Finance and Planning) Appendix i.
57 'Classification and salary plan for teachers', *Ministry Paper no. 37*, April 1973 (Kingston: Ministry of Finance) Appendix.

58   *The New Clarion*, Annual & Conference no., vol. ix, no. v (December 1973), p. 33.

59   After 1920 the Education Department expanded with nine assistant inspectors of schools and these posts were mainly held by some of the best elementary schoolteachers seeking promotion. The criticism was frequently levelled that the Department used these posts as means of co-opting some of the best teachers of the JUT, See, R. N. Murray, *op. cit.*, pp. 66-7; Cf. 'Interview with Mr A. A. MacPherson' 16 January 1974.

60   Murray, *op cit.* p. 13; 'Annual Report Business Section', presented to the JTA Conference January 1974; also, 'The financial statement and Auditor's Report on the accounts of the Jamaica Teachers' Association, as at 31 August 1973', *The files of the JTA.*

61   E. S. Jones, 'Pressure group politics in the West Indies: a case study of colonial systems, Jamaica, Trinidad and British Guiana' (Unpublished Ph.D. Thesis, University of Manchester, 1970).

62   Involved as the bureaucracy was in both political and administrative functions it was far from the Weberian ideal type; Jones noted also that there was a clear difference of interests between higher and lower echelons. See, Jones, *op. cit.*, pp. 115-117; Cf. B. St. J. Hamilton, *Problems of administration in an emergent nation: a case study of Jamaica*, (New York: F. A. Praeger, 1965), ch. 1.

63   Quoted in Jones, *op. cit.*, p. 139.

64   'Board of Education, Report for the year ended 31 December 1920', *The Annual General Report of Jamaica together with the Departmental Reports for 1920* (Kingston: Government Printing Office, 1922), p. 21.

65   *W.I.R.C. 1938-9*, C.O. 950 no. 82, J. 117, Oral Evidence p. 54ff.

CHAPTER 5 | The JUT and the colonial order

Throughout its more than seventy years' existence the JUT remained true to its original aim of representing the interests of schoolteachers and being a moderate organization. It never achieved the aim of representing teachers in other spheres of education and from the 1930s teachers in secondary schools and teachers' colleges began to found their own organizations. Little of importance to elementary education and schoolteachers passed without comment from the JUT and it is therefore necessary to look, in this chapter, at some of the issues raised by the Union and the results achieved, if any, within the constraints superimposed by the colonial political order upon an already repressive social system.

Doubtful as it may seem, the years selected (1928-31) for analysis of the JUT's activities were chosen largely at random. The issues, activities and outcomes were not particularly unusual. Some of these existed before the years 1928-31 and continued to exist thereafter. Any other years could have been chosen because although there is some unevenness in availability of material (partly due to the JUT's own defective records), there is an abundance of useful material to be found in the newspapers, government papers and sundry publications of the times. Indeed, the usefulness of selecting particular years for more detailed treatment arose from the very repetitive nature of teachers' demands, protests, etc. Moreover, it is the view that this approach may be more revealing than an alternative one which would be thematic in its selection of issues and activities.

The years 1928-31 none the less had their own peculiarities. After all, these were times of crisis internationally. In parts of Europe, chiefly Weimar Germany, the new wave of crisis in capitalist enterprises reached its nadir, affecting all levels of society. In Britain and the USA, the societies of the advanced world with which Jamaica had everything to do, the impact of the breakdown was being severely felt. It was to be expected, therefore, that in this situation of general economic hardship, the Government in Jamaica would be concerned to cut public spending,[1] given pre-Keynesian economic thinking upon which policy-makers operated. In Jamaica like the rest of the Anglophone Caribbean these developments were to be important in setting the stage for the events which started in Trinidad and Tobago from 1935 and by 1938 amounted to a challenge of the repressive social order which the colonial state had not done enough to change.

It is true that in these years the State's concern to curb public spending did not affect recurrent expenditure on education. None the less, the Government was not willing to spend more on it. Expectedly, most of the issues raised by the JUT entailed increased state expenditure.

In their attempts to influence the Director of Education and the Governor, who were the effective decision-makers with respect to education, the JUT's leaders did not depart from the Union's original moderate tactics. Of course, this was in no way unusual. It must be remembered, first, that only in recent decades have professional and semi-professional groups started to adopt the tactics of blue-collar workers, such as the strike, and generally such groups tend to eschew militancy. Second, the JUT for part of its life operated within the constraints of an authoritarian political order in which trade unions were illegal. Even when they did become legal in 1919 unions continued to suffer from very severe restrictions such as responsibility for damages during a strike. It took the events of 1938 to force the colonial and Whitehall governments to recognize formally that the victories of the British, European and American working classes were universal.

The spirit of moderation – tactics and activities

To demonstrate its moderate stance the JUT made special efforts to declare its rejection of militant tactics. There is no evidence that the leaders of the Union ever contemplated in these years or any other, the use of the strike, for example, as a tactical weapon or even a threat. In the spirit of moderation they sought to avoid antagonism of any kind between themselves and the Government and to minimize potential conflicts. Expressed in other terms, the JUT was behaving in a manner that one researcher in the English urban context of Kensington and Chelsea found interesting and is of relevance here. Dearlove argued that councillors in the Royal Borough found some groups to be 'helpful' and others 'unhelpful'. The former type had what was regarded as a 'proper communication style' whilst the latter had 'an improper communication style'. Councillors, therefore, tended to treat these groups according to their styles of communication. Dearlove found too that councillors categorized the demands groups made on the council and that 'because the Councillors' categorization of groups is known to many of the groups themselves, this has an effect on group life within the borough'.[2]

Groups which persisted in being 'unhelpful' were likely to go out of existence. In other words, the perceptions of decision-makers are likely to have an important effect on the existence of groups and their behaviour. The point may be expressed another way: because the teachers' leaders sensed that their voices were not likely to command the same respect as those of the churches by decision-makers, the leaders of the JUT sought to make the Union a 'helpful' group and to develop what would be seen by decision-makers as a proper communication style.

It was tactically useful, therefore, for the JUT leaders to continue repeating the policy of eschewing militant tactics which had been declared from its founding. It may be useful to illustrate this point from examples in the years 1928-31. Addressing a meeting of teachers in 1929 E. S. Jarrett, the treasurer of the Union, stressed that

> The JUT did not exist to fight the Government, the Education Department, the Education Officers nor any other organization, as some people thought. It existed for the purpose of bringing the teachers together and to give them the chance to interchange ideas and build up themselves.[3]

J. J. Mills likened the JUT to guilds which existed for self-improvement rather than trade unions. The founders of the JUT did not want the Union to be 'aggressive' and leaders thirty or more years later were keeping to this original intention. Throughout the history of the JUT and certainly during these years, leaders wanted to distinguish themselves from groups which sought to use less moderate tactics than the Union, and so they made a special effort to stress the non-trade union aspect of the organization. This was less offensive to the authorities.

The Board of Education, through which most demands had to be channelled before they reached the Governor who was for all practical purposes the central state institution, did not draw much criticism from the Union. This was not because leaders were unaware of the Board's limitations. The awareness of its limitations and the desire to avoid open criticism were echoed by H. B. Monteith, the retiring president, in 1928. He told the Annual Conference:

> Whether it is the function of the Board to be very consider-

ate about and sympathetic towards the question of the country's financial position, or whether, as one of its members declared, it is the function of the Board to make recommendations and leave the financial side of the matter to the Legislative Council, is a question which I do not propose discussing ....[4]

It was perhaps best to leave the question alone, not only because the Board filtered the Union's demands to the Governor but also because the Union wanted the support of the Board against the churches. At the very least, it was not wise to alienate the Board in the face of the often strong opposition which came from the churches. It was important therefore for leaders to develop a 'proper style of communication'. It was in this spirit that J. J. Mills addressed the Annual Conference in 1930 in the following terms.

Several recommendations passed by the Board of Education bearing on pressing educational needs have not come up for consideration in the Legislative Council. Thus it appears that whilst practically every other branch of government or semi-government service has received deserved consideration, especially in respect of salaries and pensions, education must wait for the last. *But we must not be unreasonable over this extreme caution. The present government has striven to improve all sections of the community economically and socially; we believe that in time the government will turn its attention more closely to the needs of education.*[5] (emphasis added)

As a moderate Union the JUT attempted also to make maximum use of the established though limited channels of access to decision-makers. These included petitions and deputations to the Legislative Council and the Governor. It argued its cases in moderate tones and attempted, sensibly, to justify most demands by saying that they were in the interest of the public good. The Union's leaders often argued their cases in strong moralistic terms instead of concentrating on giving an objective tone to their briefs. But this approach had its advantages in an overtly religious society where it was useful for leaders to demonstrate that the JUT was not concerned exclusively with the interests of its members but was also aware of the general needs of their communities.

To these ends, the mass media, such as existed, were important for teachers. Their leaders, therefore, sought, and quite often received, extensive coverage in the press for the JUT's activities. The

Annual Conference in January of each year, the various meetings of local and federal associations throughout the island and statements by leaders throughout the year, were reported in the *Daily Gleaner*, as a reading of these papers through the period from 1894 will show. Sometimes even the executive meetings of the Union were items of news in the paper. D. T. Wint's *Jamaica Critic* (later, *The West Indian Critic and Review*) also publicized the Union's views and activities, though less so than the *Daily Gleaner*. In 1928 the JUT started its own publicity organ, the *JUT Magazine* (hereafter, the *Magazine*) which boldly stated that it was

> intended to foster and promote the educational interests of the Colony as its (the *Magazine*'s) aims are identical with the aims of the JUT – aims which we make bold to say are approved by every intelligent member of this community – (and) we feel confident that it will receive from the public the approval and support it deserves.[6]

Although there was no large electorate to be influenced, as a group concerned with education the JUT sought to broaden the discussion on educational matters so that it could claim to have a hearing in the community. But leaders were also concerned to influence the relatively few who were electors so as to affect the results of the elections for the legislature, which were being held in 1930.

At the Annual Conference for that year, J. J. Mills made it known that,

> it was not an official task of the JUT to take sides in the general election movement going on. Nevertheless, every member of the profession knows that his duty is to see that the candidate getting his support fully understands and sympathizes actively with the cause of education.[7]

His speech also revealed that candidates saw education as an important vote-catching item on their platform:

> The manifestos of many aspirants to the Legislative Council, though mentioning the subject, reveal quite a crammed and hurried acquaintanceship with this important public question, or a shallow promise of nothing in particular. Our conviction is that no would-be reformer who thinks of leaving popular education to take care of itself can do much good for Jamaica at any time.[8]

It would be expected of any group concerned with education to provide a platform for discussions on educational matters, but the general weakness of the JUT as a group and the desire of its leaders to project an image of the Union as 'helpful' tended to exaggerate this aspect of its work. Although the *Magazine* was important in this regard, it was used, not surprisingly, almost entirely by teachers themselves and occasionally by inspectors of schools. The Annual Conference was by far the most important occasion for different sides to meet. By the 1920s and 1930s it was quite common for the Mayor of Kingston to welcome teachers to Kingston and for the Director of Education, the Bishop of Jamaica and other prominent citizens to address the Conference. From this platform the JUT leaders gave notice to Government of the Union's intentions on specific issues and government officials also made announcements on education.

The Bishop of Jamaica, an influential friend of the JUT, an honorary member of the Union and member of the Board of Education, told the Conference in 1929, that

> when sitting on that Board I always listen with much interest to any recommendations that come from my Union. Usually those recommendations are sound and practical and I believe I am correct in saying that invariably they receive the most careful consideration of the Board, though we do not always concur on what is suggested.[9]

The Bishop then went on to disagree strongly with the Union's proposals to the Government for the 'nationalization' of the schools (which, of course, would hurt only the churches). Much of this was meant to 'exhort' teachers to do 'good works', 'to civilize', but what is particularly interesting is that both Vaz, the Mayor, and the Bishop of Jamaica attempted to indicate that they were behind the teachers.

The Union depended greatly on influential friends who were appropriately placed from the standpoint of the JUT. Groups always depend to varying degrees on such contacts but since the JUT was repeatedly denied the continuous access it desired, such as having one of its members, chosen by the executive of the Union, on the Board of Education, this was usually important. In these years the JUT was fortunate to have the support of some of the most prominent members of the Legislative Council and the Board of Education. The supporters on the Board were F. Meyers, an elementary schoolteacher who, like all the other members, was appointed by the Governor, and D. T. Wint, a former elementary schoolteacher. In the Legislative Council, support came from D. T.

Wint himself, L. Cawley and J. A. G. Smith. Wint and Smith who were very prominent men gave their strong support to teachers although they were often critical of each other.

'Jag' Smith, a famous barrister coming out of the Clarendon hills, dominated the political scene from the time he entered the Legislative Council in 1916 until the events of 1938 pushed him into the background of public life. He remained, however, in the Legislative Council until 1942 when he died. Throughout his political career Smith enjoyed the support of teachers in the Parish of Clarendon which he represented in the Legislative Council and it was well for him to assure them, particularly since there would be elections for the Council in 1930, of his continued support.

Wint, a former president of the Union and one of the first elementary schoolteachers to be elected to the Legislative Council, was not only prominent in the Council, but he was also a journalist of some standing.[10] He was frequently asked in these years to sit on committees of the Council and the Board of Education of which he was a member. In these capacities – member of the Legislative Council, various committees and the Board of Education, and as journalist – Wint served the cause of the JUT.

If the strike action is taken as an example of overt political action and the reliance on influential friends as an example of covert political action, then the tactics and activities of the JUT in 1928-31, as before and after, were of the latter type. By being an extremely 'helpful' group the JUT avoided the possibility of any overt confrontation with the authorities which would have entailed the use of militant tactics. It is important to see what implications being a 'helpful' group in the colonial political system had for the issues the JUT raised in the years under consideration.

It is not necessary, however, to give an exhaustive treatment to all the issues the JUT raised between 1928 and 1931. Many of these were very trivial and of little general importance. To avoid over-generalization and to ensure against over-elaboration, therefore, it is perhaps best to treat one or two representative issues of different kinds in the hope that this will give a satisfactory picture of the general behaviour of the Union in these years. There were three kinds of issues – technical or trade union, professional and political – each of which may be treated separately.

Trade union issues

The more salient issues of the technical type were of a trade union nature and I propose to outline two of these here: the conflict between schoolteachers and managers and the question of salary increases for teachers. The Union also raised 'technical issues' which were not primarily trade union issues, for example, publishing the results of pupil-teachers' examinations in the papers, and medical treatment for children at school.[11] Of course, these could develop into trade union issues, depending largely on how the authorities responded to the representation of the teachers but in the first instance these could hardly be described as being trade union issues affecting conditions of work or remuneration.

Article 40

The Code of Regulations (under the Elementary Education Law of 1892[12]) reinforced the existing unfair advantage of the school manager over schoolteachers. The employment of teachers (article 38) and the termination of their services (article 40) remained the tasks of the manager in elementary schools. Teachers therefore often complained that too much power was left in the hands of the manager who frequently acted arbitrarily in his relations to them. They were particularly bitter over what they saw as frequent and unfair dismissal of colleagues by a manager acting without the knowledge of his assistants (these were referred to in the Code as co-managers and visitors) who were supposed to ensure a minimum of fair-play. Such incidents were reported to be particularly frequent in the church-run schools which were by far the most numerous. For similar reasons the machinery which existed for complaints and redress was under the influence of the manager, which made it inadequate as an instrument of justice, as far as the teachers were concerned.[13]

The Union saw Article 40 as being 'The Article that provides (sic) THAT THOSE WHO EMPLOY SHALL NOT PAY, AND THOSE WHO PAY SHALL NOT DISMISS OR EMPLOY.'[14]

For it was the Department of Education which actually paid the salary of the teacher, but the manager was responsible for employing and terminating employment. Such a situation was bound to lead to personal resentments and later to conflict as teachers became more aware of themselves as a distinct group.[15]

The mix of the formal and the informal in the nature of the relationship which existed between the teacher and the manager caused conflict and resentment, because the relationship worked against the interests of the teacher. For example, the manager was responsible for distributing the salaries of teachers in the schools under his jurisdiction and this could lead to irregular practices.[16] The supervision and general conduct of these schools were also under his purview. When he visited them he was directed by the Code to comment about these matters and the teachers in the log books. These would be sent at the end of the year to the Department to assess the teachers' grades upon which their salaries partly depended. To communicate with the Department the teacher also had to do it through the manager or the local inspector of schools who was likely to be more friendly with the manager than the teacher. There was therefore, on the one hand, a definite and formal relationship between the teacher and the manager which was officially sanctioned but not always impartially regulated. On the other hand, there had grown up an informal relationship sanctioned by custom. Nearly all managers were clergymen.[17] Indeed, it was by virtue of this that they became managers of the schools owned by their denominations. Since a minister could not always preach at all the churches under his ministry on Sundays, it was taken for granted, from the early days when the churches became involved with education, that the teachers under his management could be called upon to deputize either as preachers or as Sunday School teachers. This had worked well in a society where teachers were closely tied to the denominations by conviction and doctrine. It became a tacit understanding that, on recruitment, the teacher would be prepared to undertake such tasks, often without pay and irrespective of personal beliefs, if and when called upon by the manager-minister. As noted in an earlier chapter, many ambitious teachers could use this as a route into the ministry or thereby improve his social and financial standing. However, this was very likely to lead to a situation of conflict, as teaching became distinct from preaching. If a teacher were of a different denomination from the one owning the school in which he taught or if he had no strong faith the possibility of conflict became even stronger. But the manager had both official and customary sanctions on his side while the teacher who was bold enough to question the situation jeopardized his chances of promotion and his salary.

The JUT called upon the Department to remedy the situation by placing managers under its more stringent and direct control. The Union did not demand that article 40 be revised completely. Rather, in the spirit of moderation, its leaders called for an amendment to the article. This was not a demand for fundamental changes in the relationship between the teacher and his immediate employer, the manager. It was simply a request for the establishment of means whereby misunderstandings and injustices could be smoothed out amicably.

In support of its proposed amendment the spokesmen of the

JUT argued that the strained relations between teachers and managers worked against the best interests of both. One teacher, writing to the *Magazine*, correctly identified the issue as arising out of the dual control of the schools although he could not see why, 'under Article 40 there is no dual control manifested with respect to the dismissal of teachers'.[18]

Inevitably, the Union was staunchly opposed by the managers who were the cornerstones of the churches in the local communities. To challenge the position of the manager was therefore openly to challenge the position of the churches. What the churches wanted the Government to participate in more actively was not the control of the managers or of the schools but the financing of education. It may be recalled that the 1892 education laws for both elementary and secondary schools, particularly the former, were victories for the denominations, not for schoolteachers.

In brief, the managers countered by agreeing that there were grounds for concern but their identification of the cause and their recommended remedy differed from those of the JUT.[19] The basic problem, they argued, was a shortage of voluntary personnel. They pointed out that since managers were not paid functionaries of the Government, if it were to assume full responsibility for the local administration of education it would be very costly to the State to have to pay for such voluntary services. Of course, neither the Government nor the JUT suggested that managers should vacate their place in the local administration of education, but by posing the issue in such an extreme way the managers were able to remind both, but in particular the Government, of their indispensablity. If the manager refused to co-operate with the Government the education system would most likely collapse. They maintained that in any case the manager was held in check by his denomination and the community he served. The abuses about which the teachers were making a hue and cry were greatly exaggerated.

On this issue the teachers gained very little satisfaction from the authorities. In 1928/9, most pressure in the form of writings and speeches was directed at a committee of the Board of Education which was set up in October 1928, to investigate and recommend changes in the Code of Regulations.[20] The JUT was fortunate to have three 'influential friends' on the Committee of six, A. J. Newman, principal of the Mico Training College and a former president of the Union, F. A. Meyers and D. T. Wint. The recommendations which eventually emerged from the Board of Education went before the Governor-in-Privy Council on 14 June 1931 and were introduced in the Legislative Council on 17 November 1931.[21]

Although teachers gained some minor concessions on the less important Articles the crucial issue of Article 40 was lost to the clergy despite the determined fighting on the Board by Meyers and Wint. Wint had submitted a Minority Report which called for Article 40 to be strictly adhered to by ensuring that managers were not able to dismiss teachers without the notice of dismissal having the signature of at least one assistant manager.[22] The Majority Report, which was also signed by Newman and Meyers, recommended that the manager's power to dismiss a teacher remain but that the teacher should have the automatic right to ask the Department to carry out an investigation. At the decisive Special Meeting of the Board in May at which both the Majority and Minority Reports were given detailed consideration the manager/clergymen on the Board such as the Revs W. B. Esson, Cowell Lloyd, John Currey and Fr Francis Kelly won a resounding victory.

The Revised Code was to allow the manager to lay a heavier hand on the teacher guilty of 'professional misconduct' (a question which was never disputed by teachers) but the Department was also to exercise a more formal control over the manager. More responsibility was placed on the school inspector who was to investigate any matter of this nature which was reported to the Department in the schools in his Parish. The manager was reminded that he had to notify the Department of any summary dismissal of teachers within a week of doing so. Overall, the teacher's position remained much the same as before. The power of the Department to exercise a tighter control over the manager was most likely never exercised for it lacked the resources to keep a close check on the activities of the manager,[23] and the structural imbalance, or bias in favour of the manager/clergyman remained.

Salaries

Another important trade union issue frequently raised by teachers was the vexed question of salaries. Leaders correctly maintained that teachers were very badly paid. The 1920 reforms improved their general conditions and placed their salaries on fixed scales for the first time but as noted in chapter three of this study, teachers' leaders were not entirely satisfied with this settlement. The maximum a headteacher could earn was £200 per annum and relatively few earned this. The assistant teacher with a first class certificate could hope for no more than £100 per annum while at the other end of the scale the annual salary was as little as £25. Pupil-teachers who made up a significant number of the teaching force received considerably less.

In 1928 the JUT Annual Conference made a demand for a new minimum salary for all grades of teachers. The Union called for a minimum of £105 per annum for the lowest paid headmaster and for a new maximum for headmasters of £240 per annum. Assistant teachers should start at a new minimum of £30 per annum with a new maximum of £120 per annum.[24] There was also a demand that the minimum grants given to pupil-teachers should be raised from £6 to £8 per annum. In support of its claim the JUT pointed out that it was high time the teachers received an improvement in salaries, particularly in the light of the rise in the cost of living, the unfavourable comparison of teachers with others in government service and the fact that the Government was considering giving civil servants an increase. The point was repeatedly made that teachers deserved the consideration of the Government because of the nature of the work they did. At no point however was the demand put very forcibly by the JUT. No doubt this was so because the Union did not want to appear to be a mere trade union making demands for its members at a time when there was general hardship in the country.

At the special meetings of the Board of Education which decided on the recommendations of the Code Committee, to which this issue was referred, Wint argued, often successfully, in support of teachers. The Majority Report of the Committee suggested that the number of grades of headmasters should be lessened from five to three but that the five grades of schools should remain. Wint convinced the Board that such a scheme would result in confusion. This would be particularly so since teachers were paid, not on the basis of the grades they had achieved, but on those of their schools which, in turn, depended largely on the number of children in attendance. The Majority Report also suggested that the salary scales of all teachers should be slightly improved without raising the ceiling of £200 for headmasters except those in schools in Kingston, Montego Bay and Port Antonio. Wint disagreed with preferential treatment for teachers along these lines but agreed that the ceiling should not be raised, and again succeeded in carrying the Board. He agreed that all teachers should be upgraded, and also drew attention to those at the lower end of the occupation.

The Board of Education eventually recommended that the salaries of teachers should be upgraded but the Government found that, in its weak economic position, it could afford no more than £8,000[25] while the whole demand of the JUT would have cost an estimated £26,340 per annum.[26] It was decided that the proposed upgrading of assistant teachers should be partly met but that an increase for headteachers should be postponed. The assistant teachers received increased amounts of only about £7,700 per annum.

In the circumstances, the JUT saw this as a worthwhile victory; the *Magazine* said of the settlement, 'We are glad that at least those badly paid servants of the government and the people have come in for some consideration.'[27] On the Government's deferring the proposed increase for headteachers the *Magazine* commented,

> Well, the head teachers must wait a little longer and pray that no calamity befall Jamaica which would of necessity aggravate the financial depression now being experienced.[28]

The JUT could understand the limitations of the Government and since it was a 'helpful' and 'reasonable' group it would act responsibly in the light of the colony's weak economic situation. The next salary increase for teachers did not come until over ten years later.[29]

Professional issues

In the years 1928-31 the JUT's 'professional' demands reflected a desire on its part to influence Government's policy and to promote certain policies itself. None of the demands, however, would involve exercising control themselves of education in the manner of fully professional groups. Some of the very important issues in this category raised by the Union were the question of agricultural teaching in schools and pre- and post-elementary education, all three of which were closely related.

Agricultural teaching in schools

The question of agricultural instruction in schools dated from the days immediately after slavery. It came in for particular attention during the debate on educational matters accompanying the passing of the Elementary and Secondary Education Laws of 1892 as noted earlier in this study and was thereafter raised by officials of the Education Department, the press and various commission reports – even commissions not necessarily concerned with education.[30] The attempt to have the subject taught in secondary schools had failed before the end of the 1890s[31] but the members of the Board of Education continued to bring the matter up for discussion and for enforcement in the elementary schools.

The argument was advanced, especially in the late 1920s and 1930s, that since the State could not afford adequate facilities for all the children of school age, the most should be made of the available resources and facilities. The main purpose of the elementary school in an agricultural society should therefore be to prepare the pupil to make the most of the land.[32] Education in these schools was criticized as being too 'bookish' and too 'literary' and not sufficiently 'practical'. In some respects these critics were correct in pointing to an education which would be of practical use to the child on leaving school but they were quite wrong to pose this as an absolute alternative to basic elementary education. Teachers correctly understood this argument to be a threat to their social and 'professional' status and sought accordingly to defend the occupation. This defence of established educational norms reflected some of the social values of a society experiencing a transition of a conservative nature – groping forward whilst holding fast to what is believed to be worthwhile from the past.

In the view of the JUT elementary schools were not places to equip children with the training needed for a career; these schools were not intended to provide specialized but general knowledge at a very basic level. They existed in the words of one of the Union's spokesmen in 1929, for the

> purpose of so developing the intellectual facilities of the child that it will be fully equipped on leaving school to specialize in that branch of industry to which it has decided to devote its energies.[33]

The Union admitted that there was a problem to get the child, on leaving school, to go onto the land, but the solution was not more agricultural instruction in elementary schools. There was nothing per se, leaders argued, in the school curriculum to alienate the child from agricultural work. In their view the nature of land tenure, unavailability of land, and low wages for farm labourers, unfavourable conditions of work and the uncertain market for small crops were the real factors which kept the youth off the land.

The promotion of agricultural training in elementary schools was presented, they argued, as a panacea for the island's ills in much the same way as bible lessons were seen immediately after slavery. The Union thus hinted at deeper social problems and suggested that when these were solved the problem of alienation from the land would also be solved. This was elaborated by another writer in the *Magazine* thus,

> Let the boy feel certain that he will not share the fate of his father, whose acre of stone was forfeited by the Crown

because he could not make enough from it to pay the taxes and support a family, or whose provision ground was destroyed by the landlord because the rent was seven days in arrears; let him feel satisfied that adequate measures for the encouragement and protection of agriculture are existent, and it will need no application of physical or verbal force to get him 'back to the land'.[34]

Furthermore, agriculture was already being taught in schools but from the reports received from teachers it seemed that it was a failure, partly because the State could not or would not give adequate facilities to teachers (who were not necessarily trained agriculturalists).[35]

In periods of economic hardship such as the 1930s, the matter received great publicity, but the JUT was able to oppose 'successfully' government officials largely because the State could not afford to enforce such a policy even if it had become law. Besides, the necessary co-operation of the teachers was not likely to be forthcoming. It remained therefore very much a matter for general debate for the remainder of the colonial period and although it has received occasional government attention since independence, the problem has not been adequately tackled by either the PNP or the JLP administrations.

Infant education and continuation schools

Instead of promoting agricultural instruction in elementary schools the JUT made counter-proposals that the Government should take an active interest in infant education and in extending post-primary schools. At its 1929 Annual Conference, the JUT passed one of its routine motions calling on the Government to establish infant schools wherever possible. The refusal of the State, in 1898 when the matter was last seriously discussed, to make infant education free, resulted in the JUT constantly raising it as an issue. It wanted the State to make provision for the child to come into the educational stream from a much earlier age than seven. By this age, the Union argued, it was too late for the child to derive much benefit from education. If the State would not lower the entry age for elementary schools then the Union called upon the state to establish centres where children under the age of seven could receive some instruction.

It was argued that the late entry of the child into school life perpetuated ignorance, encouraged illegitimacy and crime and helped to mould an evil character.[36] Part of the work of the teacher was to mould the character of the child in his care but this task was made nigh impossible because by the age of seven evil influences were well established. This was bound to have an unwelcome effect upon the future, for too many children spent

> their earliest years in environments which are not at all conducive to the future interest of our future citizens and with playfellows and companions whose actions are not always worthy of imitation.[37]

Whereas the parents were neglecting these children by leaving them at home unattended while out at work, the State was also wasteful and careless with the limited resources available.

But more than infant schools were needed, if social ills were to be arrested and the youth take to the land for a living. It was also necessary to establish continuation schools so that children leaving elementary school at the age of fourteen could go on to something worthwhile. A vacuum existed in the life of the child on leaving school for there was nothing for him beyond working on diminishing family land – if any. The best description of this post-school situation was given by the JUT to the Moyne Commission in 1938 and although this date is later than the years under consideration it is worth quoting because of its poignancy:

> For the majority of those leaving school between twelve and fifteen, there is no apprenticeship, no work, nothing within reach of learning, no lands to cultivate, no moral discipline, no ambitious promptings. They swell the ranks of the worthless and irresponsible becoming fathers and mothers of illegitimate children and a number of them degenerate to mischief and crime. There is a great barren period between leaving school and their finding some kind of regular work some four or five years later on. At eighteen many of them have forgotten what they learnt at school, and have learnt nothing that can help them.[38]

This description reflected not only the moral attitude of the JUT towards the problem but also that teachers were deeply concerned about the situation. The general arguments they advanced in support of instituting continuation schools were often similar to those for infant education.

But one of the main points to be made is that the Union was promoting a cause to defend an interest. It did not want the State to attempt to implement a policy of teaching agriculture in elementary schools but at the same time the Union saw the need for imparting such knowledge. By promoting continuation schools the Union was defending the existing curriculum and leaving the traditional role of the elementary schoolteacher intact while creating more sources of employment for a potentially expansive occupation.

Just as the State could not afford to implement a policy of agricultural instruction in schools so it could not afford to lower the school age below seven years, nor establish continuation schools, to the extent the JUT wanted. To the demand for lowering the school age, the Board of Education made a stock reply to the JUT: 'The Board is not prepared to recommend the proposal.'[39]

The Government saw the need for infant centres but it could not afford to set them up and decided instead to make a grant of £500 towards the early beginnings in this direction by the Department. In 1932 the Director of Education, H. B. Easter, admitted that elementary schools were not the most suitable places for teaching any trade.[40] He also recognized that there was a glaring need for suitable centres where these could be taught but again reiterated that the Government could not afford it.

Although there was general agreement between the JUT and the authorities on the question nothing could be done because of lack of resources. But the colonial government and the JUT were confronting the outer limits of the colonial state which operated within confines established by the dominant class through the imperial government at Whitehall. The events of 1938 were to loosen some of the constraints but only temporarily.

Political issues

It should be noted that the word 'political' is being used in this context to mean issues which involved some significant changes in the socio-economic and political system before they could be met and or where party-political preferences are deeply involved. The issues the JUT raised in this period were of the former because no modern political parties existed in the period 1928-31. I want to look briefly at two of these issues here: the questions of compulsory attendance at school and the 'nationalization' of schools.

Compulsory attendance

Like so many of the issues the JUT raised in the years 1928-31, the demand for the State to enforce compulsory attendance at school had a long history. The provisions of the 1892 Elementary Education Law for phased compulsion and accompanying penalties[41] were never enforced. The optimism of the early 1890s gave way to gloom as the island's imports rose above its exports and the call came (from within the island and from Whitehall) for retrenchment.[42] This did not however deter the JUT and from year to year it continued to make the demand that the Government should introduce compulsion throughout the island. In 1911 and 1914 this demand met with limited success.[43] Fourteen areas were prescribed for experimenting with compulsion, presumably with the intention of extending it to the rest of the country if the exercise was successful. After 1914 the JUT did not cease to argue that the whole island be subjected to the same law.

During 1928-31, as before and after, the Union argued in much the same way as it had done on other issues considered: there was a necessity to rid the country of illegitimacy, illiteracy and crime; compulsion would help to develop a healthy and frugal peasantry. Education was the best way of arresting many of Jamaica's ills but these would continue as long as education was not made compulsory. Too many children who had registered were staying away from schools and nothing was being done about this. If the State had no intention of extending compulsion to the whole island then it was showing that 'it is anxious to be regarded as being unworthy, and undeserving of the loyalty and confidence of its citizens'.[44]

The Union admitted that if compulsion were to be introduced then the schools would not be able to absorb all the children of school age in the country. But this was itself only pointing to the main problem, that is, that there was a glaring need for the Government to build more schools for the school-age population. The core of the Union's argument was stated in the following manner:

> We contend that the state should provide schoolrooms for the accommodation of every child; we contend that the state is guilty of an unpardonable crime against itself when it allows 40 per cent of its future citizens to grow up in utter DARKNESS AND IGNORANCE – the great preparatory school for the Penitentiary, the Alms House and the Hospital, the great nursery of Vice and Disease and Poverty.[45]

The realization that the State could not spend the necessary amount on compulsory attendance throughout the island had some effect on the formulation of the demands in these years. In 1929 the Annual Conference passed the motion that, 'Government be asked to extend compulsory attendance at schools to districts outside the compulsory areas, where there are schools with sufficient accommodation'.[46] This was an attempt to frame a demand in terms which could be acceptable to the Government and capable of implementation by it.

In his Report for 1930 S. A. Hammond, the Director of Education, gave a critical appraisal of the educational system in relation to compulsory attendance.[47] His major point was that the State could not afford the high costs. Jamaica would need over 1,500 more teachers and an additional £400,000 on the annual education vote, and this would still be within the grants-in-aid system. (This contrasted sharply with the additional amount the Government allocated to education in the years 1930-1 – that is £10,000 equally divided between the church-run and the government-managed schools. This was far from adequate but in the circumstances it was welcomed. Hammond also pointed out that should compulsion be enforced, there would be an additional need for more and better-paid attendance officers. The costs of these and the general improvement of education such as lessening the high pupil/teacher ratio, improving salaries and school accommodation were not accounted for in his projected figures.

Hammond's second main point was that compulsion was not a success in the prescribed areas. The average rate of attendance for these areas was 66 per cent while that for the rest of the island was as high as 60.5 per cent; in areas where attendance was exceptionally good it could not be attributed to compulsion but to broader social factors. Additional reasons for the relative failure of the experiment were that attendance committees were not doing their work and attendance officers were badly paid.

Lastly, he argued that compulsion could not really be expected to solve the problem of bad attendance. In Britain where there were all the necessary pre-requisites present, the result achieved was only 80 per cent attendance and the most Jamaica could reasonably hope for, if the British example were to be taken at face value, was 80 per cent effectiveness which would not warrant the greatly increased expenditure.

Hammond therefore made an alternative suggestion. The education system was generating waste since only about half of the school-age population registered and only about half of this number actually attended school regularly. The solution therefore was that the State should make elementary education free only on the basis of attendance; if the child did not appear at school after a certain period he was to be struck off the register. This, Hammond thought, would force parents to appreciate the schools more and attendance, without the aid of attendance officers, would improve. In this way, he hoped, the education vote could be more usefully allocated and a step in the right direction towards reforms of the system would be made.

Within the limitations of the colonial system and an unfeeling dominant social class, this issue could be at best a continuing one. It could not be met even where the authorities saw the problem as clearly as the teachers because taxation for this purpose could not pass the legislature and Whitehall had little or no interest. The insistence on the citizen's right to free elementary education for his children in the face of the overwhelming scarcity of resources tied all to an inefficient education system.

The nationalization of schools

The JUT called upon the State to assume the full responsibility for elementary education and thereby put an end to the duality of ownership and control of schools. In these years the word 'nationalization' was frequently used in different contexts and since it was in currency the JUT called for the 'nationalization' of the school system. The Union argued that it was possible for the State to do this since it was already standing most of the costs of elementary education.[48] Although the community was paying for the upkeep of the schools the public often could not, leaders argued, make use of them for community purposes whereas the churches could. Moreover, the churches, in their present condition, found it increasingly difficult even to meet the limited costs of their part of the 'concordat'. In a very real sense therefore, the argument continued, the schools were not truly 'denominational' because public funds kept them going for the benefit of the churches.

This was a very important issue because it hit at the very heart of the education system. In effect the Union was calling for the State effectively to put an end to its long co-operation with the churches and establish a fully national system of education. Because it was so fundamental an issue, 'nationalization' was linked to most of the other issues the Union raised in the years under consideration.

The importance of this demand was clearly understood by the Bishop of Jamaica who strongly opposed it in his address to the JUT Annual Conference in 1929. He pointed out that if the State were to attempt to carry out such a policy it would lose the funds and voluntary services of the denominations. More importantly, he argued, the churches could put the whole system out of operation because they owned most of the schools. Although he refused to use 'moral' argument against nationalization, the Bishop's concluding remarks on the issue made it clear to the Conference that his denomination, the Anglican Church, would stand firmly for dual ownership:

> Let us say this quite definitely, the Government has not yet approached the denominations with any particular offer or request. I am not sure that it has any to make. Meanwhile let it be understood if we are 'holding on' it is that we may be faithful to the trust committed to us by those who, in generations gone by, struggled and sacrificed for the education of the boys and girls of this island who otherwise would have been untaught and uncared for.[49]

These remarks also indicated the attitude of the Government which was made even more clearly at the same Conference two days earlier by the Acting Director of Education, G. H. Deerr. He made it clear that education in Jamaica would remain 'a denominational grant-in-aid system'[50] because of the indispensable contribution of the churches. The policy of the Government was, it seems, basically that since the denominations were no longer building schools while the State was doing so, eventually the education system would be a fully 'national' one.

The reply from the Board of Education to the JUT on the issue therefore was that the Government was 'doing all it can'.[51] For the JUT this did not amount to much.

Conclusion

The JUT therefore made demands and raised issues some of which had the general characteristics of either being pertinent to its immediate needs or, seemingly unwittingly, calling into question aspects of the colonial system. Most were never wholly or even partly met. It is not necessary therefore to look far for the effectiveness of the Union. It was not very effective as a group seeking to influence the direction of government policy or in raising issues which were authoritatively resolved. Being neither a powerful nor an influential group the JUT was not likely to succeed against the powerful clerical interests which were well represented on the Board of Education and which effectively controlled crucial areas of education.

Even in democratic systems groups such as the JUT rarely win their briefs but it would be expected that those which have been in existence for a considerable time will have made some important gains. The issues on which the Union won concessions were also not likely to be of great significance but the apparently small victories of the JUT account partly for its long existence within the colonial political system. It gained some concessions on some of the technical and professional issues which it raised but it was unsuccessful with issues which were of a 'political' nature, largely because of the strong and pervasive influence of the churches and the limitations imposed on the colonial state both by the imperial government itself, acting as a vehicle for more powerful interests, and by the strength of the dominant social class in Jamaica which had no interest in the education of the ordinary Jamaican.

At another level the JUT was blocked by a well established and competing group (composed of the churches) from the more effective and established channels of communication with decision-makers and this forced its leaders to rely significantly on the support of 'influential' friends. This became one of the main tactics of the Union. There is no doubt that in many circumstances groups behave in this way, but the general weakness of the JUT forced it into this pattern of behaviour in order to survive in the colonial system.

The Union was also greatly influenced in the manner in which it raised issues. It sought to present its demands in terms acceptable to the authorities, stressing that it was a 'reasonable' body. As a group seeking to exercise some influence the JUT understood the 'nature of the game', acted 'sensibly' and sought to be helpful to the authorities but with only minimal pay-off. Although a 'union' with very limited, if definite and clear, trade union concerns its leaders sought to give the impression that the JUT was not just another 'selfish' organization making claims on Government for improvement but one vitally concerned with the general welfare of the community. Most, if not all, the cases were argued in terms of what was believed to be good for the country and some general principle was always brought into the discussion as a point of reference. Formal procedures such as frequent meetings, exhortations to good works and strong moral values became almost as important as the very issues themselves. Teachers felt, quite clearly, that by highlighting issues they were performing a useful citizenship role in the community. And, undoubtedly, they were doing so. In an age of few social commentatators, this role by elementary schoolteachers constantly pointed to some of the inherent limitations of colonial rule and the kind of society which was emerging from the restrictions of slavery.

Notes

1   Cf. 'Report of the Commission appointed to enquire into the staffing of government offices and the emoluments of public officers and employees', *The Minutes of the Legislative Council of Jamaica for the year 1929* (Kingston: Government Printing Office, 1930), Appendix xiv, p. 1.

2   J. Dearlove, *The politics of policy in local government* (Cambridge University Press, 1973), pp. 169, 173.

3   *The Daily Gleaner*, 8 November 1929, p. 32.

4   *The Daily Gleaner*, 3 January 1928, p. 10.

5   *The Daily Gleaner*, 7 January 1930, p. 16.

6   *The JUT Magazine*, December/January 1928-9, vol. i, no. i, p. 1.

7   *The Daily Gleaner*, 7 January 1930, p. 16.

8   *The Daily Gleaner*, 7 January 1930, p. 16.

9   *The Daily Gleaner*, 11 January 1929, p. 14.

10 J. Carnegie, *Some aspects of Jamaica's politics, 1918-1938* (Kingston: Institute of Jamaica, 1973), p. 73; Wint also edited a publication, *The Tribune*, from as early as 1904, see R. N. Murray (ed.), *J. J. Mills: his own account of his life and times* (Kingston: Collins & Sangster (Jamaica) Ltd., 1969), p. 125. He published and edited the *Jamaica Critic*, which changed in 1929 to *The Jamaica Critic and West Indian Review*.

11 *The Annual Report of the Jamaica Union of Teachers for the year ended 30 November 1929*, pp. 16-17.

12 *Jamaica Laws, certified copies of Acts*, 1889-93, 1894-6 and 1897-1900 C.O. 139, nos. 106, 107 and 108.

13 The conflict which could arise from this was well illustrated in the publicized case of R. A. Thompson, the headmaster of an elementary school in Spanish Town and one of the JUT's delegates to the Moyne Commission in 1938. The case ran from 1906 to well after the First World War and involved the inspector and the school manager plotting, as far as teachers were concerned, against Mr Thompson. See, *W.I.R.C. 1938-9*, C.O. 950, no. 82, J. 117.

14 *Ibid.*, p. 3.

15 There was a marked failure on the part of the JUT to document or keep records of such cases in detailed form; this does not mean that there were no problems of this nature, rather this points to the weakness of the Union. This is demonstrated by the fact that it had to take a case such as Thompson's to the Moyne Commission in 1938; the case was a dead one by this date.

16 'Interview with Mr A. A. McPherson' 16 January 1974. Mr McPherson, a former president of the JUT was the Treasurer of the JTA until 1974; he started teaching soon after the First World War. He recalled, for example, that a manager would sometimes use the teacher's salary and pay him days later after making a collection at church on Sunday.

17 For example, of the 216 principal managers in Jamaica in 1930, not even one was a layman, see 'Education Department, Report the year ended 31 December 1930', *The Annual General Report of Jamaica together with the Departmental Reports for 1930* (Kingston: Government Printing Office, 1931), p. 259.

18   *The JUT Magazine*, vol. i, no. i (December/January, 1928-9), p. 3.
19   *The Daily Gleaner*, 31 May 1929, pp. 6-21.
20   *The Daily Gleaner*, 25 April 1929, p. 18.
21   *Minutes of the Legislative Council of Jamaica for the year 1931* (Kingston: Government Printing Office, 1932) Discussions were repeatedly postponed during the year until 1 December, cf. 'The Hon. Legislative Council', *The Daily Gleaner*, 18, 19, 27 November 1931.
22   Yet the Government, as indicated by Hammond, recognized some of the problems involved. Hammond pointed out that one of the 'sources' of the weakness of the dual system was the dual function of the teacher, common in some country schools, where he has sometimes church as well as school duties and may be retained for their fulfilment in spite of his inefficiency as a teacher. 'Education Department, Report for the year ended 1 July 1929', *The Annual General Report of Jamaica together with the Departmental Reports for 1929* (Kingston: Government Printing Office, 1930), p. 476.
23   *Minutes of the Legislative Council for the year 1928* (Kingston: Government Printing Office, 1929), p. 33.
24   'Report of the Salaries Commission,' 1929, *op. cit.* Appendix A.
25   'Board of Education, Report for the year ended 31 December 1930', *op. cit.*, p. 15.
26   *Minutes of the Legislative Council, for the year 1928*, p. 33.
27   *The JUT Magazine*, vol. ii, no. iii (April/May, 1930), p. 4.
28   *The JUT Magazine*, vol. ii, no. iii (April/May, 1930), p. 4.
29   *The JUT Magazine*, vol. xxviii, no. 1 (January/April 1956), editorial: 'History of elementary schoolteachers' salaries', pp. 1-2.
30   For example, *The Report of the Commission appointed to enquire into housing conditions of the poorer classes of the community*, (Kingston: Circulars of the Office of the Colonial Secretary, no. 11 of 1926), p. 1.
31   'Schools Commission Report, 31 March 1899', *The Annual Report of Jamaica together with Departmental Reports, 1899* (Kingston: Government Printing Office, 1900), pp. 42-4.
32   See for example, *The Daily Gleaner*, 3 January 1928, p. 10; also *The JUT Magazine*, vol. i, no. ii (April/May 1929), pp. 1-2.
33   The *JUT Magazine*, vol. i, no. ii (February/March 1929), p. 3.
34   *The JUT Magazine*, vol. i, no. ii (February/March 1929), p. 2.
35   *Ibid.*, p. 2 and *W.I.R.C. 1938-9*, C.O. 950, no. 17, J. 154, Oral Evidence. Teachers who were qualified to teach the subject adequately could receive better salaries from the JAS.
36   See, *The JUT Magazine*, vol. i, no. ii (February/March 1929).
37   *The JUT Magazine*, vol. iii, no. i (December/January 1930), p. 3.
38   *W.I.R.C. 1938-9*, C.O. 950, no. 82, J. 117, p. 8.
39   'The Board of Education, Report for the year ended 31 December 1929', *The Annual General Report of Jamaica together with the Departmental Reports for 1929* (Kingston: Government Printing Office, 1930), p. 211.
40   'Education Department, Report for the year ended 31 December 1932', *The Annual General Report of Jamaica together with the Departmental Reports for 1932* (Kingston: Government Printing Office, 1934), p. 290.
41   Law 31 of 1892, *op. cit.*, First penalty – 5/– (five shillings: 25p); –

second penalty – 10/–; third penalty – £1; failure to pay would result in 7 days (max.) imprisonment and cases were to be heard before two JPs.

42 Sir David Barbour, *Report on the finances of Jamaica* (Kingston: Government Printing Office, 1899), p. 4.
43 'Law 35 of 1914', *Jamaica Laws, certified copies of Acts*, 1914-18, C.O. 139 no. 112. The penalties were to be those set out in the 1892 provisions.
44 *The JUT Magazine*, vol. i, no. i (December/January, 1928-9), p. 2.
45 *Ibid.*
46 'The Annual Report of the JUT for 1929', *op. cit.*, p. 16.
47 'Education Department, Report for 1930', *op. cit.*, Appendix A.
48 *The Daily Gleaner*, 23 May 1929, p. 21; 9, 11 January, 1919.
49 *The Daily Gleaner*, 11 January 1919, p. 14.
50 *The Daily Gleaner*, 9 January 1929, p. 14.
51 'The Annual Report of the JUT for 1930', p. 7; also *The Daily Gleaner* 7 January 1930, p. 18.

CHAPTER 6
Teachers in the age of party politics

In the circumstances of the 1960s, especially after political independence in August 1962, teachers were bound to respond to the rapid changes of the times by taking steps to strengthen their position in the social order and thereby ensure that the occupation continued to enjoy its relative prestige. Understandably, leaders wanted to make sure that the occupation had a secure base from which to defend and promote teachers' interests as well as influence the course of educational developments in a society seemingly poised to change. In this regard it must, of course, be remembered that these were the first years of political independence and all social services seemed ready to take off from their hitherto stagnated positions towards long-expected developments.

To achieve these general goals it became necessary to adopt and apply a more systematic strategy than all previous organizations, including the JUT, had done hitherto. For, with political independence and the largely intolerant Labour Government of Bustamante, the Ministries of Education and Finance as well as the Prime Minister, became the relevant power-targets for teachers. The Minister replaced the Director of Education, and the Prime Minister, as noted earlier, acted, at first, as if he believed that he was a new type of Governor for Jamaica. Quite clearly, new tactics had to be adopted while making maximum use of traditional ones developed by the JUT. This dual aim was of particular importance to a society exhibiting essentially conservative values and practices.

The spirit of anger – the JTA's tactics and activities

The very coming together of the various teachers' associations in 1964, including the JUT, to form the Jamaica Teachers' Association was more than an end in itself, it was also a tactical move by leaders to create a force capable of influencing government and defending teachers. The new association, at first, continued to rely on tactics used by the JUT in the colonial period. For example, the JTA appealed to public opinion and parliament and presented its briefs in terms acceptable to the authorities. Not unlike groups elsewhere and in other conditions, the JTA also sought to cultivate influential friends. But in the changing and uncertain circumstances of the 1960s, new slogans and tactics were needed. The JTA eventually had to employ the ultimate weapons available to similar groups, the boycott and the strike, in order to establish continuous access to, as well as machinery for negotiations and consultation with decision-makers.

Like the JUT, leaders of the Association saw public opinion as an important force in national politics as is clear from the many attempts made to influence it. They ensured that wide publicity was given to its activities and throughout the years covering the remainder of the period of this study, the JTA enjoyed more than adequate coverage in the press.[1] Most of the issues it raised and which were emphasized in meetings, interviews, conferences and deputations were reported. The main issues of these years – the Byfield case, the Education Bill and the Code of Regulations, the question of salaries, the strike and boycott of some Ministry of Education programmes – were all well publicized. The JTA was constantly before the public for it seemed that whatever the Association did was newsworthy. Leaders also made extensive use of the radio. In the confrontations of 1963 and 1966 they made a number of important broadcasts on the issues affecting teachers.[2] They also made frequent use of the medium of the public meeting, both at national and local levels and particularly during periods of acute tension between the Minister and the Association. By securing maximum publicity for its activities the JTA's leaders were able not only to mobilize members but also to gain the sympathy of parents.

The JTA, like the JUT, sought to present itself as an organization concerned with issues affecting both teachers and the public. Examples of this concern with general public issues of the day which distinguished the JTA from other semi-professional groups in Jamaica were the firm positions taken at the 1965 Annual Conference on the problem of hooliganism and public disorder,[3] and the confiscation of Dr George Beckford's passport by the Government in 1968.[4] On the first of these the JTA adopted an outraged moral stance and on the second it posed as a defender of academic and political freedom. In pressing the cause of education, the Association called upon the whole community to participate at different levels and initiated projects such as the Council on Education.[5] Such ventures, whether intended or not, certainly gave a good impression of the JTA as being responsible and concerned not only about issues affecting teachers, but about broad social and moral problems of the community.

In an attempt to influence the public, the Association sought to make the public aware of educational issues. It stimulated debates which sometimes led to confrontations with the Government and these kept education in the public view. By constantly appealing to the public, the JTA also forced the Government, particularly the Minister of Education, to make statements regarding his and his Ministry's activities and policies. Not unlike elsewhere, the electorate may not have been able to intervene directly to influence the outcome but it was observing the confrontation and the Government had to bear in mind that, unlike the colonial regime, it had to try to secure the vote of parents in general and parish elections at regular intervals. In any event, the Opposition was likely to make political capital of 'mistakes' by the Government of the day.

Although the JTA, like the JUT in the colonial period, never actually waged a 'parliamentary campaign' in the way teachers, for example, have done in Britain,[6] some use was made of the legislature. The existence of political parties in the independence period provided the JTA with party political support in the House of Representatives. The Association received unreserved support from the PNP which was in Opposition from 1962 to 1972. Even its leader, Mr Norman Manley, Q.C., often spoke on behalf of the JTA; Mr F. Glasspole, the Opposition spokesman on education (and later Governor-General of Jamaica), never failed to be critical of the Minister of Education, the late Edwin Allen. Of course, both the JTA and the PNP Opposition gained from this support, but it was also to contribute to the delay of the JLP Government's recognition of the Association.

As a body concerned with education the JTA, like the JUT before it, sought to provide a platform for discussion on educational and related matters. The Annual Conference was in the 1960s seen as an occasion of national importance, not only for teachers but also for the community at large. At the official opening of Conference influential individuals would be invited to sit on the platform. These would cover a much wider spectrum than in the days of the JUT, including not only such dignitaries as the Bishop of Jamaica (representing the spiritual life), and the Governor-General (representing neutrality), but also representatives of teachers' associations abroad, (to enhance prestige). The latter included groups such as the WCOTP, the NUT and the CUT. In its attempt to appear nonpartisan, the Association also welcomed on to the platform leaders of both political parties.[7] On such occasions Ministers of Government might make statements regarding the Government's intention with respect to education.[8] (In the 1970s the PNP Prime Minister, Mr Michael Manley, was to use the platform to announce, for the first time, his government's policies in areas not in the least related to education.[9] This, of course, reflects the extent to which the JTA had come to be regarded as important, an achievement never imagined by JUT leaders.) The Association acquired not only legitimacy by providing a platform for discussion on education but also considerable prestige through the composition of its platform. Thus, in times of open confrontation its leaders have felt free to call upon influential persons who patronized the organization, for their support.[10] In itself, this fact significantly distinguished the JTA from the JUT in terms of gained respectability.

Issues were sometimes placed in categories which were readily understood by the Government and the public alike. When the JTA denoted certain actions of the Government to be of a 'political nature' or to be an attack on the 'professional' rights of teachers, it was of course reflecting the different concerns of teachers, but these terms were also used to convey certain impressions about a democratically-elected government.

It is not uncommon for middle-class occupational groups to respond to government activity by pointing to attacks on 'professional' status.[11] The JTA on the one hand was struggling to be recognized as a profession in the sense that lawyers and medical men are members of professions and on the other hand it was defending itself by saying that the teaching 'profession' was being attacked. What is important is not whether teachers were correct in their perceptions of themselves, but that they had this perception at all and used it to their advantage. By adopting this stance the JTA was able sometimes to put the Minister of Education slightly on the defensive and he was sometimes forced to explain why he wanted to belittle the 'professional' status of teachers.[12] To fulfill its trade union responsibilities, the JTA had, of course, to defend its rights which included such activities as strike action. The labels 'professional' and 'political' which the JTA attached to issues were therefore sometimes more than mere slogans, reflecting as they did for the Association the types of threats teachers had to face from the Government.

In 1966 teachers took the important decision to abandon their traditional, moderate tactics and adopt the strike weapon and to boycott certain programmes of the Ministry of Education. These were attempts to show to the Labour Government that the JTA was not willing to co-operate if the Government would not meet the demands for higher salaries and negotiate with leaders over the controversial Articles 35 and 36 of the Code of Regulations then before the House. The JTA was able to demonstrate to the Government that the Association had the overwhelming support of the teaching community and the sympathy of parents. Some worthwhile concessions were gained from the Government after this and the events marked a turning point in the relations of the JTA and the Government with a lessening of the tension which had existed since 1963. Because the strike and the boycott were important innovations in the behaviour of teachers in Jamaica, and since the situation provided a good opportunity to see how the JTA was able to use a number of tactics simultaneously, it is worthwhile to give a brief description of the events of 1966.

The strike and the boycott came only after the leaders of the JTA felt that there was no chance of gaining satisfaction from the Government on the issues of a salary increase and negotiations over the Code of Regulations. The boycott involved a deliberate refusal by teachers, at the direction of the JTA, to attend certain technical educational programmes organized by the Ministry of Education but which did not immediately affect the day-to-day work of the Ministry or teachers. It lasted from April to September 1966, when relations between the Government and the JTA had improved. The strike started later and lasted for three days. On 27 May, Mrs Fay Saunders of the Action Committee (set up to co-ordinate the strike effort) presented a programme of activity to the executive of the JTA aimed at achieving maximum coverage. The programme included lobbying of members of parliament; press conferences to be covered by the media; phone-in by JTA members to both radio and television programmes; notifying the teachers' organizations within the Caribbean (the CUT), the United Kingdom and North America. Efforts were to be made also to inform parents throughout the country of what the JTA was about so that teachers would not alienate them.[13]

Telegrams were also to be sent to the Acting Prime Minister, Mr Donald Sangster, the Minister of Education and the Leader of the Opposition, Mr Norman Manley. This was certainly a much wider range of activity than could have been possible in the colonial period. But although the scene was being prepared for an island-wide strike, the JTA leadership still hoped that the Government would respond favourably to their representations and make the strike unnecessary.

When on the following day, however, the Manchester Teachers' Association (MTA) angered by the Government's refusal to negotiate and also by the Minister's handling of the German Case,[14] declared its intention to call a strike in the parish, the JTA leadership had to take decisive action.[15] Efforts were quickly made to capture the initiative from the MTA whose actions were later described by the JTA executive as 'immature' and needing to be put into 'proper perspective'.[16] Of course, these accusations simply reveal the fact that the MTA was the faster on the draw and the national leadership was trying to steal the thunder in the situation.

Although the strike only lasted three days, the events of the following ten days were momentous for the Association. Over the last weekend of the month, the General Council of the Association met in Mandeville, Manchester, with the MTA executive and succeeded in working out a common strategy, with the national executive assuming general leadership. The executive was to try again to negotiate with the Acting Prime Minister, Mr D. Sangster, and Mr Edwin Allen. If this were not possible or if talks broke down, then the JTA would call a country-wide strike to last for three days. When Sangster and Allen refused to negotiate, this plan went into operation between 2 and 6 June with, as the JTA claimed, a 99 per cent response from 'all teachers including private schools'.[17]

At this stage the Minister retaliated by announcing his intentions to make teachers subject to the regulations of the civil service; they should then, he believed, be able to spend all their time teaching rather than going on strike.[18] This increased the tension and the activities of teachers to defend themselves. Daily meetings of the executive were held and the president, Mr Desmond Gascoigne, made a number of important broadcasts over the radio. On the 10 June a special meeting of the executive was convened and it was decided to hold a mass meeting at Excelsior School on the following day. It was estimated that over 3,000 teachers attended the meeting and the call by the MTA to introduce a 'rolling strike' whereby the various Parish Associations would lead teachers on strike one after the other, was defeated.

It was at this meeting also that the president, Mr D. Gascoigne, called for the launching of the 'Great Offensive' and for diligence against 'demagoguery and pint-sized dictatorship'[19] at both district and parish levels. Quite clearly, once the confrontation had begun other issues surfaced. But the JTA leadership was anxious not to continue the strike beyond the three days and succeeded in getting the membership to reject the MTA's militant proposals. Perhaps leaders feared a backlash from parents or they were satisfied with the results. Having made their point they did not wish to prolong the confrontation.

The tactics the JTA used were not always employed simultaneously nor were they rigidly separated in application. The changes in the behaviour of teachers in the 1960s were quite clear: in 1963-4 the various associations united to defend and promote their common interests largely as a result of political independence and the activities of the Labour Government. The Association first made maximum use of traditional tactics with which teachers were familiar but when these failed significantly to influence the Government it became necessary for leaders to adopt militant tactics in order to achieve the desired formal and continuous access to decision-makers.

In the years 1964 to 1967, there was a tendency for the leaders of the JTA to argue their briefs in political terms and under the cloak of 'professionalism'. This was not surprising for in the highly charged party political atmosphere of the 1960s most of the issues raised required political solutions although this did not always necessitate overt political activity on the part of the Association. Because of the political situation, resolution of issues in one category often influenced issues in others. As in the case of the JUT in the colonial period, it is possible and useful to categorize the issues which the JTA raised into trade union, professional and political issues and give examples of each of these for the years 1964 to 1967.

Some trade union issues

For the greater part of the 1960s the question of salaries and regrading remained a point of contention between the Government and all categories of teachers. In December 1965, the JTA's claims were presented in a detailed memorandum to the Ministry of Education calling for a 25 per cent point-to-point increase for all teachers and a 50 per cent increase for headteachers.[20] From time to time between then and July 1967 the demand seems to have changed marginally but it was this memorandum which formed the basis for negotiations with the Government.[21] The JTA had been instrumental in gaining a 10 per cent increase in salary for teachers in 1964, but this was far from satisfactory. The Association wanted improvements based on the 1957 regrading (that is, point-to-point[22] as opposed to an overall increase) which had been made by the PNP Government.

In presenting their case the JTA leaders argued that the increase of 1964 was viewed both at the time and later as a mere stop-gap; it was only an 'adjustment' pending a more satisfactory settlement. Education, they declared, was vital to the development of the country if Jamaica were to make much use of its newly acquired independence. The JLP Government's indifference to teachers' salaries not only damaged education but also endangered the future of the whole community; the prosperity of the society was therefore at stake. The Government's attitude was described as being 'shortsighted, unimaginative, reactionary and contradictory'.[23] One prominent JTA leader contended that the work of the teacher was treated little better than that of sweated labour. Furthermore, the cost of living, they argued, was rocketing ahead of salaries and the starting salary of a trained teacher compared unfavourably with that of a school-leaver entering the civil service. New senior posts and scales were needed so that those who saw teaching as a career could have prospects of promotion. They would also have the desired effect of attracting the young and able into the occupation.

This issue had arisen in the early 1960s and it had helped teachers of the various associations then in existence to see their common problems, but only after the strike of 1966 did teachers gain satisfactory concessions from the Labour Government, in July 1967.[24] Throughout these years negotiations between the Association and the Government on this issue was intermittent because the Government repeatedly refused to establish a machinery for continuous negotiations over salaries and conditions of service. Even after July the demand was not fully met, but teachers, particularly their leaders, were satisfied. It would appear that most teachers gained an increase of about 15 per cent while some had as much as 20 per cent and new scales were introduced so as to attract young and well-qualified people into teaching.

By 1969, however, teachers were again making the demand for another increase. The Annual Conference of that year was asked to support a motion (from a local association) calling on the Government 'to effect immediately a substantial increase in salaries of teachers of the island'.[25] The Special Resolution of the Conference, supported by 'several associations', reflected the widespread concern of the JTA members over the question. In 1971 teachers received another salary increase but it was not until 1973 that they received an even more significant one from the PNP which had returned to office in 1972.[26]

In 1967 success was not due entirely to the strike and boycott of the previous year. Undoubtedly, the success owed much to these events for the JTA executive had demonstrated that it had the overwhelming support of teachers, but there were also other causes. The general election of 21 February 1967 ensured a JLP Ministry for another five years but before this victory there were attempts by the Government, particularly the Ministry of Education, to placate the JTA. Perhaps, this was because the Government was having its internal problems over the question of who should succeed the flagging veteran 'chief', Sir Alexander Bustamante, and it felt in these circumstances that it had better help to end the long bitterness between itself and the teachers. Immediately after the elections, Mr Donald Sangster, the Acting Prime Minister and Minister of Finance, supported amongst others by Mr Allen, was elected Prime Minister by his party in the place of the ailing Bustamante. Soon after this the new Prime Minister died suddenly in Canada and another struggle ensued over the leadership. Much jockeying followed and eventually Mr Hugh Shearer, Bustamante's nephew and one-time heir-apparent, narrowly succeeded to the premiership.

It must be remembered also that the new Labour Government from 1962 operated within a relatively hostile environment. The PNP had established strong support within the various institutions of the State, such as the civil service, the police and the army and consolidated its long-standing association amongst groups such as teachers during the party's administration from 1955. The Labour Government found itself at loggerheads with all these groups during much of the 1960s and at one time or another one or more of these groups, including the police, went on, or threatened to go on, strike to register protest at government policies. In addition, these years, especially leading up to the 1967 general elections, saw the first outbreaks of systematic violence between the supporters of the PNP and the JLP which was to become commonplace in the 1970s. In the view of some observers the Rodney Riots of October 1968, sparked off by the Government's banning of UWI historian the late Walter Rodney, was a culmination of the growing repression of the Labour Government.

The relations between the teachers and the Labour Government must not be seen as unique. The antagonism was a widespread one and until Shearer took over the reins of his party's government, the administration tended to adopt the tough-man posture first set by Sir Alexander. Shearer made it clear from the outset of his leadership that he would be 'a no-nonsense prime minister'[27] and in his attempt to contain widespread violence earned the name 'Pharaoh', symbolizing oppression. None the less, the importance of Shearer's leadership with respect to teachers is that he attempted to lessen tension between his government and the various sections of

society and state with which his party had previously been at loggerheads. He started to cultivate support for the JLP but this was too
late to save his party from electoral defeat in 1972. There was time
enough however for the new leader's friendly approach to ease
tension.

First, important changes were made in the Ministry of Education, although Allen remained. Mrs Esme Grant who had annoyed
teachers by her public pronouncements was replaced by Dr Arthur
Burt of the University of the West Indies (UWI) as parliamentary
secretary and Hector Wynter became Minister of State for Education. Teachers' leaders admit that these changes brought about a
healthier atmosphere for co-operation between the JTA and the
Ministry. These changes also marked an important change in the
tactics of the Government. Wynter began by establishing machinery
whereby teachers and ministry officials would meet regularly to
resolve technical problems such as conditions of service and salaries
and every effort was made to ensure co-operation between Allen
and leaders of the JTA.

Secondly, senior ministry officials such as the senior chief
education officer, Mr Cousins, attended the JTA executive meeting
to explain Allen's 'New Deal for Education'.[28] The new Prime
Minister himself adopted a friendly posture towards the JTA. On 24
June 1967, he attended the executive meeting of the JTA to explain
his government's attitude towards the issue of salaries. He told
teachers that

> he and his Government regarded education as one of the
> top priorities in Jamaica and were willing to do their best
> for education within the limits of the country's financial
> resources, and the demands upon public funds by all other
> sectors of society.[29]

Here was a very different attitude from that adopted by Bustamante and Mr Sangster from 1963, which the JTA welcomed.

This general change of attitude on the part of the Labour
Government also made possible the resolution of issues in a number
of other areas. One of the most important of these was the vexed
trade union issue of the employment of teachers. The Byfield case
was still before the courts and teachers were at loggerheads with the
Minister over his Bill.

In 1964, JTA leaders maintained, the Minister assured them
that there was nothing to fear from the wide powers entrusted to
him by the Education Law. The Code of Regulations which was to
follow would ensure against any possible abuse of such powers and

teachers could feel secure in their work. But when the Proposed Code of Regulations was published in 1965 for public debate the teachers felt confirmed in their fears that Mr Allen wanted wide and extensive powers so as to be in a commanding position over them. The Byfield case seemed only a foretaste of things to come. 'Political victimization' would be the order of the day.[30]

The JTA was particularly opposed to Articles 35 and 36 of the Proposed Code which provided for the employment of head and assistant teachers. The Association presented over forty amendments to the Proposed Code to the Select Committee of the House appointed to enquire into and to hear public views on them, but its opposition was especially directed against these Articles.

The Proposed Articles (35 and 36) suggested that when headteachers were appointed the local school board concerned should send its final choice to the Minister for confirmation. If the board could not arrive at a definite decision it should send the names of three shortlisted candidates to the Minister to choose one. If disagreement arose between the Minister and the board at this stage the procedure would be repeated until the situation was amicably resolved or the Minister imposed a solution.[31] A slightly less elaborate procedure was proposed for the appointment of assistant teachers. The leaders of the Association became, however, extremely suspicious of the Minister's motive with respect to the appointments of both head and assistant teachers. It seemed to them that such procedures could lead again to situations such as his treatment of the Kingston school board in the case of the appointment of Byfield.

The nature of the arguments put forward against the proposals came out best in the JTA's memorandum to the Select Committee of the House set up to look into the Proposed Code in 1965. The proposals, in the view of the writers of the memorandum, reflected an attempt to make the Minister 'headmaster of every school, a position impossible to attain'; it was a reflection of 'a police-state mentality and an attempt to introduce a fascist approach into our democratic society'; the proposals were harking back to 'a long dead colonial era'.[32] The proposals were 'backward' and 'authoritarian'. A Code of Regulations in the Association's view should,

> Above all ... completely remove the minister from the type of dealings with professional personnel which will expose him to any form of political pressure or suspicion of political favouritism.[33]

Although originally a technical trade union type issue, these arguments of the leaders show how the question of employment developed into one requiring a political solution.

In a letter to the Select Committee, the secretary-general, Mr Ben Hawthorne, elaborated the difficulties which would arise as a result of the Minister being involved with administrative tasks.[34] The school boards, he went on, should be accepted as competent to appoint assistant teachers after consulting with headteachers. The appointment of headteachers would warrant, however, the setting up of a body which should be autonomous except where it was in conflict with the Minister and Hawthorne suggested the establishment of an Appointment Authority for this purpose. The Minister would thus retain his authority to have the last word on certain appointments without being tied to day-to-day administrative matters. The Authority should, of course, he argued, be composed of non-political but prominent citizens.

The general concern of the JTA leaders was to avoid the possible stranglehold of the Minister over the teaching occupation. They therefore wanted to see authority dispersed so as to ensure a measure of democracy in the administration of education which would then safeguard the teacher from 'political victimization'.

The JTA was not to be as successful on this as on the salary issue. In the House of Representatives, the Minister had promised to go towards the 'half-way house' in the Select Committee but from the concessions made to the JTA, he certainly did not. Apart from reversing the order of the Articles, the government members of the Committee were only prepared to recommend that a small concession be made. The Majority Report which they signed stated that 'only applicants for the post of Principals whom the Board is willing to appoint and the minister is willing to approve will be appointed.'[35]

The Minority Report of the Committee reflected the support the JTA received from the PNP Opposition on the issue. It pointed out that the approval of the Minister for the appointment of assistant teachers was 'unnecessary and cumbersome' since there was going to be a Registration Board to ensure that a school board would have easy access to the records of candidates. The procedure was also wasteful. Particular dissatisfaction was expressed at the retention of the Minister's right to reject the advice of the Committee of the Education Advisory Council on the appointment of principals. It commented:

This unfettered right of the Minister despite the advisory service of the Education Advisory Council's Committee still opens the way for political patronage as well as victimization to be practised by any person holding the political office of Minister in any Government.[36]

The Minority Report pointed to the state of affairs between the Ministry and the JTA and saw this strong ministerial policy as a way to make matters worse. Those who signed the Report agreed with all the other amendments accepted but they maintained that they could not possibly accept Articles 35 and 36.

But even a strong group and the Opposition itself could not force the Government to make more significant concessions on this issue. The Minister was quite determined on the matter and he had the support of the Cabinet. It was partly this failure in 1966 which forced the JTA leaders finally to consider using the strike and boycott as weapons. Militancy of itself did not bring about changes, but with the relaxation of tension between the Labour Government and the JTA during the last months of 1966 and early 1967, an atmosphere was created in which both sides could return to the negotiating table.[37]

Professional issues

Unlike the JUT, the JTA raised some professional issues which reflected a desire not only to influence the process of decision-making but also to get the teaching occupation recognized as a fully-fledged profession. This difference in the nature of issues raised by the JUT and the JTA reflects the growing maturity of the teaching community's awareness of itself, but it also reflects the more widespread democratic sentiments of the post-1938 period. It is, therefore, very relevant to look closely at two issues which may be categorized as being of a 'professional' nature in the early years of the JTA. These were the JTA's opposition to registration of teachers and the demand to be recognized in the new Education Bill.

The 1964 Education Bill proposed a systematic registration of teachers who would be recognized by the Ministry of Education. The JTA initially welcomed this and in its memorandum to the Select Committee of the House the Association gave its reasons for supporting the Bill:

i) It (the Bill) recognizes and implements the Ministerial System in Education and gives the Minister the necessary power for full and effective control.

ii) It integrates the whole of the educational system of the island.
iii) It paves the way for the effective enforcement of compulsory education.
iv) It establishes a system of regulating independent schools.[38]

As noted earlier, the JTA was to change its tune as its attempts to influence the Minister failed. Even at this stage, however, the Association was firmly opposed to the powers being reserved for the Minister which could lead to possible abuse by the individual holding the office. Not only should certain safeguards be written into the Bill, but the JTA wanted also to make sure that it was actively involved in important aspects of educational administration. On the question of the registration of teachers the Association wanted to see that those who had been in teaching before the enforcement of the new measure, be exempted from producing a medical certificate as a condition of registration; they should be registered automatically. Of much more importance, however, was the desire of the leadership to have the JTA responsible for the registration of teachers. It argued that the JTA

> support fully the proposal to institute the registration of teachers, and believe that this will do much to raise teaching to the status of a major profession. We point out however that in countries in which registration of teachers is carried out, registration is the function of the teachers' association itself, and that in Jamaica in the legal and medical professions, registration is carried out by boards which have a majority membership elected by the profession itself.[39]

The Association went on to propose that the Board should consist of two representatives of the JTA nominated by its council, two appointed by the Minister and a chairman appointed by the Chief Justice. Filling vacant positions should be subject to prior approval of the nominating body. The Chief Justice should be responsible for setting out the procedural rules and provisions should be made for legal representation and the right of the accused to call witnesses.

The main argument for this was, of course, the fact that the JTA represented, in the words of the memorandum, 'the integrated teaching profession in Jamaica'.[40] Since this and the demand to be recognized as the body nominating representatives on relevant bodies are closely related, the results achieved may best be considered together.

From its position of unity and strength the JTA made the bold step of asking the Minister of Education that

> The 'Council of the Jamaica Teachers' Association' be
> recognized in the Education Law as the body to nominate
> representatives for the teachers' organizations whenever
> such representatives are called for in the Law.[41]

The Association argued that there were precedents for this: the
medical and legal professions were so recognized in law and so there
was no reason why teachers should not be accorded the same
privilege. After all, the JTA was the body representing the whole
teaching community from elementary schools to teacher-training
colleges.

This would, of course, not only make the JTA's position strong
in its relations to the Government but also in its relations to
teachers who would find it extremely difficult to effect a split in the
JTA or to form rival organizations. Leaders were also very sensitive
to the centralizing tendencies in the administration of education and
viewed this as a threat to the status of teachers. To escape what they
saw as possible strangulation by the Ministry the JTA's leaders
promoted policies which would make the occupation more of a
profession, not only in its own eyes but also in those of the public.
The demand represented a dashing attempt to get teachers into
an unquestionable position of control over some aspects of the
occupation.

The JTA did not succeed in this nor in persuading the Government that it should adopt the Association's proposals about the
registration of teachers. Allen refused to have the JTA recognized
in the Law and, as he told parliament when introducing the Report
of the Select Committee, he would have to remember that there
were various interests concerned with education when he came to
appoint members for the Registration Board. He pointed out that
the JTA was already recognized by the Government and the Ministry as the body representing teachers. It was the body with which
the Government 'do business'.[42] Since not all teachers were members of the Association, however, if the Government were to agree
to the demand of the JTA that it be recognized in law then he as
Minister would be practically forcing teachers to become members
of the JTA. This was something he was not prepared to do. The
Government did not want to give the impression that it was forcing
individuals to join any particular association. He indeed recognized
the important role the JTA would play in advising the Ministry and
himself but this was no reason for creating yet another statutory
body alongside the Education Advisory Council.

Later in the debate the Minister, following the Leader of the

Opposition's bald definition of a 'profession' (which included the idea that members are 'trained') pointed out that not all teachers were in fact trained. This, by implication, made it impossible for the teaching occupation to be recognized as a 'profession' and for the JTA to be accredited the status it demanded. If the JTA were to split and another association arose how would the Government then treat such an organization, the Minister asked. It was his intention to keep education out of politics and he was determined to avoid committing the Government to such actions. He stated:

> I say that for all practical purposes this Government recognized the Jamaica Teachers' Association as the mouthpiece of teachers and whatever representation they make to us we regard as coming from the teachers. But to go as far as legislating I am afraid that we cannot do that at this moment.[43]

Three prominent members of the Opposition spoke on these issues, Glasspole, Jones and Manley himself. They were satisfied with the general outcome of the Select Committee except on these particular issues. It was their general agreement which led Glasspole and Jones to sign the Majority Report but they felt bound to submit a Minority one also. Glasspole stressed that when he had first drawn up the Bill in 1960/1 he did not include the JTA in it because at that time there were several associations in the country. Now that there was only one teachers' association the Minister should not hesitate to recognize it in law for 'the picture has changed'.[44] The Ministry had indeed recognized the JTA and since this was nearing 'kissing terms' there were no grounds for not extending this recognition in the law. He saw immediate benefits accruing from this for both the Government and the teachers:

> The fact is that in terms of the present position, nothing could inspire greater confidence in the relationship between the teachers and Government than the recognition of the JTA in a Bill of this sort.[45]

Jones reiterated these points, but Manley, the Leader of the Opposition, spent a longer time speaking in support of the JTA. In his view the teaching occupation qualified as a profession and the recent unification of the teachers' associations into the JTA demonstrated that the teachers were themselves aware of this. The unity of teachers was a prerequisite to the unified system of education which the Bill was seeking to establish. It was, in his view, an unsound argument to say that the law could not recognize the JTA because of a fear that it might break up into separate associations later. This argument he pointed out, was never put in the case of the legal and the medical occupations. He felt that teachers would, inevitably, become totally responsible for their actions, meaning presumably by this that the Association would become responsible for disciplining and controlling teachers – and this might as well start from their Association being recognized in law. He was, of course, correct in his argument that until the occupation could regulate itself it would not enjoy the 'dignities' of professional status. But this did not shake the Minister who was quite certain that it was not correct to comply with the request. This was, therefore, yet another important issue on which the JTA failed to persuade the JLP Government in spite of strong support from the PNP Opposition.

Political issues

Indeed, most of the issues raised by the JTA during these years became highly political because of the party political situation which had developed after 1938-44. It is, therefore, sufficient to examine just one overtly political issue of the period. Undoubtedly, the most deserving of attention is the Association's resistance to the threat from the JLP Government to make all teachers civil servants.

In the post-independence 1960s Jamaican teachers maintained that although they were paid by the State this fact of itself did not make them civil servants. They are subject to the Code of Regulations which is operated by the Ministry of Education, but not to the civil service regulations. In the colonial period, elementary schoolteachers were very proud that they were not regarded as civil servants and, in the same form, teachers in the 1960s in Jamaica saw no reason why they should be subjected to the constraints of the civil service. When in May and June 1966 the JTA called teachers out on strike with an overwhelmingly favourable response, the Minister retaliated by threatening to make them subject to the regulations of the civil service. Naturally this appeared to teachers to be the Government's attempt to control their freedom so as to make their actions predictable.

The JTA, and teachers generally, reacted quickly to the Minister's statement. Meetings were called, publications abounded and broadcasts were made on the 'threat' in June 1966. The leaders were able to consolidate the Association further for it became increasingly clear to the pedagogic community that the Minister was intent on defeating them. The views of teachers on the issue were most clearly stated by the staff of the Calabar High School in a document they sent to the JTA executive, in June 1966. The gist of their argument was that a great wrong would be done to teachers if they were made civil servants. Teachers, after all, were better able than the Ministry to judge how teaching should be carried out. As a civil servant the teacher would no longer be a teacher but a mere transmitter of knowledge. He had to prepare the child for life and this task entailed duties to the child which the Ministry could not properly regulate. In defending the 'professional' relationship which existed between the teacher and the child, the writers pointed out some prerequisites if the teacher were to execute his tasks to the best of his ability:

i) The teacher must function in an unregimented and flexible atmosphere where he can use his initiative inside and outside the classroom.
ii) He must be free to participate fully in the life of his community. He must strive to understand fully the problems and needs, and help to give expression to the aims and aspirations of the people in his community.
iii) The teacher must be free to choose his place of work without external pressure and according to the dictates of his conscience.
iv) The teacher must enjoy security of tenure.[46]

Because of these 'necessary conditions' the writers asserted that the teacher must remain free of the civil service regulations which would undermine his freedom and, thereby, his professionalism. The teacher would lose some of his 'trade union' rights such as holidays. He could be transferred from one place to another regardless of his preference. The hours of duty for a civil servant were fixed whereas the teacher did much of his work, unpaid, after teaching hours. But of far greater importance than these would be the limitations placed on teachers, such as not being able to contribute to newspapers, take part in radio and television broadcasts which involved free comment on the policies, etc., of the Government of the day and the administration generally. The writers saw the threat as being 'part of a dangerous tendency to concentrate control and the elimination of voluntary service and enthusiasm'.[47] This posed a threat to democracy, for local initiative was being undermined and the right of teachers to participate in political activities was being curtailed. A great danger was therefore lurking, for,

> The body of citizens who have until now been the leaders
> of democratic opinion in this country because of the very
> nature of their work would thus be effectively silenced.[48]

Leaders took the threat seriously and there was hardly a meeting of
the JTA during the months after June 1966 at which the issue was
not given serious consideration.

Eventually the threat was dropped by Allen but this was not the
achievement solely of the JTA. The Government and particularly
the Minister, retreated because of more general developments in the
country during the months following his statement. It was largely
a retaliation and it was to some degree tangential to the main
problems between a Labour Ministry and the teachers. So, once
these were resolved the threat fell into its proper place. The lessening of tension between the Minister and the JTA in the last months
of 1966 and early 1967 cleared the way for this issue to be forgotten
by both sides. The crucial issues had been Articles 35 and 36 of the
Code of Regulations, salaries and the general attitude of the Minister towards the teachers and the JTA. Agreements on these meant
that the potential threat would lapse. In June 1967 the JTA, at the
intervention of the churches, relaxed its stubborn attitude towards
the Code. Since it was now law the teachers had little choice but to
work by it but the JTA in proper constitutional style decided to
continue to press for its revision. Thus, when the senior chief
education officer asked the JTA for its proposed revisions these
were immediately sent.[49] The point is that the situation was defused. Both sides were prepared to drop their threats – teachers
would no longer belligerently oppose the Code and nothing more
was heard about Allen's threat.[50]

The immediate aftermaths of 1967

As an association representing a semi-professional body in an
ostensibly democratic and competitive party political system, the
JTA was a fairly successful group capable of defending its members'
interests, initiating and promoting policies and commanding respect
from both the public and the Government of the day. Between 1964
and 1967 it had to struggle for this position and in doing so established order and coherence to teachers' grievances and aspirations.
The JTA was therefore to become a force in the educational system
of the country for the remainder of the 1960s and in the 1970s.
Before, however, concluding this discussion of teachers and politics
it is relevant to indicate in general terms the changed circumstances

of the 1970s which tended to curtail the seemingly unassailable position which the JTA had achieved by the end of the 1960s.

First, the JTA gained, or, in the view of the Government of the day was granted, access to the relevant decision-making bodies established by the Ministry of Education. These included the teacher-training committee, the teacher-registration board, and the education advisory council and its various sub-committees. The Ministry and the JTA agreed to the appointment of a liaison officer with an office at the Association's headquarters and another at the Ministry of Education.[51] As part of the new peace of 1967 a salaries and conditions of service committee was established for teachers and officials to meet on a regular basis. As is typical of successful groups, therefore, the post-1967 situation was one in which neither the Association nor the Government appeared to have won or lost outright. But in substantial terms the Association had gained what the JUT never managed to achieve, that is, continuous access to relevant decision-makers.

Second, the allegiance of the JTA leadership to the PNP paid off handsomely after 1972 when the party was returned to office. During the election campaign itself the JTA behaved very much like other groups which wanted to see a change in the governance of the land. After all, the JLP had been in office from 1962 and the changes expected after a decade of political independence did not seem forthcoming. A reading of the *Gleaner* throughout the election year reveals widespread support for the PNP which had as its motto 'it's time for a change'. After the PNP won the elections Florizel Glasspole returned to the Ministry of Education for a brief while before being 'kicked upstairs' as Governor-General by the radical new Prime Minister, Manley the Younger. Both Glasspole and his PNP successors in the 1970s had a listening ear for the advice of the JTA. Indeed, in 1974 the invitations to Mrs Fay Saunders and Dr Errol Miller to join the Ministry as senior members were indications of the distance the JTA had covered in its attempt to be where decisions which affect teachers were being taken.

Teachers were no longer outsiders depending entirely on influential friends in the right places. Nor was their union trying any longer to frame demands and requests in a manner which would demonstrate to decision-makers that teachers were having to go out of their way to be a 'helpful' group in the way that the JUT had to. As a matter of course the Association was concerned not to be confrontational with the Ministry. But its leaders no longer had to bow unduly to a vastly superior and essentially undemocratic establishment.

Perhaps the most significant development in the post-1967 period, however, was the formation of the National Union of Democratic Teachers (NUDT) in 1975. This was a development not expected by the leaders of the Association. The event, however, confirmed Allen's fear that the JTA could split and the Government of the day would be faced with the problem of recognition. It was as well, therefore, for the PNP Government that the JLP had refused to recognize the JTA formally in the Education Act as the sole body to represent teachers' interests. Had Norman Manley succeeded in his support for the Association, his son's government in the 1970s may have had to face the embarrassment of what to do about the NUDT whose leaders' political and ideological thinking were close, though not identical, to the new radicalism of the PNP.

There are several factors which help to explain the emergence of the breakaway union. The first of these must be the very success of the JTA in bringing together all categories of teachers. Having achieved this and the desired access to decision-makers the Association became the victim of its own success. Its original militancy naturally gave way to moderation. This was, of course, the mood of teachers before the confrontation with the JLP Government in the 1960s but success may have given rise to a degree of complacency. As often happens with groups in this position, the once militant leadership became, in the eyes of some younger members, too 'reasonable' with, and too understanding of, bureaucrats and the new PNP Ministry.

At the JTA Annual Conference in December 1973, it was evident, from discussions with younger teachers, that they felt that the moderation of the leadership compromised the interests of the lower ranks in the profession. The predominance of headteachers and principals in the leadership, it was believed, led to there being insufficient promotion and defence of the interests of those lower down the occupational ladder. The leadership, on the other hand, tended to see such criticisms as a demonstration of disloyalty, or lack of appreciation, of the unity which the Association had achieved.

Moreover, the settling down of a conservative leadership of the JTA occurred just at the time when young Jamaica was being radicalized. From the late 1960s the intelligentsia was beginning to examine the achievements of independence and it was finding these lacking in important respects. Radicalism at the UWI offered a critique of the neo-colonial economy which Jamaica and the rest of the Commonwealth Caribbean had inherited. The country's dependence on foreign capital, the ownership by North American companies of natural resources such as bauxite and land, the increasing social and material distance between the rich and the poor, and so forth, were examined. As may be expected from academic intellectuals, this critique from the *New World Group* remained highly academic.

The militant Black Power movement in the USA was another source of the increasing radicalism of the time. Not surprisingly, this movement affected West Indian students in North America as well as in the Caribbean. In Jamaica this led to a rapid transformation of academic radicalism into a fairly widespread political disaffection with the socio-economic and political structures of the country. One result was the formation of the more populist and dynamic *Abeng* group which replaced the *New World Group* and quickly became the vehicle for the new militant radicalism, which now moved away from the university campus.

One of the events which triggered off this development was the demonstration in Kingston over the banning of radical UWI lecturer the late Dr Walter Rodney in October 1968. Rodney's crime was that he had been teaching African history to the outcast Rastafarians in the ghettoes of Kingston and, simple as this now sounds, in those days this was heresy for the majority of the Jamaican population. The Jamaican post-colonial society of the 1960s had not undertaken an immediate questioning of its inheritance and was, indeed, loth to do so. Rodney's teachings posed a direct challenge to the received values which denigrated the African heritage of the vast majority of Jamaicans. By the 1970s, therefore, the new radicalism began to be felt in various sections of the young intelligentsia, which had grown because of the expansion which took place at all levels of education from 1948 when the UWI was founded.

The new radicalism was significantly to affect the PNP Government. Under the leadership of Michael Manley, D. K. Duncan and the second and third generations of PNP leaders the party at first slowly moved to embrace much of the radicalism preached by the *New World Group* intellectuals. Economists such as Norman Girvan, George Beckford and Owen Jefferson and political scientists such as Carl Stone and Edwin Jones became active supporters and advisers to the Government. By the end of its first term in December 1976 the PNP had moved significantly away from the traditional middle ground of Jamaican politics over which both the PNP and the JLP had fought since 1944. The party and the Government embraced the radical Third World critique of both the economy and the international situation, and during its second term, 1976-80, succeeded in alienating significant numbers of traditional supporters.

The point is, however, that during the 1970s the radicalism which had been developed by the *New World Group* (and to a lesser extent aspects of the radicalism of the *Abeng* group also) became party principles and began to affect government policies.

Younger teachers were far from being immune to these developments. Indeed, their principal complaint was that internal democracy in the JTA was inadequate for the demands of the moment – hence the deliberate emphasis on the 'democratic' in their title. In the view of John Houghton and his radical colleagues the JTA was led by members of the occupation who did not have a great deal of sympathy with the aspirations of the younger teachers and insufficient numbers of these were moving into the leadership.[52]

The new militancy was not, however, necessarily in support of the PNP. It was much more in tune with the then emerging radicalism which the *Workers Liberation League*, under the leadership of Dr Trevor Munroe, was advocating. This was a Marxist-oriented group which later developed into the (Soviet-oriented) Jamaica Workers' Party.

The emergence of a new teachers' union, of course, opened the possibility for teachers' political support to be divided between the parties. With more than one organization representing teachers, the PNP could no longer simply take for granted the support of organized teachers in the country. This did not mean, however, that the JLP could count on the breakaway union's support either. The breakaway was not to the right but to the left of the JTA leadership. None the less, the existence of more than one union offered an opportunity to leaders of the semi-profession as well as governments of either party to avoid making education and the behaviour of teachers as highly political as in the 1960s.

Conclusion

Whereas the JTA was seen at that time by the JLP as being a mouthpiece for the Opposition PNP, everything Allen did made the teachers suspicious. A situation of mutual suspicion existed, with the Minister and the Prime Minister mistaking teachers' demands for PNP mischief. During the first part of the 1970s the close relations between the PNP Ministry and the JTA appeared to confirm this view of their activities but the presence of a new union made this less likely and therefore helped to depoliticize the context in which teachers had to promote and defend their interests and the education system of the country.

Notes

1   There were times, according to some teachers' leaders, when the *Daily Gleaner* would refuse to publish their material, but generally the paper gave a very good coverage of the activities of the Association. Unlike the 1970s, there was no national daily to compete with the *Gleaner* and its circulation was, and is, wide. Although it was against the strike in June 1966, the paper nevertheless gave publicity to it. Its editorial for 2 June 1966 read (p. 10):

> The decision of the Jamaica Teachers' Association to call a strike of all teachers in primary and secondary schools, starting today, is a deplorable decision. There is no point to the strike whatever. This is no stand for democratic rights. It is an ill-considered and ill-conceived directive that takes the current silly season in Jamaica's life a bit too far.

In the view of the editor the JTA was 'spoiling for a fight'.

2   There were over seven of these in June 1966 when the teachers and the Government were in open confrontation; see, for example, *The New Clarion*, Annual & Conference No., December 1966, p. 10.

3   *The Minutes of the JTA Annual Conference, 1965*, pp. 21/2; also, *The New Clarion*, vol. i, no. i (February 1965), p. 4.

4   *The Jamaica Teachers' Association, Memorandum Re. Passport, 12 January 1968* (Kingston: Farquharson Institute of Public Affairs, n.d. but presumably 1968).

5   See for example, the JTA's collection of papers, 'National conference on education, Jamaica Hilton, 23-26 April 1970' (n.d.) also 'National Conference on Education, 26 February 1965', *The files of the JTA*.

6   Cf. R. D. Coates, *Teachers' union and interest group politics: a study in the behaviour of organized teachers in England and Wales* (Cambridge University Press, 1972).

7   At the opening of the 1974 Conference there were, for example, Mr Allen and Mr E. Matalon the then Minister of Education, the Mayor of Kingston, Councillor Brown, and Mr D. Coore the Minister of Finance and Deputy Prime Minister.

8   For example, in 1966 Mr D. Sangster, Acting Prime Minister and Minister of Finance, led the Conference, teachers held, to believe that they would be given an increase in salaries. When later in the year the Budget was presented and there was no mention of a salary increase for teachers they became extremely angry with Mr Sangster, and used this as one of the reasons for going on strike. Cf. *The New Clarion*, vol. ii, no. ii (March 1966), p. 4.

9   Also *The JTA Annual Conference, December-January, 1973/4.* (Mico College, Kingston, 3 January 1974); Mr Manley spoke mainly about his government's policy on foreign affairs, particularly on the oil crisis.

10   Letters from the JTA's President, Mr D. Gascoigne, to the Bishop of Kingston, 11 February 1966; to J. A. Rhynie, 3 February 1966; to the Moderator, United Church of Jamaica and Grand Cayman, 2 February 1966; Also, 'The Minutes of the JTA executive meeting' 24 June, 'The Minutes of the JTA General Council', 25 June 1966, and 'The Minutes of the JTA executive meeting', 22 July 1966, *The files of the JTA*.

11   Terence J. Johnson, *Professions and Power* (London: MacMillan, 1972), ch. 6; and Imperialism and the professions: notes on the development of professional occupations in Britain's colonies and the new states, *Sociological Review Monograph*, no. xx; Paul Halmos (ed.) *Professions and Social Change*, (1973); also, D. C. Lortie, 'The Balance of control and autonomy in elementary school teachings', Amitai Etziono (ed.) *The semi-professions and their organization: teachers, nurses, social workers* (New York and London: The Free Press & Collier-MacMillan Ltd. 1969), p. 1ff.

12   Jamaica Hansard, Session 1966-7, vol. i, no. i, May 1966 (Kingston: The Gleaner Co. Ltd., 1966) p. 161; also Session 1967/8, vol. i, no. i (14 June 1967), p. 69.

13   'The Minutes of the JTA executive meeting', 27 May 1966, pp. 1-2, *The files of the JTA*.

14   Mr G. German, headmaster of the Manchester Secondary School in Mandeville, was accused by parents and by the school board of using his position to promote in the area the PNP Opposition which he supported. Eventually, he was dismissed from his post by the board; it was widely believed that pressure was being applied by the Minister. The Ministry carried out investigations and confirmed the dismissal but since the Report is still considered to be the internal concern of the Ministry I was not able to secure a copy. Mr German, before the affair was over returned to Britain. Being very popular with teachers in the area he quickly gained their support and this came at about the same time as the breakdown over the negotiations between the JTA and the Ministry. Cf. 'Interview with Mr Clinton Muschette' 22 February 1974; Mr Muschette was President of the Manchester Teachers' Association in 1966 and he became President of the JTA in 1973; also 'Interview with Mr Ben Hawthorne' 29 March 1974.

15   Statement of the Manchester Teachers' Association, Thursday, 2 June 1966, *The files of the JTA*, p. i; also, *The Daily Gleaner*, 2 June 1966, pp. 1-2.

16   *The New Clarion*, vol. ii, no. iii (May/June 1966), p. 2; *The Daily Gleaner*, 2 June 1966.

17   *The New Clarion*, vol. ii, no. iii (May/June 1966), p. 2.

18   *The Daily Gleaner*, 4 June 1966, p. 20.

19   *The New Clarion*, vol. ii, no. iii (May/June 1966), p. 2.

20   'Report of the salaries and conditions of service committee of the JTA, Salary Proposals, 1965', *The files of the JTA*.

21   'The Minutes of the JTA executive meeting, 28 October 1966', *The files of the JTA*. At this meeting some members spoke of a higher figure.

22   *Letter from Mr Ben Hawthorne* (29 January 1975). Mr Hawthorne who was secretary-general of the JTA from 1963-74 explained this system thus (p. 2):

> . . . where the teacher is on a salary scale rising by increments from minimum to maximum, a new scale would place him at a point which gives him as many increments in the new as he had earned in the old scale.

23   Cf. *The New Clarion*, vol. ii, no. ii (March, 1966), p. 1.

24   'The Minutes of the JTA executive meeting', 24 June 1967; and 28 July

1967, p. 2, *The files of the JTA*; also 'Regrading and revision of salaries of teachers, 1967/8', *Ministry of Finance Paper, no. 49*, 12 July 1967, submitted to the House by E. Seaga, Minister of Finance and Planning.

25   *The New Clarion*, Annual & Conference No., December 1969, pp. 6-7. The Special Resolution of that year was,

> Be it resolved that Government be requested to implement a salary scale for teachers related to the importance of the work they undertake, the need to recruit and retain teachers in the service, and the demands of living in a society where the cost of necessities is extremely high.

See also *The New Clarion*, Annual & Conference No., December 1969, p. 7.

26   See, *The New Clarion*, Annual & Conference No., December 1973, p. 33.

27   T. Lacey, *Violence and politics in Jamaica 1960-1970*, (Manchester University Press, 1977), p. 50; this text is also of immense value in giving a general view of the 1960s.

28   'The Minutes of the JTA executive meeting', 1 April 1967, p. 2, *The files of the JTA*.

29   'The Minutes of the JTA executive meeting', 24 June 1967, pp. 1-2, *The files of the JTA*.

30   The Gerry German Affair was also going on at the time; see 'The Minutes of the Annual General Meeting of the post-primary department of the JTA', 3 December 1965, p. 2, *The files of the JTA*.

31   The latter point was no doubt a double precaution taken by the drafters of the Code and it would seem that they too had the Byfield case very much in mind.

32   'The Memorandum of the Jamaica Teachers' Association on the Educating Code, 1965', p. 2. *The files of the JTA*.

33   *Ibid.*, p. 5.

34   Mr B. Hawthorne, 'Letter re: Education Regulations – appointment of teachers to the Chairman and members of the Select Committee on the Code of Regulations' (22 May 1966), *The files of the JTA*.

35   'Report of the Select Committee appointed by the House of Representatives to study and report on the proposed education regulations 1965 ('The Code') (18 May 1966), p. 4, *Jamaica Hansard*, Session 1966-7.

36   'The Minority Report' was signed by F. Glasspole, W. V. Jones and S. R. Pagon; expectedly, no members of the government party signed this. See 'The Minority Report', Report of the Select Committee, p. 2, *Jamaica Hansard*, Session 1966-7.

37   'The Minutes of the JTA executive meetings' and 'The Minutes of the JTA General Council', *The files of the JTA*, after September 1966, reflect these changes in attitudes; cf. 'Interviews with the officials of the JTA', (1974).

38   'Memorandum of the JTA to the Select Committee of the Legislature on the Education Bill, 1964', p. 1, *The files of the JTA*.

39   *Ibid.*

40   *Ibid.*, pp. 2-3.

41   *Ibid.*, p. 3.

42   *Jamaica Hansard*, Sessions 1964-5, vol. no. i (2 March 1965) p. 557.

43   *Ibid.*, p. 560.

44   *Ibid.*, p. 559, Although the PNP returned to office in 1972, and Mr Glasspole was Minister between 1972-3, nothing was ever done to recognize the JTA as a 'professional' body during the 1970s.

45   *Ibid.*

46   'Memorandum to the JTA from the Staff of the Calabar High School', (n.d. but presumably soon after the threat of 4 June, 1966) p. 1, *The files of the JTA.*

47   *Ibid.*, p. 3.

48   *Ibid.*

49   'The JTA's recommendations for amendments to the Code, re. Ministry's letter C 345 September 1967', *The files of the JTA.*

50   Another example of a tangential issue taking on major proportions was the insistence of the JTA that the Government should institute machinery for the continuous negotiation over salaries and conditions.

51   Interestingly enough, the first person to occupy the position was Mr D. Gascoigne who was President of the JTA in 1966 when the strike was called.

52   Shirley Romain-Brathwaite's M.Sc. thesis for the Department of Government, UWI, will shed a great deal of light on the grievances of some radical assistant teachers in the JTA in the mid-1970s.

CHAPTER 7 | Some concluding remarks

The general discussion in this study has been about the activities and concerns of organized teachers in Jamaica from the 1880s to the beginning of the 1970s. In this respect the focus has been upon specific issues and activities with a view to ascertaining the groups' resources, ideological orientation, degree of access and so forth, which would partly determine whether they were successful.

One striking difference between the JUT and the JTA which emerges throughout the discussion is the degree to which they were respectively successful in defending and promoting the interests of teachers and education. While the JTA made some impressive gains, the failures of the JUT were conspicuous. The chief explanations for these results, however, have been seen to be not only the groups' respective resources and status but, more importantly, the general political contexts within which they operated.

In these concluding remarks I want to pick up two points about education, teachers and politics in the Anglophone Caribbean which were introduced in a general way in chapter one and developed, with respect to Jamaica, in the subsequent discussion. This chapter, therefore, serves a two-fold purpose: in the first instance it is a summary of some of the main points of the study: secondly, it attempts to relate these points to the general experience of the Anglophone Caribbean.

Education in the Anglophone Caribbean

Individual Anglophone Caribbean countries are proud of their education systems and, understandably, loudly proclaim their distinctive features. The Barbadian's boast that his country has the best education record must be placed alongside the equal claim of the Trinidadian. The general view in the Eastern Caribbean Anglophone islands and Guyana that Jamaicans have been unfortunate in not having had many educational opportunities (and hence the reputed violent behaviour of the Jamaican[1]) must be seen within the inter-territorial but quiet rivalry between different sections of a people who have more in common than they are sometimes willing to admit. The Jamaican's attitude of superiority towards the rest of the English-speaking Caribbean – expressed in the phrase 'small island people' – must be seen in a similar light. The 'small island people' in Jamaican creole is as condescending as is the 'the little man' (the hard-working man who makes do but is far from being well-heeled) in the middle class' version of that still formative but expressive language.

In reality these countries have almost everything in common and can therefore afford to stress their relatively minor differences. The similarities arise naturally enough in this respect from a common tradition of education, the main features of which were outlined in chapter one. These included, to all intents and purposes, an identical syllabus, a common structure and administration of education as well as a dual system of ownership and control. This common experience is, of course, due to several factors. Only one of these need be mentioned here, however, since the matter was discussed in a general way in chapter one.

The early acquisition by Britain of her Caribbean colonies meant that there has been a long enough period of uninterrupted rule for British assumptions and presumptions to become the norm. Even countries such as Trinidad, which came late under British rule, did so as long ago as the beginning of the nineteenth century. This has been long enough for the influence of other European countries (Spain, France and the Netherlands) to give way to English educational and general cultural assumptions. After a turbulent early history of settlement, piracy and inter-European wars, some of which were partly fought out in the Caribbean sea and on the islands, the region settled down to a long and remarkable period of peace.

Unfortunately, this long peace did not bring with it rapid and transformative development for the people who had, through force or voluntary action, made the region their home. What did occur, however, was a steady evolution of institutions and norms governing social behaviour. These were later to be recognized as being distinctly West Indian. With respect to education this meant making the best of a highly divisive and under-resourced system. But for a population emerging from the inhumanity of slavery and the constraints of indentured labour the little they received from the State could be turned into much.

Whilst in general terms the development of education and the experience of elementary schoolteachers in Jamaica do not depart significantly from the rest of the region as indicated in chapter one, it may be useful to indicate some of the variations in the West Indian tradition of education at this point. Seen from a distance, the Jamaican case appears as part of the regular pattern of the Anglophone Caribbean. If we look more closely, however, we shall see differences which are worth mentioning. It is not simply a case of Jamaica being the odd man out, although in some respects this is so. Nor are the differences between countries all of a kind. It should be enough, however, to give just one or two examples of these similarities and differences here.

The educational dualism described in chapter two was perhaps the outstanding hallmark of education throughout the region. Under this system the churches continued to be the major owners of schools whilst the State paid for many of the expenses such as salaries, the maintenance of buildings and so forth. Of course, in some countries this went farther than in others and in these respects it may be useful to contrast Jamaica and the former British Guiana (now Guyana).

In the first place, the compromise which church and state achieved in Jamaica was never attained in Guiana. It was not surprising, therefore, that when in the early 1960s the radical People's Progressive Party Government led by Dr Cheddi Jagan attempted to institute what it believed would be a national system of education, the churches objected to what in Jamaica they had strongly demanded from as early as the 1880s and certainly by the 1890s. They realized that the State must provide education for its citizens. The legitimate role of the churches in education, however, was actively to guide and guard the moral training of the child whilst he or she was still at school. In Jamaica these shared responsibilities were comparatively clear after almost a century of give and take. As in England, it was understood that whilst the churches were once the bearers of education and they owned the majority of schools, it was only a matter of time before the system would come under state control. As noted, at the beginning of the period under discussion, the churches took the initiative in encouraging the State to play a major role in the education system. By the end of the First World War, however, the churches had come to recognize that only the lack of financial resources inhibited the State from assuming greater responsibility for education throughout the country. When, therefore, the State, for political rather than purely educational reasons, was able to assume nearly all responsibility for the system there was relatively little ecclesiastical opposition. At the same time the State had no desire to take over all the functions of the churches.

This was close to the experience of most Anglophone Caribbean countries. After all, such a development was very much in line with the demands of teachers and the expectations of parents. Decolonizing British Guiana, however, provided an interesting contrast. It may be useful to mention aspects of this.

First, there was a difference of degree in the operation of the dual control of schools. In Guiana the majority of both elementary and secondary schools were owned, up to the period of decolonization after World War Two, by the Christian churches. Even after World War Two, when the State acted on the realization that it ought to play a more direct and active role in education, the schools it built were handed over to the churches for management and control.[2]

In some of the countries where this was equally true it was an innocent enough practice based on the long-standing and high regard for the churches. In the case of Guiana, however, there was the added complication of religious and racial differentiation of the population. One half of a population made up of Africans, Europeans and groups of mixed ancestry were members of one or other denomination of the Christian churches. The other half of the population was of East Indian descent and was strongly attached to faiths carried from the Indian sub-continent, mainly Islam and Hinduism. Thus, whilst the prominent role of the churches in education tended to strengthen the Christian groups it worked against the non-Christians. This meant, moreover, that the school system inevitably became entangled in the quagmire of ethnic nationalist politics into which the PNC and the PPP dragged the country from the late 1950s to the mid-1960s. However damaging to the long-term good of the country, the *racial option* proved quite irresistible to the country's two national political figures, the late L. F. S. Burnham and Cheddi Japan, as the stakes of power became higher with political independence around the corner.

Where separatist schools of a racial or ethnic kind existed they marked a departure from the general West Indian norm. It should perhaps be stressed, therefore, that West Indians owe a great deal to a generation of men and women who took command in a quiet and at first unassuming manner and moulded education so that nearly all its intolerant and racial overtones have been shed or at least muted. This is no mean achievement within the constraints set by a dominant white colonial regime and a colour-conscious creole society.

If we compare this experience with other parts of the post-colonial world we will find that there are few other places where education, without too much deliberate central planning, has come to play a more unifying role. After all, the West Indian may be an African, Indian, Amerindian, European, Middle-Easterner, Chinese and so forth. In short, the population of the region has been drawn from almost every part of the world. Yet there is a distinct historical and cultural experience which makes people from such a wide variety of backgrounds West Indian. This is expressed in the music, language, cuisine, skin colour, hair texture, universalistic world outlook and much else which are common throughout the region.

The education system cannot take the whole institutional credit for this, but its claim to much of it is a strong one. In most other parts of the post-colonial world where British educational values once obtained in the schools, the results have not been the same. In some countries the education system, through selection and exclusion, reinforced ethnic, racial, gender and regional differences. Each of these groups attended distinctly different schools and even if children were being taught roughly the same syllabus, the important 'integrative' role of the educational apparatus never came into play as far as the society as a whole was concerned. East, Central and Southern Africa were, of course, the best examples of this kind of colonization. In places such as West Africa and India the educational experiences were more like the settler colonies of East and Central Africa than the West Indies.

Another common aspect of educational dualism which the Caribbean shared was, of course, the class division which elementary and secondary education represented. All the British territories had their prestigious secondary schools – Jamaica College, Harrison College in Barbados, St Mary's College in Guiana, Queen's College in Trinidad and so forth – but these were a world apart from that inhabited by the vast majority of children in the elementary sector. This division both reflected and reproduced the class division of these societies. To a large extent they also perpetuated the colour-divide described in chapter two.

For a long period of West Indian history secondary schools were attended mainly by white children. With time 'high colour' middle-class children gained a foothold. Too slowly these schools eventually came to be attended by children of nationals rather than expatriates. The important point, however, is that schools were not legally or formally racially exclusive as in the other colonies. As small as these points undoubtedly were in their individual parts, taken together they amounted to an important point of difference with the non-Caribbean British empire. This was to bode well for future post-colonial West Indian societies.

On the positive side the remarkable fact about these élitist schools was that people from all racial and class backgrounds aspired to them because they represented the gateway to a better future. When all is said and done, therefore, about the education system as it emerged and developed in the region, it cannot be said to have been an unsurmountable obstacle to the urge of the West Indian people to become part of a wider world by adapting received institutions and norms to the demands of the contemporary world.

These schools provided the region with a brilliant generation of post-independence scholars. They included, amongst others, the historian the late Walter Rodney, the economists George Beckford, Clive Thomas and Norman Girvan; in the colonial days the same education system produced scholars such as the late Eric Williams, C. L. R. James, M. G. Smith and Sir Arthur Lewis. Creative writers as diverse as Wilson Harris, the late Vic Reid, the Naipaul brothers, Andrew Salkey, Samuel Selvon, George Lamming, Eddie Brathwaite and Derek Walcot also came through this education system.

In terms of elementary education it is important to note that several of the persons who became professors in the University of the West Indies either commenced their careers in, or were products of, that sector. The late Aubrey Phillips, Errol Miller and a number of individuals throughout the university as well as former vice-chancellor Sir Philip Sherlock, have been examples of this contribution of the elementary sector to current higher educational developments in the region. It is doubtful whether any other semi-profession or profession in the region has contributed more to the development of educational awareness and maintenance of the high standards for which the region is known.

It must now be quite obvious that education in the British West Indies has been an important field for class and as well as racial struggles. The relatively open educational system which appeared from at least the 1880s to the present had to be fought for and won. In particular, secondary education had, as in Britain in an earlier period, denoted a middle-class location in the social system. In the Caribbean there were, additionally, the racial and colour factors. First the racial obstacle was overcome and this made the West Indies remarkable societies. Colour, however, remains today as a very real question in West Indian societies, particularly in Jamaica. Even after the period of enlightenment initiated by the Ministry of Manley the Younger (1972-80), perhaps the single most crippling problem facing Jamaican society internally is the question of *colour* which informs all kinds of social existence, including education.

Teachers, educational policies and politics

This common educational experience naturally meant that elementary schoolteachers in the Anglophone Caribbean were bound to have much in common. The annual departmental reports, commissions and specific reports on education all reveal the common problems teachers faced and their common responses to them. I want to mention some of these in order to show that the main demands of the JUT and the JTA, but particularly the JUT, were not unique.

First, many of what I described as 'technical' issues formed a common stream of demand by teachers from British Honduras in the north to Guiana in the south-east. These included trade union issues such as salaries and conditions of work as well as the welfare of school children, the state of buildings and so forth. On all these issues teachers throughout the region made much the same points to the authorities. In brief, they complained that salaries were too low, classes too large, and provisions and facilities inadequate. Teachers everywhere complained about the need to enforce the compulsory attendance laws which existed in nearly all the British West Indian colonies but were never comprehensively and seriously applied.

In terms of 'professional' and 'political' issues, again, much the same demands were made by teachers elsewhere as in Jamaica. Throughout the region elementary schoolteachers opposed all attempts to curtail the teaching of the Three Rs so that planners could include vocational training in these schools. At the same time, like the JUT, they raised the demand for the State to expand education beyond this basic level and refused to see elementary education as a reason for the alienation of youths from the land. They all made demands for the teaching occupation to be improved by having more facilities for the training of teachers. In Trinidad and Tobago and Jamaica such facilities were of a comparable high standard but in most of the islands, British Honduras and British Guiana these were quite insufficient. In St Lucia, for example, Mayhew reported in the 1930s that there was only one trained teacher.

In one form or another teachers throughout the region made the demand that education should come more closely under the control of the State. Essentially, this was an attempt to loosen what many teachers saw as the stranglehold which the manager had over the teacher. Such a demand, however, could mean different specific things in different places.

For example, in Guiana this demand had an added dimension due to the racial and religious divisions discussed earlier. Until the

1960s the vast majority of schools were still controlled by the churches and since the East Indian population was, in the main, non-Christian, this meant that not many East Indian teachers were employed because the teacher was required to participate actively as a believer in the services of the church. The call for greater state control over the school, therefore, meant different things for the African and Indian populations. The latter stood to gain more immediately. In Jamaica the demand for greater state participation – the 'nationalization' of schools – was 'political' in that it required the change from colonial to independent political status for it to be met. In Guiana, however, the demand involved additional political factors. The jockeying for power led national leaders to exploit racial and ethnic differences for political advantage. And after political independence the issue remained a highly contentious one because resolution one way or the other entailed differential benefits for the Indian and African populations.

Of course, teachers from the different countries varied in the emphases they placed on issues which they raised. For example, in their representations to the Moyne Commission in 1938-9, whilst all teachers' associations raised or alluded to the general conditions of their countries, this allusion was stronger in some statements than in others. The St Vincent teachers spent most of their time describing the plight of the island and the region and making recommendations for their common improvement. The Hondurans were most concerned about the absence of provisions for teacher-training and facilities for teaching retarded children.

Nor did all the teachers' organizations in the region have the same resources with which to attempt to influence educational policies. In the first place, in most of the British West Indian colonies unions did not emerge as early as in Jamaica. The awareness of a corporate spirit amongst the majority took much longer to develop. In the larger territories, such as British Guiana, there were 'associations' from as early as the 1890s but it does not appear that these developed into the kind of robust union the JUT did. In others, such as British Honduras, the association was not founded until as late as 1932.

This relatively late development may have been due largely to two principal factors. First, the comparative size of Jamaica and the spread of elementary schools throughout the island meant the existence of a teaching force large enough to warrant awareness of sectional interest. Apart from being the single largest population in the Anglophone Caribbean Jamaica also had the lowest teacher/pupil-teacher ratio in its teaching force even though Trinidad and

Tobago was nearly twice as rich (from oil and pitch) as Jamaica before her exploitation of bauxite in the 1950s and the early 1970s.

A second factor which marks off Jamaica in this respect was no doubt the early relative centralization of education through state intervention. As noted in earlier chapters this intervention was partly at the invitation of the churches themselves in an attempt to save their schools. This had the immediate impact of forcing teachers to see their common interests both with respect to the churches and the State.

The majority of teachers in the region, therefore, had even less of a chance than the JUT and the JTA to influence educational policies. The emergence of the Caribbean Union of Teachers in the years after World War Two has meant, however, that small teachers' associations as well as larger ones can call upon regional support in their struggles. Indeed, already in the 1930s some of the associations in the Eastern Caribbean tended to frame their demands jointly with unions in different islands.

This was not particularly helpful, however, to the teachers' organizations because they still had to deal with separate island or national authorities. As small as the Anglophone Caribbean is (less than the 800 square miles of Wales when Guyana is excluded), a variety of political authorities exists. In terms of governments per head of population the region's less than six million souls are amongst the most governed people in the world. This legacy must be one of the greatest failures of British colonialism in the region. The attempt to bring these countries together on the eve of imperial departure in the Federation of the West Indies in the late 1950s was not only too late, it must have seemed cold and cynical. In both the colonial and the independence periods, therefore, teachers in the region have had to present their case in terms acceptable to separate political authorities. In several of the islands this meant that teachers' associations were too small to have any influence on decision-makers.

Finally, it is clear that teachers constituted a comparatively weak group and exercised little influence in the colonial period. After political independence they saw the demands they had made earlier become national policy, but their own social status declined. This was, of course, inevitable given the expansion in the economy and the opening of new avenues for upward social mobility. Many young and talented people who would have taken up schoolteaching could now enter the other professions such as medicine, the law,[3] or an academic career.

But the failure to influence decision-makers should not overshadow the contribution elementary schoolteachers made to the emergence of the modern West Indies. For example, the relatively democratic systems which mark off the region from most post-colonial Third World societies owe much to these teachers and their organizations. In the first instance teachers insisted, even under the essentially anti-democratic colonial regime, that matters which affect the public must be discussed openly. This insistence obliged decision-makers to explain their plans. Moreover, they provided a public forum outside the narrowly based legislative assemblies where education, as one of the most dearly held public services, could be widely and sensibly debated.

Apart from being proverbially committed to the cause of education and the interests of their pupils, the elementary schoolteacher in the Anglophone Caribbean by his or her action taught the people much about the art of compromise. In the teachers' struggles to improve education they made it a public issue and for this the Caribbean people, particularly the literate, owe them much. In a society emerging from the inhumane conditions of slavery elementary schoolteachers impressed on parents the need for educating their children and never allowed administrators and decision-makers to forget that the system could always be improved.

Notes

1 See, H. Goulbourne, Notes on explanations of violence and public order in Jamaica, *SES*, vol. 33, no. 4 (1984).
2 See, Harold A. Lutchman (1970), Administrative change in an ex-colonial setting: a study of education administration in Guyana, 1961-4, *SES*, vol. 19, no. 1 (March 1970); also, M. K. Bacchus, Patterns of educational expenditure in an emergent nation: a study of Guiana 1945-65, *SES*, vol. 17, no. 3 (1969).
3 See, S. Goulbourne, 'Access to legal education and the legal profession in Jamaica', William Twining (ed.), *Access to legal education and the legal profession in the Commonwealth*, (Butterworth, forthcoming).

Bibliographic note

This is a bibliographic note rather than a comprehensive bibliography because it is not necessary to repeat here all the texts already listed in the notes at the end of each chapter. Only the most relevant books, articles and government reports are included although my debt to the wider literature must be obvious. Most of these have, of course, already been mentioned in the notes but it may serve a purpose to bring them together here.

Books and theses:

Carnegie, J. 1973. *Some aspects of Jamaica's politics, 1918-38*, Kingston: Institute of Jamaica.

Coates, R. D. 1972. *Teachers' unions and interest group politics: a study of the behaviour of organized teachers in England and Wales*, Cambridge University Press.

Coleman, J. S. (ed.) 1965. *Education and political development*, Princeton University Press.

Crenson, M. A. 1971. *The un-politics of air-pollution: a study in non-decision-making in the cities*, The Johns Hopkins Press.

Day, G. 'An assessment of the adequacy of teacher education in Jamaica in relation to educational needs since 1938'. Unpublished M.A. Thesis, University of the West Indies, Mona, 1972.

Eisner, Gisela. 1961. *Jamaica 1830-1930: a study in economic growth*, Manchester University Press.

Figueroa, J. J. 1972. *Education, society and progress in the Caribbean*, Oxford: Pergamon Press.

Foner, N. 1973. *Status and power in rural Jamaica: a study of educational and political change*, Teachers College Columbia University Press.

Foster, P. 1967. *Education and social change in Ghana*, London: Routledge & Kegan Paul.

Jones, E. S. 'Pressure group politics in the West Indies: a case study of colonial systems – Jamaica, Trinidad and Guiana'. Unpublished PhD Thesis, Manchester University, 1970.

Lewis, Sir Arthur. 1977. *Labour in the West Indies: the birth of the Workers' Movement*, London: New Beacon Books.

Lewis, G. K. 1968. *The growth of the modern West Indies*, London: Mcgibbon & Kee.

Macmillan, W. M. 1938. *Warning from the West Indies: a tract for the Empire*, London: Penguin Books.

Moodie, G. C. & Studdert-Kennedy, G. 1970. *Opinions, public and pressure groups: an essay on vox populi and representative government*, London: Allen & Unwin.

Munroe, T. 1972. *The politics of constitutional decolonization: Jamaica 1944-62*. Institute of Social and Economic Studies, University of the West Indies, Mona.

Murray, R. N. (ed.) 1969. *JJ Mills: his own account of his life and times*, Kingston: Collins and Sangster (Jamaica) Ltd.

Philips, A. S. 1973. *Adolescence in Jamaica* , Kingston: Jamaica Publishing House/Macmillan.

Post, K. 1978. *Arise ye starvellings*, The Hague: Martinus Nijhiff.

Smith, M. G. 1965. *The plural society in the British West Indies*, University of California Press; also (1974 ed.), Kingston: Sangster's Book Store Ltd.

Stone, C. 1983, *Democracy and clientelism in Jamaica*, New Brunswick: Transaction Books.

Williams, E. (n.d. but presumably 1950). *Education in the British West Indies*, Port of Spain: Guardian Commercial Printery.

Articles and unpublished material:

Bacchus, M. K. 1969. Patterns of educational expenditure in an emergent nation: a study of Guiana 1945-65, *SES*, vol. 17, no. 3.

Beckford, G. 1968. 'Education as an instrument for development', Substance of a talk delivered to the Annual Meeting of the JTA, Kingston, 2 January 1968.

Bolland, O. N. 1971. Literacy in rural areas of Jamaica, *SES*, vol. 20, no. 1.

Collins, S. 1956, Social mobility with reference to rural committees and the teaching profession, *Transactions of the Third World Congress of Sociology*, vol. 3.

Comitas, L. 1964. 'Occupational mobility in rural Jamaica', in V. E. Garfield & E. Freidl, n.p. (eds) *Symposium on Community Studies in Anthropology*.

Cross, M. & Schwartzbaum, A. 1969. Social mobility and secondary school selection in Trinidad and Tobago, *SES*, vol. 18, no. 2.

Crowley, D. J. 1957. Plural and differential acculturation in Trinidad, *American Anthropologist*, vol. lix.

D'Oyley, V. R. 1963. The development of teacher education in Jamaica, 1835-1913, *Ontario Journal of Education Research*, vol. vi, no. 1.

Johnston, T. J. 1973. 'Imperialism and the professions: notes on the development of professional occupations in Britain's colonies and the new states', Paul Holmos (ed.), *Sociological Honograph*, no. xx, University of Keele.

Lewis, Sir Arthur. 1962. Education and economic development, *International Social Science Journal*, vol. xiv.

Lipset, S. M. 1959. Some social requisites of democracy: economic development and political legitimacy, *APSR*, vol. liii.

Manley, D. 1963. Mental ability in Jamaica, *SES*, vol. 12, no. i.

Seaga, E. 1955. Parent-teacher relationships in a Jamaican village, *SES*, vol. 4. no. 3.

Smith, N. G. 1960. Education and occupational choice in rural Jamaica, *SES*, vol. 9, no. 3.

Woolcock, J. 1984. Class conflict and class reproduction: an historical analysis of the Jamaican educational reforms of 1957 and 1962, *SES*, vol. 33, no. 4.

Primary sources:

Included here are British, colonial and Jamaican government reports as well as those of external bodies and the teachers' unions. I have excluded details of interviews partly because the most relevant ones are already mentioned in the notes to individual chapters and partly because they are too many to include in a bibliographic note.

Great Britain (listed in chronological order):

Report of the West India Royal Commission with subsidiary report and statistical tables and diagrams and maps. C. 8655. London: HMSO, 1897.

Chaired by former Governor, Sir Henry Norman, with the Fabian socialist Sydney Oliver as Secretary, the Commission was set up by Joseph Chamberlain (then Secretary of State for the Colonies) to enquire into the causes of the fall in the price and production of West Indian sugar in the 1890s. The Report gives a good picture of the economic state of the West Indies in the 1890s.

Sadler, E. M. (ed.) 1901. *Educational Systems in the Chief Colonies of the British Empire*, Great Britain, Board of Education: Special Reports on Educational Subjects, vol. iv, Cd. 416 HMSO.

Wood, Hon. E. F. 1922. *Report on a Visit to the West Indies and British Guiana*, Cmd. 1897, HMSO.

Orde-Browne, G. 1939. *Labour conditions in the West Indies*, London: HMSO.

Statement of Policy on Colonial Development and Welfare, London: Cmd. 6175, HMSO, 1940.

The West India Royal Commission, 1938-9, C.O. 950. The Commission, set up as a result of the revolts in the West Indies 1935-8, sat both in London and in the West Indies. It received representations from over 370 witnesses and groups, over 730 memoranda and about 300 communications relating to individual grievances and is therefore a wealth of information on conditions, including education and teachers, in the region.

West India Royal Commission Report, Cmd. 6607, London: HMSO, 1945.

Stockdale, Sir Frank A. 1945. *Report on Development and Welfare in the West Indies, 1943-4*, Colonial no. 189, London: HMSO.

Jamaica government: (published and unpublished material, listed in alphabetical order)

A plan for post-primary education in Jamaica (being the Provisional Report of the Secondary Education Continuation Committee), Kingston: Government Printery, 1946.

A Ten-Year Plan of development for Jamaica, Kingston: Government Printery, 1945.

A Ten-Year Plan for Jamaica, Kingston: Government Printer, 1947.

A National Plan for Jamaica, 1957-67, Kingston: Government Printer, 1957.

Annual Reports of the Ministry of Education, Kingston: Government Printer, 1958-64.

Barbour, Sir David. 1899. *Report on the finances of Jamaica*, Government Printing Office.

Board of Education Annual Reports, Kingston: Government Printer, for the years 1893-1938. *Report of a meeting of the Board of Education*, Kingston: Government Printer, 1900, 23 and 24 October, 1900. These reports are also to be found in *The Governor's Report on the Blue Book and Departmental Reports* at the Colonial Office.

Census of Jamaica 1943: Population, housing and agriculture, Kingston: Central Bureau of Statistics, Government Printing Office, 1945.

Census of Jamaica 1960: vol. i and ii. Kingston: Department of Statistics, 1963-4.

Census of Jamaica 1960: Notes on education and race. Kingston: Government Printing Office, n.d. but presumably 1963.

Census of Jamaica 1970: Preliminary Report. Kingston: Department of Statistics, 1971.

Classification and salary plan for teachers. Ministry Paper, no. 37, Kingston: April 1973.

Education Department, Annual Reports, 1893-1938. Kingston: Government Printer.

Facts on Jamaica: Education, Kingston: Department of Statistics, 1973.

Five Year Independence Plan, 1963-68: A long term development programme for Jamaica, Kingston: Central Planning Unit, Ministry of Development and Welfare, n.d. but presumably 1963.

Government Statement of the revision of salaries of public officers and employees, July 1955. n.p. but presumably Kingston: Government Printer, 1955.

Jamaica Correspondence & Despatches: C.O. 137, 1891-1900; 1920-32, *passim.*

Jamaica Hansard: Proceedings of the House of Representatives. 1959-67, *passim.*

Minutes of the Legislative Council of Jamaica, 1891-1900, 1920, 1927-32.

Minutes of the Privy Council of Jamaica, C.O. 140, 1891-1900, 1920, 1927-32.

New deal for education in Independent Jamaica, Ministry Paper no. 73. Kingston: Ministry of Education, 1966.

Numbers and types of institutions, 1964-70. Kingston: Ministry of Education, Statistical Section, n.d. but presumably 1970/1.

Regradings and revision of salaries of teachers, 1967-8, Ministry of Education Papers, nos. 49 and 60. Kingston: 1967. (The following Reports are listed in chronological order)

Report of the Commission appointed to enquire into the education system in Jamaica. Kingston: Government Printing Office, 1898.

'Report of the Committee appointed to enquire into the staffing and emoluments of government officers and employees, 1928.' *Minutes of the Legislative Council of Jamaica, 1928,* Kingston: Government Printing Office, 1929. Appendix A.

'Report of the Commission appointed to enquire into unemployment in Jamaica, 1936'. *Minutes of the Legislative Council for the Year 1936.* Appendix xli. Kingston: Government Printing Office, 1937.

Report of the Commission appointed to enquire into the disturbances which occurred in Jamaica between 23 May and 8 June 1938, Kingston: Government Printing Office, 1938.

Report of the middle-class unemployment committee. Kingston: Government Printer, 1941.

Report of the Committee appointed to enquire into the system of secondary education in Jamaica, 1943. Kingston: Government Printer, 1943.

Report of the Selected Committee appointed by the House of Representatives on the proposed Education Regulations, 1965 (The Code) with appendixes and Minority Report, 18 May 1966, Kingston: Government Printer, 1966.

Review of the development in education and social welfare in Jamaica during the period 1944-54, Kingston: Government Printer, 1954.

Schools Commission, Annual Reports, 1892-1900. Kingston: Government Printer.

The Annual General Report of Jamaica, 1927-31. Kingston: Government Printer.

The Code of Regulations, 1929 ed. Kingston: Government Printer.

The Code of Regulations, 1966, Kingston: Government Printer, n.d. but presumably 1966.

The Educational thrust of the '70s, Kingston: Government Printing Office, n.d. but presumably 1973.

The Torch, Kingston: Ministry of Education Publication, 1955-74, *passim.*

General

Newspapers and Journals:

The Baptist Reporter, Kingston 1929, *passim.*

The Daily Gleaner, Kingston 1891-9, January 1918 – December 1920, *passim,* 1928-32, *passim,* 1974, *passim,* 1947-66.

The Colonial Standard and Despatch, Kingston, January – December 1892.

The Bulletin of the Educational Supply Co. Ltd., Kingston, vol. 1, nos. xvii and xxi, 1901.

Journal of the Jamaica Agricultural Society, vol. i, no. i, January 1897.

The Jamaica Branch of the British Medical Association: Bulletin, no. i, 1928.
K. A. McNiel (ed.) *Directory for 1956.*
The Jamaica Catholic Educational Association: Statement by the Jamaica Catholic Educational Association on its philosophy of education, May 1973.
The Jamaica Critic, Kingston, 1927-9.
The Jamaica Journal of Education, Kingston, vol. v, nos. iii and iv, 1905, vol. viii, no. iv, 1909.
The Jamaica Manufacturer, official organ of the Jamaica Manufacturers Association vol. i, no. i, 1964.
The Jamaica Times, Kingston, 1929, *passim*.
The Jamaica Weekly Gleaner, (U.K. ed.), 1972-5, *passim*.
The Teacher, Kingston, 1901-1904, *passim*.
The West Indian Critic and Review, 1929-30.

Miscellaneous Reports etc.:

The Jamaica Branch of the British Medical Association: Presidential address, 15 October 1931.
The Jamaica Catholic Educational Association: proposed constitution, n.d.
The Jamaica Civil Service Association:
The Report of the Managing Committee of the Jamaica Civil Service Association, to be presented at the Annual General Meeting to be held on Tuesday 22 July 1920.
Jamaica Civil Service Association, 54th Annual Conference, 21-25 May, 1973.
Jamaica Council of Human Rights, Report 1973.
The Jamaica General Trained Nurses Association, Annual Reports, 1947-52, 1961-4.

Teachers' Organizations

(i) **The JUT:**   – *Annual Reports*, 1895-1939, 1948-1963, *passim*.
                    – *Minutes of the Executive* 1909-29 *passim*.
                    – *The JUT Magazine*, 1928-34.
                    – *The JUT Clarion*, 1948-63 *passim*.
                    – *The Revised Rules of the JUT*, 1936.

(ii) **The AAMM:** – *The AAMM News*, 1947
                    – *The AAMM Journal*, 1955-64.

(iii) **The JETA:** – *Files of the JETA*, 1961-1963/4.
                    – *The Minutes of the JETA*, 1961-1963/64 *passim*.

(iv) **The JTA:** – *Annual Reports*, 1965-74.
                    – *The constitution of the JTA*, 1964, 1967.
                    – *Minutes of the Executive Committee*, 1965-68 *passim*.
                    – *Minutes of the Annual Conferences*, 1965-8.
                    – *Minutes of the Finance Committee*, 1965-8 *passim*.
                    – *The files of the JTA*, 1964-8.
                    – *The New Clarion*, 1964-74.

Index